Losing Hold

Losing Hold

By

Kellie Doherty

Desert Palm Press

Losing Hold
Cicatrix Duology – Book 2

by Kellie Doherty

© 2017 by Kellie Doherty

ISBN (trade): 9781942976363
ISBN (epub): 9781942976370
ISBN (pdf): 9781942976387

Desert Palm Press
1961 Main Street, Suite 220
Watsonville, California 95076
www.desertpalmpress.com

Editor: CK King (https://www.facebook.com/RavensEyeEditing)
Cover Design: Rachel George
http://www.rachelgeorgeillustration.com/portfolio/)

Printed in the United States of America
First Edition April 2017

Acknowledgements

There are so many wonderful people I'd like to thank! First, to Lee and the Desert Palm Press crew for helping me craft this story into what it is today. Second, to all my friends who cheered me on during the process. Third, to my family who always encouraged me to do my best and supported me in more ways than I can count. And last but not least, to my budding fanbase who offered kinds words about this adventure of mine. I write this for myself and for my characters and for the world inside my head, but I finish it for all of you. Thank you.

Dedication

For my parents
Ed and Deb

For my sister
Jessie

Chapter One

THE DARKNESS LASTED A few moments, but the pounding in Mia Foley's chest seemed to last an eternity. The base of the escape pod brightened, glowing with a steady white light. It chased the darkness to the top of the pod and threw shadows onto the hull.

Mia took in her surroundings. With smooth paneling, concave ceiling, slightly domed deck, the escape pod wasn't pretty and certainly not comfortable. They barely had enough space to stand, even less to sit, with the holoimager fused in the center. At least the harnesses—freezing metal arms that had snaked tightly around their bodies—had sunk back into the hull. With no noticeable hatches or bulbs, it remained a mystery where those long arms had gone. Or if they'd even come back again. She rubbed her nose at the tangy scent permeating the air. Something in the air purifier. The deck flashed red, green, and purple. It ended on light blue, the color of a cloudless sky, disconcerting as the color glowed beneath them. It made Mia feel like she was falling. Which, in a sense, wasn't far off the mark.

Mia shook her head. This couldn't be possible. She'd escaped from Charles Donavin, gotten off his abhorrent Acedian ship. She hadn't wanted to leave her crew, hadn't wanted to sacrifice them to save herself. She had chosen her crew over her own life. Chosen Cassidy Gates. Her gaze shifted up from the deck and onto the viewport. Her silver eyes glinted back. How was it possible she was still changing? She couldn't be disappearing like this. Not now, not here. Not anymore. And yet, Mia knew she was. From the way Cassidy now stared at her, wide-eyed with her back pressed against the hull, it became apparent Mia's first mate knew something was changing, too.

Mia shifted her weight forward, just a bit. "Please, Cassidy, it's me."

Cassidy's lower lip trembled. She wiped her hands on the ripped fabric that barely covered her thighs. "How am I supposed to know that? Your eyes—"

"Are the only thing that's changed."

Cassidy's gaze skittered away. "You attacked us."

"Cassidy, please. Listen." Mia paused, waiting until Cassidy's eyes met hers. "I wasn't thinking straight. Donavin controlled me."

"And I'm supposed to believe he's not controlling you now?"

Mia spread her arms, palms up. "Yes."

She was glad for the clarity of her voice, even though her emotions warranted a different pitch altogether, a pleading tone. Cassidy had to understand. Of all people, she had to. She didn't. Instead of relaxing, Cassidy seemed more tense, more scared, if that were at all possible. Her entire body shook. It took all of Mia's control to not stretch out her hand a little farther and comfort the one she loved. Instead, her gaze drifted to the viewport again, and the silver eyes staring back at her claimed her vision. Surely, there was a way to make Cassidy believe her. Surely, she didn't think the kiss, of all things, was Donavin's idea.

Static from the comm system interrupted her thoughts. Cassidy started from the sound and stared at the speaker behind her head. The static crackled.

Skyler Jones' voice filtered through the white noise. "What's happening over there?"

Cassidy didn't reply, so Mia did for her. "My eyes turned gray."

Silence. Mia caught a glance from her first mate and tried to hold it, but Cassidy's eyes flitted toward the deck instead. It seemed she found the colors of this pod especially fascinating.

At last, Skyler's voice erupted through the static. "Do you feel differently?"

"Differently? As in?" Mia expected the nurse to be more descriptive than that.

"Emptier."

A chill raced through her body. She certainly wasn't empty, not anymore. "No."

"When did you last feel him?"

Mia grimaced, thinking back to their hurried escape. "On the Acedian ship, right before you told me to get into the pod."

"And nothing since?" Even through the static, the panic in Skyler's voice rang true.

Mia hesitated. Now wasn't the time for dishonesty. "Only once, for a short time, I heard a snippet of his thoughts." The three words seemed to echo in her head. *I'll be waiting.*

Silence, again. It dragged on this time.

She was about to say something more when Skyler asked, "And

what did he say to you?"

"It's not important." Cassidy frowned at those words, and Mia immediately regretted saying them. It seemed like she was holding back, and she rushed to add more. "He just said that he'd be waiting."

A scowl probably painted the nurse's face, but in separate escape pods, Mia would never know. Skyler's voice deepened. "A threat like that from an Acedian is always important."

Mia frowned and ran a hand through her hair. She waited, expecting another question, maybe something from the Dee brothers, or Harrison even. The comm was full of static.

Yes, Donavin's last words were a threat. Of course they were. She wasn't naive enough to believe the Acedians would leave her alone. Their ship was damaged, though. These escape pods hurtled away from them faster than any other shuttle. She had her crew to help her. Her eyes may be silver, but she wasn't turning. Not yet. A sigh escaped her lips. This wasn't the celebration she wanted after escaping her enemy.

She leaned back against the hull. The Acedians had always been following her. Ever since the attack on the *Hekate*, the same brawl that left her parentless, she had moved constantly. She had to. She hated every terrible deed she had to commit to keep one ship away from them, away from him, the scarred man that murdered her parents, the one called Charles Donavin. A trail of destroyed ships and people drifted in her wake. A heavy pit formed in her stomach. She tried to rub the feeling away. It didn't help.

Instinctively, she looked at Cassidy. Her gaze lingered on how her torn shirt lay on her shoulders, how swatches of her dark pants had been entirely removed. How she still looked bold and proud even when fearful of her own captain.

Mia had bonded with this crew, found a new life with these people, but it was her decision that had gotten them captured and tortured. Their ship blew up, and her crew, plus a few stragglers, was on the run. She left Cassidy and looked out into the black instead. The stars passed by the viewport in a blur. She didn't mind. The escape pod must have turned; now she could see the two other pods traveling beside them. The third pod contained those stragglers. Harrison, a Paradousian officer, was adopted into the crew as the ranking military presence on her ship. Skyler, though? Mia frowned. She still wasn't sure whether or not to trust the ex-Acedian, but the woman had helped her get out of a tricky situation. Still, the raven-haired nurse was hiding something.

A voice cut into Mia's thoughts, Cassidy's voice, "You were acting strange when we tried to escape." Cassidy kept her eyes on the deck.

Mia stared at her. "Well, I was being controlled by a homicidal maniac at the time."

The words came out harsher than she intended, and they caught Cassidy's attention. Finally, she lifted her gaze. Her eyes didn't hold their usual spark, but Mia could get lost in those dark depths all the same. She made sure to keep her distance, though. Her first mate still shivered. Though from fear or loss of blood Mia couldn't quite tell. The wound on Cassidy's shoulder seeped red, and her other injuries needed attention, the fracture especially.

Mia nodded at Cassidy's arm. "Will you let me manage the fracture?"

Cassidy didn't answer at first. Instead, she took a deep breath, held it, and let it out. It seemed as if she steadied herself for something. Finally, she shook her head and spoke into the comm system, "Are you sure it's safe?"

Cassidy didn't have to explain any further. Both Skyler and Mia understood what she was really asking.

"She's fine for now," Skyler replied. "The farther away we get, the harder she'll be for him to control. The worst she'll do is become apathetic."

Cassidy's eyes narrowed. "What?"

"She could be stripped of emotions, but if we fly right, Donavin won't have time to finish his plan."

Mia almost asked "what plan" then decided against it. Right now, she needed to fix Cassidy's wounds. Questions would come later.

Cassidy gave Mia a long, searching look, one that drifted down and up her body but never once met her gaze. Twisting the silver ring on her middle finger—a nervous habit of hers—Cassidy repeated, "She's safe?"

"Yes."

She still didn't look convinced, her eyebrows furrowing. Taking in another deep breath and letting it out, Cassidy's next words were directed at Mia. "Just don't do anything Acedian, okay?"

Mia nodded. "I'll try not to." She spoke into the comm. "Skyler, you mentioned a medical kit somewhere in this pod?"

"Yes, it should be directly under the holoimager. Pry open the front panel. You're looking for a little white box."

Mia crouched down the best she could, one knee on either side of the holoimager, and loosened the panel. Sure enough, a white box about the size of a book lay inside. Grabbing the kit, she placed the panel back onto the imager and stood. The medical kit clicked open, revealing a small array of healing technology nestled inside. Mia pulled out ones easily recognizable: clotting pills, a roll of gauze, a scanner, and a bubble heliogun, and one she didn't: a tiny container full of clear liquid. She set the kit down and glanced at Cassidy. Obviously, they would have to be closer in order for Mia to help. Cassidy clutched her arm tighter, but the blood now dripped from her shoulder and couldn't be ignored. Mia slowly scooted over. Cassidy didn't shrink away.

Mia twisted the top off the jar containing the clotting pills and held out the container of dark capsules. "You should take a few of these to help with the bleeding. Your arm should be dealt with first. I want to check if that fracture got any worse."

Cassidy nodded. She plucked a few pills from the jar and chewed, making a face at the taste.

Mia grimaced. "Bitter, right? Will made me take some when he fixed my leg."

Cassidy didn't reply. Apparently, this was going to be a quiet healing. Mia settled herself against the hull and held out her hand. Cassidy hesitated, only for a moment, before she offered her arm. Her wrist trembled in Mia's gentle hold. Mia tried to ignore how soft Cassidy's skin felt. Tried to ignore how charged she felt being this close to Cassidy. Tried to ignore the thudding of her heart. Tried, and failed, but the task at hand made it easier. Mia lifted Cassidy's arm to the scanner. It blinked on, humming softly. The orange light shimmered as Mia moved it over Cassidy's arm.

A small holoimage materialized on the back of the device, an image of the fabric binding Cassidy's arm, her muscles and veins, her bones beneath. The darker crack of the fracture. The hair on Mia's neck stood. Her stomach clenched. The image was eerily similar to Mia's when Donavin had peered inside her, though Cassidy's veins pulsed red where Mia's had shone silver. Spirals and spikes peppered the area beneath the holoimage, but Mia couldn't understand the Acedian symbols. The gist of the wound seemed simple enough, though.

Mia put the scanner down, and the light blinked off. She turned to Cassidy. "The fracture seems okay. It's still just a hairline, which will make healing easier. I'm going to have to unwrap this bandage in order to put a better one on."

Cassidy tightened her jaw and looked away. Her hair fell in waves over her shoulder, the strands of purple highlighting her darker tones. An ache formed in Mia's chest at that simple reaction. Finally, Cassidy nodded.

Mia reached over to the white box. "There are pain pills in the med kit if you want them."

When Cassidy shook her head, Mia worked on her arm. It must have hurt, unwrapping then binding her arm up in the white fabric, but Cassidy never made a sound. She didn't even glance in Mia's direction.

"Done."

Cassidy gave a cursory look at her newly bandaged arm and continued her scrutiny out the viewport.

The silent treatment annoyed Mia. She was, after all, healing her first mate. "I need to patch up your other wounds. May I?"

After a slight jerk of the head, which Mia took to be a nod, she continued, putting the scanner back into the box and taking out the tiny container full of liquid. She hoped it was antibacterial, and one sniff of the sharp scent proved her right. At least this would help clean the wounds. The one on Cassidy's shoulder had stopped bleeding, but that was only because of the clotting pills. She lifted a piece of clean cloth from the med kit and dipped it into the liquid.

"This will sting," she said. When Cassidy didn't reply, Mia placed the soaked cloth onto the wound.

Cassidy yanked away. "Quasar, Mia, that hurts!"

Mia pulled Cassidy back and began dabbing the cut. "I told you it would be painful."

Cassidy frowned. Their eyes met. "You said it would sting, not feel like a hoard of angry Skadian wasps impaled me."

Mia smirked, and warmth flooded her chest. That's the Cassidy she knew. "I thought Skadian women had a higher tolerance for pain."

Her first mate scoffed. She rubbed a hand over her thigh, as if doing something like that would help ease the pain. "I thought you actually knew what you were doing."

Mia lifted an eyebrow. "And what made you think that?" She went back to concentrating on her work. This time she could feel Cassidy watching her, and her neck prickled from the attention. With the blood wiped off and the wound as clean as she could get it, Mia decided to use the bubble heliogun. She pointed the tip at the base of the cut and pulled the trigger. At once, a bubble formed and met Cassidy's skin, creating a translucent, gleaming dome over the wound. The bubble popped, and the gleaming liquid covered the entire cut, holding it together and protecting it from harm.

"Where did you learn how to use that, then?"

Cassidy's question hung in the air for a few heartbeats before Mia answered it, "I got pretty banged up after *Luminaria* and ended up on the planet Shade. They had these types of healing guns there, and I found a bubble one works best on cuts like these."

Cassidy shifted her weight. "You learned a lot in your...travels."

"I had to." Mia repeated the process on the other wounds, and soon Cassidy's skin was decorated with the gleaming liquid. There was only one wound Mia had not touched. A gash on Cassidy's cheek still needed tending to. Heat rose from the back of Mia's neck, creeping toward her ears. She would have to get mighty close to her first mate to bubble that wound. Before, it might not have been a problem, but would Cassidy even allow it now? She searched her first mate's face for the answer.

Cassidy turned her cheek toward Mia. "Go ahead."

Mia swallowed the lump forming in her throat. She flipped the cloth around in her hand and dipped the cleaner section into the liquid. Slowly, she placed one hand on the side of Cassidy's face while the other dabbed at the cut. Her thumb lay over the corner of Cassidy's lips. The softness of Cassidy's skin, the warmth of it, caused a jolt deep in Mia's core and the tickling of butterfly wings in her stomach. *Did Cassidy still feel the same?*

Cassidy's eyes remained transfixed on the viewport, not on her. Within moments, the gash was clean. Mia used the heliogun and intended to move away, but Cassidy placed her hand atop Mia's and twined their fingers together. She traced Mia's knuckles, and the gentle touch sent the butterflies swarming. Yet Mia kept still, not wanting to push too far and spook Cassidy. For that brief moment, even though Cassidy still hadn't looked at her, they were connected.

Static burst through the comm system, again. Both women jumped and let go. Mia focused on the speakers, while Cassidy folded herself against the hull and did the same.

"How's it going in there? Is our patient doing well?"

Skyler. Of course. "Yes." Mia coughed to clear her throat. She looked at Cassidy. "I did the best I could."

A small smile played on the corner of Cassidy's lips, as she tucked her wounded arm against her chest. "Mia did a good job."

"Still, I'd like to look at you when we land." Skyler's statement came a bit too quickly for Mia's taste.

"Of course," Cassidy replied.

Mia moved closer to her speakers, letting Cassidy reclaim one side of the escape pod. "Where are we landing?"

"There's a small planet this escape pod seems to be heading toward. A light keeps flashing over here. It just started a few moments ago. Hasn't yours done the same?"

Mia started to answer, but a sudden light on the imager distracted her, flashing a solid yellow. "Ours just started. Jeff, Will, what about yours?"

The brothers had been oddly quiet during this escape. Jeff's voice came through the speakers. "Ours came on now as well."

Cassidy peered at the light. "How are we supposed to know what it means? It could be saying we're low on oxygen or something."

Harrison's murmur came through next, finally joining the broken conversation. "Low oxygen would probably warrant a red light, not yellow. And our pod still has the holoimage of our trajectory. Like when we first got out of the Acedian ship? It never turned off."

"Here," Skyler said. "I'll turn yours back on."

The holoimager blinked to life, projecting three little blue lights amid a dark backdrop. A section of the image seemed missing but appeared after Mia removed the medical kit. The lights—their pods—did seem to be heading toward a red planet in the center of the image.

Jeff's voice came through. "So we're landing on that planet. Do we know what planet it is?"

Worry spiked through Mia, and she butted in. "If the pod is headed there, won't the Acedians just follow us?"

"I've masked our engine trail." Skyler's voice seemed harried, as if that had been a dumb question. "As far as they're concerned, we're just a few comets."

Mia's jaw tightened, disbelief washing through her, and she shook her head. "How do you know how to do that?"

"You pick up a lot of things living with the Acedians."

A pinging noise followed by a steady whooshing sound caught Mia's attention. She scanned the pod, trying to find the source. The noise came from the comm system. A shout came soon after. Will.

Mia placed her hands on the hull, the smooth paneling cold to her touch. "Will, what's happening? Are you okay?"

Jeff's voice was urgent. "Something punctured our hull. Micro asteroids maybe. I'm trying to find the sealant. Skyler?"

Punctured? Mia glanced around at their tiny enclosure. The brothers would only have a few minutes, probably less, before all the air was sucked out of their tiny pod. The darkness, the emptiness, the icy death of space loomed around her even though their pod seemed intact. Her chest tightened. Surely they'd make it. They had to.

"Breach it!" Skyler yelped. "We just got hit, too. Look where the deck panels meet, one of the panels should open. You can find a sealant in there. Plug any holes you can find."

Mia stared at the comm. Skyler's voice held fear, a panic that she hadn't heard from the nurse before. A panic of things going out the airlock fast. She could barely breathe as the hurried voices shouted back and forth.

"I can't find it," Jeff shouted.

"Try the second panel to the starboard side of the holoimager."

"Get out of the way, Will. The panel isn't moving."

"Then do the next one." Skyler's voice was sharp. "I've found mine. These pods should be similar."

"I've tried all the starboard ones, and there's nothing. Nothing!"

Helplessness washed over Mia. She felt paralyzed, her thoughts muddied. She couldn't do anything.

Cassidy, however, sidled next to her and spoke clearly and calmly into the speaker. "Jeff, ours was under the port panel closest to the viewport."

Mia gaped at her. Cassidy held a coned tool with blackened edges and a bulbous backing. "The sealant?" she mouthed.

Cassidy nodded, noting the loosened deck panels.

Jeff's voice came through the speaker. "I found it."

Cassidy pushed the lever by her thumb. Clear liquid oozed out and dripped onto the deck. "Good, now push the lever down, hold it, and stick the sealant into the punctures."

Silence. Cassidy moved closer to the speaker. "Jeff, did you do it?"

Silence. "I've done it. Did yours get hit?"

Relief flooded her, and Mia sighed. Her thoughts solidified once more, and she dropped her hands. "No, ours didn't. Why didn't the holoimager tell us we were going through an asteroid belt?"

Skyler answered. "Maybe it wasn't designed to sense those types of anomalies in space."

Cassidy scoffed, putting the sealant down. "It can detect a planet but not an asteroid belt?"

Before anyone could answer, the escape pod jerked sideways. Hard and sudden, the motion caught the two women off guard. Mia crashed into the holoimager, her right thigh taking most of the force. Cassidy started to fall. Her hands flailed for something to grab onto. Mia caught

9

her good arm and pulled her upright.

Cassidy tensed. "Asteroid?"

Mia nodded. "And not a micro one either."

Another asteroid hit their pod, sending both women sprawling. Pain spiked up Mia's shoulder from the blow, but she planted her boots against the base of the holoimager and pushed her back against the panels. *Maybe we can just ride it out?* Another asteroid hit, and another. Soon their pod quaked and creaked under the barrage. A section crumpled inward, toward them.

Metal screamed and so did Cassidy. Mia pulled her away from the danger. Cassidy shut her eyes. Mia almost did the same when the crumpled section grew bigger, inched closer. Someone was speaking through the comm system, though she couldn't distinguish the words or recognize the voice. The only thing Mia heard were the frightened breaths of Cassidy standing next to her. *It would not end like this. Not in an escape pod. Not now.* A heartbeat later, the barrage stopped. The pod ceased shaking. Cassidy held her breath, but all was silent and still.

Mia looked around. Where Cassidy once stood, the hull was bashed in almost to the holoimager. Thankfully, there were no hull breaches. *Had the others made it through?* As if in reply, panicked voices came through the comm.

"Mia? Cassidy?" The brothers.

Skyler spoke next, her voice steady. "We're okay. The hull will fix itself, but we're going to have a bumpy ride."

The holoimager flickered. A blurred image of two pods going one direction and the third heading a few degrees south appeared then vanished.

Cassidy gasped and pointed at the now-empty space. "Ours turned off. Are we at the planet?"

For a few harried moments, no one replied. Finally, Harrison's garbled voice came through. "We're here. Entering atmos—"

The pod jerked once more.

Chapter Two

IT WASN'T THE FACT they were hurtling toward a planet she knew nothing about that aggravated Mia, nor that when they landed they wouldn't be with the others, nor the simple truth that the Acedians would follow. No, what pushed Mia over the edge was the white noise empty of the usual dips and pitches of human speech. Even when she yelled into the comm, no one answered. She pounded her hands onto the hull. The sharp pain in her palms felt good. It kept her focused almost, radiating up her arms and down her fingers.

Cassidy started, turning away from her inspection of the buckled plating. "Did that help at all?"

"I'm not going to die in here," Mia muttered.

Cassidy scooted over to their section, away from the damaged side. "Well, we'll survive the entry, at least."

"And how do you know that? How do you know we won't burn up entering the atmosphere or impale ourselves on some treetop? That blasted section alone will be the first to weaken and rip off." She jabbed her finger at the plating and glared at the comm system again. She wanted to talk to her crew, to Will and Jeff at least. What if the sealant didn't hold?

"That blasted section is fixing itself, just like Skyler said it would." Cassidy nodded to the other side of the pod. Mia followed her gaze and her jaw went slack. "The escape pods are made from the same material as the Acedian ship."

Of course. With a quiet sucking sound, the crumpled section receded and smoothed, forming a perfect imitation of the opposite hull. A shiver rippled through Mia, and she rubbed the back of her neck. The Acedian tech never failed to amaze her.

Cassidy scooted over and ran a hand along the new section, looking over her shoulder. "We should be glad they did. They probably saved our lives."

Despite the truth in Cassidy's words, Mia scowled. There was no way in Helix she would be thankful for anything the Acedians did. The pod bucked. She hung on to the holoimager. Cassidy did the same.

"Just in time," Cassidy murmured.

Mia eyed the new paneling, then grabbed Cassidy and pulled her closer. Their shoulders bashed together from the sudden movement. At Cassidy's questioning glance, she said, "I don't trust that side will hold."

Mia tightened her grip on the holoimager and looked out the viewport. The planet was right beneath them, a burgundy sphere. The pod bucked again. They entered the upper atmosphere, and the planet disappeared behind a wall of flames. The lights dimmed. Static still played in Mia's ear. Gooseflesh tickled her skin, prickling her arms and neck. The pod vibrated now. Her muscles tensed against the motion, and she pushed her back against the hull to steady herself.

Mia looked in Cassidy's direction. "The pod might survive, but we may get banged apart first."

Cassidy nodded, her eyes wide, her features washed red in the fiery light. Another jerk, and the pod stilled. The viewport cleared, giving them a closer view of the planet. Lakes and land masses flitted by, but the pod was still too high and the sky too dark to see if a civilization had been established on this planet. Mia had been to many planets; this one didn't look familiar. Not from up here at least. She couldn't see the other two pods but forced herself to assume they got through the entry okay. She would accept no other conclusion. A steady thrum entered the space, blocking out the white noise and filling her ears.

Cassidy leaned closer, bumping their shoulders together again. "Where's that noise coming from?"

Mia shook her head. "Maybe a propulsion system?"

The pod jerked again, and the thrumming stopped. The viewport now showed the curve of the dark horizon and the dual moons rising above it. The horizon slowly shifted, rising steadily above them and disappearing as the pod turned once more. Her boots lifted off the deck. At first, she didn't understand. Then it clicked. Falling. They were actually falling. Mia's stomach lurched.

Cassidy gasped and grabbed onto Mia's arm. "What happened to the pod's gravity?"

Mia didn't have an answer. The viewport spiraled shut, the pod pitch black now. The metal bands appeared and snaked around Mia's body before melding back into the hull. The bands pulled her close to the vibrating surface, metal pushing on her arms, chest, stomach, and legs. A smaller one slithered over her forehead and pulled her into the padded headrest. A yelp beside her confirmed the same was happening to Cassidy.

"We're freefalling," Cassidy whispered, panic clear in her voice.

"Try to stay calm," Mia muttered, gritting her teeth against the sudden nausea.

"Can't. We're—"

Mia looked at her first mate. Or at least in the direction of where her first mate was. If only the lights would return. She wanted to see Cassidy. She shifted a little, reaching out the best she could beside her. Their hands touched, and it only took Mia a heartbeat to realize that Cassidy was trying to do the same. A momentary thrill warmed within her. She grabbed what little of Cassidy's shaking fingers she could reach. "We will make it through this."

Cassidy's voice drifted through the black. "I know."

Mia closed her eyes against her fear and swallowed. At this height, it would be impossible to survive. Her stomach lurched again. She wanted this to be over, willing it to be done, ended.

And then it was. They no longer fell, but she hadn't felt the impact. Where was the crushing of metal? The slowing of speed? The viewport spiraled open more. Light spilled into the pod. She blinked, and slowly the outside world came into view. The dusty surface, trees looming overhead. It all seemed like what she had seen during their entry and yet, something seemed off. Delicate strands interlinked just outside the viewport, forming a blue webbing. The bands slithered off her, and she stumbled over to the viewport, pushing her hands against the heated glass.

"What kind of unorthodox way is that to get to a planet's surface?" Cassidy grumbled.

Mia hardly heard her. "I don't believe it."

"What?" Cassidy came up beside her, taking in a view of the outside. "What is that?"

A hiss erupted behind them. They spun around to face it, and Mia balled her hands into fists as the side of the pod slid apart. A sliver of moonlight appeared on their side of the pod, from deck to ceiling, growing until it reached shoulder width. She crouched, ready to spring, just in case someone, or something, waited outside. The hissing stopped. The opening seemed complete. Cassidy moved as if to go outside, but Mia held her back. She put up a hand, signaling Cassidy to wait, and made her way toward the narrow opening.

Dust still settled to the ground, leaving behind a dry, cracked scent. Leaves littered the ground beneath the clump of trees surrounding them. Two full moons hovered in the dark sky, illuminating their clearing. Mia sensed no danger. The webbing remained just out of reach. It had to surround the entire pod, a sphere of some sort.

Mia hesitated. If she stepped out of the pod, her boot would surely hit the webbing and there was no telling what that would do to her or to Cassidy. She held her breath and held her boot outside of the pod. Stupid, maybe, but if something were to happen, let it happen to her not Cassidy. Mia waited a heartbeat, wondering how strange this would look to anyone outside—a single boot sticking out of the door. The hull of the pod expanded and flattened, creating a walkway for them. She motioned Cassidy to follow. Mia took two small steps and reached out to touch the blue strands. A strange humming sound emitted from the force field.

"Wait." Cassidy grabbed her shoulder. "We don't know what it will do to us. Look what it did to the ground." She gestured behind them.

The pod floated above the ground. The dirt beneath it had been disturbed, not by the actual machine but by the force field it had created. The webbing molded the dirt, creating a dimple in the once-flat surface. The escape pod hovered inside this webbing, upright and unblemished. Not even a scratch etched its outer hull. Mia had to admit this tech was far beyond what she had seen before. Still, her stubbornness took hold.

"It's not like we can stay inside this bubble forever." Mia reached out and touched the web. A shock ran through her, and she jerked back. It hadn't hurt, not really, but energy seemed to have bounced over her skin. The webbing flickered and disappeared. Two hands shoved her in the back, and Mia stumbled onto the dirt and spun around.

Cassidy leapt off the walkway beside her, staring at the vibrating pod. It listed to one side, crashed into the ground, and split apart with a resounding crack. The segments melted into a pool of liquid metal. Only the wiring and padding remained intact. Shock rippled through Mia, curling around her midsection. Her eyes widened.

Cassidy gawked at the wreckage. "All because you had to touch the force field?"

Mia shrugged. "How could I know that would happen? Why would the Acedians destroy their single means of escape?"

"To cover up the fact that they're Acedians, maybe." Mia glanced at Cassidy in surprise. That would be a perfect reason to destroy their pod. Cassidy rubbed a hand over her face and sighed. "At least I grabbed this before we left." She leaned down and grabbed the medical kit off the dirt, then looked pointedly at Mia. "We should go. If this planet is inhabited, someone, or something, probably heard that."

Cassidy took the lead and strode into the dark forest. Mia hesitated, her fists pushed into her hips, staring at the pool of gray matter that used to be their pod. What if they had still been inside when it happened? A quiet crackle behind her signaled that Cassidy had moved farther away. She sighed, pursuing Cassidy into the darkness.

The trees twisted far above her. Their limbs splayed outward and upward, their roots jutting up from the dirt. Even the trunks seemed to be connected. She had to climb the branches just to get through. The lack of light didn't help the matter either. Whatever moonlight filtered through the trees certainly didn't reach the ground below.

"Cassidy," Mia huffed, "how are you even getting through this?"

No answer. Not even the sound of Cassidy's footsteps crunching over the bark anymore. Mia reached for the next branch, the bark rough on her palm, and pulled. The branch snapped. She fell, catching herself on a nearby trunk. The bark scraped off a thin layer of skin and a smear of blood stained the bark when she let go. Sharp pain flashed in her hand, and she wished she still had her gloves. At least they'd offer some protection from the rough bark. Swearing, she pulled herself up again and gasped. The woods ended abruptly only a few paces away, and an oval lake lay beyond the trees. Cassidy seemed transfixed by it. Just one more tree blocked Mia's way. She pulled and pushed her way through, hands grasping at the branches, her boots pressed hard against the trunk. She ended up next to Cassidy in a matter of heartbeats, breathing more heavily than she would've liked. Something hummed by her ear and she swatted the tiny bug away without a second thought.

"Cassidy, how did you..." Mia's question trailed off.

Cassidy didn't move. Her lips were set in a line across her face. Her jaw so tight, a muscle twitched in her cheek. She didn't brush away the strands of hair blowing across her face or unclench the fists at her sides. She simply stared, and finally, Mia followed her gaze. The lake, brightened by the twin full moons rising in the sky, would have looked beautiful if it weren't for the beast currently drinking it.

The creature's huge, streamlined back ended in a long narrow tail. Clawed, webbed feet peeked from beneath the heavy bulk. Mia swallowed the fear thickening her throat. It had to be as big as all three escape pods combined, maybe bigger. The moonlight glinted off this creature's back. With jagged, scarlet lines running down its flank, spilling into gray and black, the creature seemed to melt into its surroundings.

It gulped the water, lapping and splashing as if it hadn't a care, which could be the case considering its size.

Cassidy's eyes flitted toward her. "We should go back."

Even though Cassidy whispered, Mia tensed. A bead of sweat traced a path down her back. "How do we know if it's carnivorous? Maybe it eats vegetation?"

Cassidy balked, her eyes widening even more. "Would you like to ask what its preference is?"

"If that thing chases us, we won't get far," Mia replied through clenched teeth. "Those tree branches are insane and your arm—"

"I managed before. And if we can't get through easily, maybe that thing can't either."

Mia shook her head. "It could probably crash its way through. A branch broke in my grasp earlier."

The creature shifted but didn't turn. It kept up a steady pace when drinking. Cassidy leaned back anyway. She wanted to run. "You punched a hole through a metal wall, Mia."

Mia flashed back to that Acedian ship. Cassidy's screams filled her mind and she pushed them away. "Under different circumstances. You know that."

The creature lifted its head and sniffed the air, water sloshing from its jaws. Its oval eyes glinted in the moonlight. Cassidy took a step back, her foot crushing a twig. She froze, mouth slack, as she stared. The creature had frozen as well. Mia squeezed Cassidy's arm, reassuring her and trying to reassure herself as well. Eye's shifted toward them, black against reddish skin.

Water dripped off fangs onto massive feet. Huge. It was huge. Mia let out a breath and sucked in another just as fast, fear tightening her chest, making it painful to breathe. The creature lifted itself onto its hind legs, clawing at the air with its front. Rivers of water streamed down its mauve belly, and Mia recognized the washarian...wash for short. Deadly and there was only one planet she knew of that washes inhabited. Mia backed away. Her pulse pounded in her ears. The creature roared through gaping jaws. Louder than any engine, the sound vibrated her bones. A cold sweat broke out over her skin. The creature snorted and fell forward, landing with a thump that rattled the ground.

Cassidy took a deep breath, ripped her arm free of Mia's grasp, and bolted. The med kit thumped onto the dirt. Her boots pounded the ground, as she headed for the tree line. Mia spared one more glance at the creature before fleeing as well, matching her pace with Cassidy's. They jumped onto the nearest branch, slipped deeper into the forest, and looked back. Mia cursed under her breath, as the creature loomed closer. If only she had her dagger. If only she had anything to protect them.

The creature towered over them, its massive bulk slamming into the forest, reducing the trees to timber. It roared again. Water droplets flew from the beast's jaws, splashing onto Mia's shirt. The overpowering stench of rotting fish and heat rolled over her. The creature slashed at Cassidy. Mia grabbed Cassidy's waist and yanked her sideways, pushing her against the tree and covering her as the claws raked downward. Their eyes met for an instant, stilling time. Cassidy's wide, brown eyes shimmered with fear. Then the wash's claws ran through air, missing them both. The creature's foot landed on the tree next to them and shoved it over. Shards of broken branches pounded around them. Cassidy yelled as one slammed into her side, and Mia shifted her body to protect her from any others. If they stayed in this forest, chances were they'd be speared by the branches instead of the creature. The beast swiveled sideways, its massive head turned toward them.

Mia did the only thing she could think of and punched it between the nostrils. Her fist sank into the thick skin. The creature didn't seem injured, but it reared its head back, giving Mia the chance to grab Cassidy and leave the trees behind. They ran hard on the packed dirt beside the lake. The creature snarled, smashing its way out of the trees and chasing after them.

The forest completely ended halfway down the lake. Beyond that, barren flatlands reigned. She had no idea what to expect, although at this pace they wouldn't make it far anyway. The lake rippled with every step the beast took. A root jutted into their path ahead. She hopped over it.

"Mia," Cassidy yelped.

Mia swiveled around just in time to see Cassidy falling onto the dirt. She threw out her hands to stop herself. Both hands. The fractured arm crumpled beneath her, and she curled to one side, holding her injured arm tight. Mia rushed back, stepping in front of Cassidy and widening her stance. If she had to, she would fight. Even without her dagger, she did have one thing she could use against this wash. The creature, nearly on top of them now, halted and drew back up to its full height. Heart pounding, Mia readied herself, calling up the cold within and the strength that came with it.

A spear whizzed past Mia's head and embedded itself into the creature's belly. Black blood splashed out around the metal shaft, and a rumble came from deep within the beast. It worked its jaws open and closed, claws slashing at the air. Cassidy crawled back, and Mia moved with her. The creature teetered, eyes flashing yellow. With one last weak snarl, it tumbled to the dirt. Relief washed over Mia, but there was no telling what calling the cold had done to her. Probably sped up the Acedian process, if anything. For now, she could still shove it away.

A voice called out from the remaining trees beside them. "You really should not challenge a wash."

Mia helped Cassidy up and searched for the speaker, startled by the formality in the voice.

A man clad in black and armed with a second spear stepped out from the shadows. "Most do not win."

Chapter Three

THE MAN SMILED, HIS teeth an eerie, shining white. "The wash was distracted. You posed little threat. That is why it showed its stomach. You would not have survived without my spear."

Mia moved around Cassidy to stand in between her and this man now, since the wash no longer threatened them. She folded her arms and tilted her head at the stranger. "Then I gather introductions are in order?"

"First the encampment, then introductions. This way."

Before Mia could say anything else, the man disappeared into the darkness. She eyed the fallen beast. Gray markings decorated the corners of its eyes, mud splattered across its narrow head, and its skin seemed to glisten. They might not have won had the man not thrown his spear. Mia hadn't seen a wash in long time, and even now, she didn't quite remember how to incapacitate them. Aside from a spear to the heart, of course. She turned away and focused on Cassidy instead.

Cassidy groaned and stared at the forest. "My arm feels worse, and I don't want to encounter another one of these creatures anytime soon."

Mia shook her head. "Neither do I."

After a moment, they followed the stranger. Mia usually didn't trust someone so readily, but it felt as if she knew this man. He waited for them, just inside the first clump of trees. Tall, broad shouldered, he stood straight-backed with his arms folded across his chest. Muscles etched deep into his dark skin. Dirt covered the fabric from his shirt collar to his scuffed boots. His dark, graying hair was tied back with a single piece of string, and he searched the forest with narrow, green eyes. None of these traits stood out, and yet there was an overwhelming sense of familiarity. Even his formal way of speaking seemed to nudge something in Mia. His pathway through the forest of tangled branches made the going simple. Even Cassidy breathed easily.

Cassidy twirled her ring and surveyed the massive tree before her. Her eyes followed the trunk up and up as it twisted into the darkness.

"Why didn't we just leave the forest and walk on that flat land by the lake?"

The stranger smiled but didn't look at Cassidy. For some reason, he kept his eyes on Mia. It unnerved her though not as much as she would've thought. The dirt caked across his forehead, down his cheeks, and over his nose obscured his features too much for her to recognize him.

"That land is dominated by wash. It is their dwelling spot. We will be on level ground soon. Just place your hand here, your foot there, and leap over." The stranger mimed his words, putting his hands on the twin branches closest to him and his boot on the limb halfway up. The tree loomed above the man. Its limbs stretched into the sky and disappeared into the black. The ground was lost beneath its leaves, and crisp foliage scent filled the air. "Gravity on this planet is less than others, you may have noticed."

Mia bit her lip, a blush heating up her neck. She hadn't. A novice mistake. A quick glance Cassidy's direction confirmed that neither had she.

The man grinned wider. "The dirt on the other side is solid and free of roots."

With that he tensed, leaned back, and shoved off the ground, leaping high above the heart of the wood and through the opening in the branches. Higher than a man should be able to at normal gravity. At any gravity Mia remembered anyway. A subtle thump came from beyond.

Cassidy swayed, and a slight green tinge crept up her face, ebbing slowly into her cheeks. She let out a high-pitched bark of a laugh and turned to Mia. "I can't possibly do that. Even with the lower gravity and a healed arm, I doubt I could."

If the gravity was truly lower here, maybe the leap wasn't that bad. He had certainly taken it in stride. Mia held out her hands. "I think I can manage for both of us."

Cassidy went suddenly still, as if regretting her words. She glanced back to the tree and gave a stiff nod, cradling her injured arm to her body. "Don't do—"

"Anything Acedian, I know," Mia interrupted, softening the blow with a smile. She moved closer, slowly gathering her first mate into her arms. Cassidy still tensed against her, but that would have to do for now.

"Ready?" Mia's breath fogged around them both. The air had

grown colder since they landed. Significantly colder. Cassidy gave another nod.

Mia moved to the tree and pushed off with her feet like the man had showed them. Lower gravity or no, the jump demanded all of her strength. She cleared the gap in the branches and gasped at the sight that now lay before her—dirt and darkness. Holding Cassidy closer, she landed as gently as she could, absorbing the impact with her legs.

Cassidy slid out of her grasp and stumbled forward. Her voice came out higher than normal. "Why is it so dark?"

The man had already walked a distance away before he turned. "The forest hides the moonlight for a good while. It will return."

Cassidy twirled the ring on her finger again, twisting it around and around until Mia caught her hand and pulled her forward. Cassidy's jaw tightened, her nostrils flared, and she turned away panicked.

Mia tightened her grasp. "Come on, Cassidy, we have to follow him."

Cassidy shook her head, eyeing the stretch of land that lay before them. The darkness seemed to stretch forever here. Mia knew that was a lie. A trick of the eye. It would be easier to see once they started walking. Surely, Cassidy knew that. Still, when Mia looked back, Cassidy squeezed her injured arm and tried to back away.

Was she afraid of the dark? Or something worse? Mia moved forward, not too close. "Nothing will hurt us, Cassidy."

"How do you know?" Cassidy's lips pressed together. Her gaze darted down to her own arm.

"Because I won't let it." And, even if Cassidy didn't believe her, Mia meant every word. She squeezed her first mate's hand. "He found us in the middle of nowhere. There are probably more people at the encampment, maybe one of his friends found the others. Maybe we can find a way off this rock. Now, come on." Cassidy didn't move. "Do I really have to make this an order?"

A ghost of a smile lit Cassidy's face. "Probably."

"Then it's an order," Mia replied, happy to see her panic break, if only for a moment.

Mia started in the direction of the stranger, and Cassidy shuffled behind her. They looked back. The forest's limbs stretched far into the sky, tangling together. The wall of wood had captured the light of the moons, blocking them both from view.

Nothing jumped out at them, but it still seemed as if something pushed in on Mia, as if the air itself lived. A gust of wind blew past.

Goosebumps rose on Mia's arms. She rubbed them away. It took a few moments for Mia's eyes to adjust to the darkness and, when they did, barren landscape stretched out around them. What a place to crash land into. Mia's stomach clenched. If the Acedians came here they would find her crew in no time.

Creases lined Cassidy's forehead, so Mia shook away the fears and took another stab at comforting her. "Look, the forest is throwing these shadows onto the ground. It'll get lighter as we move further away. I'm sure, once the moons rise a bit higher, this whole place will brighten, okay?"

Cassidy nodded. She tightened her hand around Mia's then let go. The walk was lengthy and silent after that. The stranger leading them never looked back, never checked on them, and never hesitated in his stride. He didn't even speak. Dust billowed up from their boots with every step, irritating their eyes.

Cassidy coughed a few times. The shadows surrounding them slowly ebbed away as the moons rose, and the place brightened. Something small and narrow slithered over her boot then burrowed into the dirt. Even with that small encounter, a flash of recognition came to Mia. She had seen a creature like that before. Just as she had seen the wash before. Before she could place where or when, Cassidy tugged her forward and they continued on. The desert stretched far around them, with nothing breaking its flat surface. It seemed as if they would never reach the encampment.

Finally, the man stopped. Mia drew up next to him. Cassidy studied their surroundings, but Mia scrutinized this stranger. Formidable, though she could take him if necessary. He turned to her and muttered, "You would not win." Confusion must've crossed her face, because the man continued, "You may not recognize me, Foley, however I recognize you. And one of the comrades you fly with."

Mia shifted uncomfortably. *How does he know my name?* She wanted to scrub the dirt off of this stranger's face to see who he really was. "How do you know me? And who else do you know?"

The man didn't answer but instead searched the horizon.

Cassidy nudged her, so Mia turned. "What?"

It seemed they had reached the encampment. Dwellings rose in clumps, ranging from only a few paces wide to twenty-five or thirty. At first, Mia thought the homes were made of a rustic material—perhaps wash or other animal hide—yet as they drew closer, the metallic shimmer told her otherwise. These were housing units like ones the old settlers used when first landing on a planet, before the actual buildings were constructed. Probably the same materials they had been transferred to the planet with. It was better here than on Helix, where the prisoners were dumped on the planet with only the clothes on their backs and a small set of food rations. No housing units, no tech, not even water purifiers. She snuck glances into the makeshift, metallic houses they passed by. The smallest stored food and weaponry, and the sharp baying of animals filtered from the larger ones. A shrill sound echoed in the night. Small fires burst into life around the perimeter, while a much larger one started in the center of the camp. A few small orbs lit up as well, held aloft by sticks jutting from the ground. Those orbs had to be solar powered, what else would these prisoners have? Reminded her of Pargon. Reminded her of something else, too. Something she couldn't quite place. The moonlight burnt away. Men and women stared at them, spears raised high and glinting. She stiffened.

The man called out. "I have found more wayward brigands. Put your weapons down."

A voice drifted back. "The others were in 'tary garb, as is one of your girls."

How they could tell Cassidy wore a military uniform was beyond Mia. Cassidy's clothes had been torn, after all. But that person had spoken of others. Mia narrowed her eyes, trying to see past the light and strange people. There. Skyler, Will, and Jeff huddled inside a cage, if one could even call it that. It seemed to be a large storage pod, with four metal plating walls and a cover that faced out instead of up. The cover had been badly damaged, however. Burn marks blackened it and something had torn an entire section off the front, which now served as a hole for the prisoners to stare mournfully out of. Only Harrison lingered outside of it. He smiled and half waved. Cassidy grabbed Mia's arm. She had seen them.

"She is injured. We must help her." The man who saved them started into the camp.

"We cannot trust them, Clin. They could be spies."

The man who saved them—Clin—laughed. "Spying on what? A smuggler's camp hunkered down on a prison planet. What did they think we would do, start a Fissurian revolt?"

A what revolt? Mia took a step back. It felt like she had been punched in the gut. Recognition of Clin, this camp and it's glowing orbs, this planet Fissure finally dawned on her. Of course he seemed familiar.

He was the one who saved her so many cycles ago. The Peri family.

Clin Axion Peri interrupted her thoughts. "Besides, this young lady might as well be one of our own."

He pulled Mia in front of him and pushed her closer to the fire. Heat washed over her skin. At first, no one reacted, but Sheyla, Clin's wife, stumbled forward. Her dark dress was ripped at the hem, the torn fabric wrapped around her bare shoulder, a dark stain in the center of the cloth. "Mia? My little Mia."

Sheyla engulfed her in a bear hug. Surrounded by warmth, Mia instinctively buried her face into Sheyla's hair, not caring about the dirt clumped within it or what the others would think. Sheyla Peri had been like a mother to her for a little while, and tears tickled the back of Mia's eyes at the hug. She squeezed them shut, both to keep the tears from falling and to keep Sheyla from noticing how her eyes had unexpectedly changed color. When Mia met Sheyla's gaze, the woman grinned and pulled her deeper into the camp. Clin strode beside them. He wiped his face free of the grime and smiled at her. Of course it was Clin! He had the strongest arm on all of Fissure. Only he could've speared that wash in one throw. Worry niggled at the back of her mind over where Cassidy had disappeared to, but the footsteps treading close behind them had to belong to her.

They ended up beside the cage. A rusted locking mechanism twisted around the cover, securing it closed. Mia eyed her crew. Jeff and Will seemed fine, some scratches bled on their dark skin, nothing too deep. Skyler, it seemed, had suffered no injuries. Harrison stepped away from Clin, but the lackey didn't look scared. Awed, perhaps, would be the better description of the smile spreading across his face. Mia shot him a questioning glance, and Harrison didn't respond.

Jeff spoke up first. "And how was your adventure down to this lovely prison planet?"

Skyler waved that question away. "They're obviously okay. Did your pod disintegrate?"

"Cassidy's not okay." Will shoved a hand through the bars and pointed to Cassidy, who had just stepped up beside the cage.

"It's worse," Cassidy said, holding her arm.

Skyler frowned, her gaze locked onto the bandaged limb. "What happened?"

A crowd of smugglers huddled around them, forming a semi-circle around the cage. They watched their captives closely, as if haggard appearances and ripped outfits fascinated them in some way. Whispers floated like the slight drone of insects. Mia eyed them warily, but Sheyla glared at them and hugged Mia tighter. The woman knew no boundaries.

Cassidy, too, shuffled closer to Mia. "Can we just fix it, please?"

Mia disentangled herself from Sheyla's embrace and looked to Clin. "Why are they inside this cage? And why is Harrison outside of it?"

A gruff voice she didn't recognize came from the mass of people. "Jer Harrison is perfectly safe, even in the abhorrent garb the 'tary hands out these days, but we don't know the other three."

Mia cocked an eyebrow at Harrison again, and he whispered, "Later. We should get Skyler out, at least, so she can fix Cassidy's arm."

Of course, Mia agreed. She searched the faces of the crowd for one she recognized. None jumped out at her. Apparently, people had moved on from this little encampment, everyone except for Clin and Sheyla. A stab pinched her heart as she recalled their daughter, Viv. Had something happened to her? Perhaps later she could find out. She turned to Sheyla. "What'll it take for my friends to be released?"

Sheyla beamed and placed a thin hand atop Mia's shoulder. "Only the knowledge that they are your friends."

The woman nodded to the crowd. Clad in boots, thick pants, and a shirt made of shimmering scales, a girl freed herself and produced an older archivist from the folds of her clothes. She slipped between Mia and Clin and pressed a few buttons to unlock the cage.

Harrison scoffed. "I tried to tell them that, but they waved me away."

The girl turned, her long, blonde hair loosening from its bun. "Look at your garb, Harrison. We did not know if you changed your tack and flew that way. Mia would never do such a thing."

It took a few moments for Mia to recognize the girl. Barely over nineteen cycles old, her green eyes glimmered in the firelight and a mischievous smile played on her lips. "Viv?"

The girl nodded.

Mia gasped, and the pinching on her heart released. Relief filled her instead. "How have you gotten so blasted tall? The last time I saw you, you were up to my hip."

Viv Peri backed up and let the cage door swing wide. "That was ten cycles ago, Mi-mi."

Jeff clambered out of the cage and gave them both a smirk. "Yes. Come on now, Mi-mi, you don't want to upset our kind and gracious hosts, do you? Say hello to your old friends and let Skyler do her work."

Mia punched him on the shoulder. He rubbed the spot and made way for the others, dragging his brother with him. Clin motioned for the crowd to disperse. Where there once was silence, noises drifted from the huts, the hum of conversation, a musical tone heavy with drums, snorts of animals. Somewhere beyond the fires, a beast bellowed a cry into the night. Mia allowed herself a small smile.

Skyler made a straight line for Cassidy. The nurse shared a few quick words with Sheyla, who pointed them to the healing house, and Skyler pulled Cassidy toward it, both disappearing behind a bronze metal door. Last to exit the cage, Will didn't look in Mia's direction or thank Viv for letting him out. Instead, he lingered beside Jeff and Harrison. After a few concerned glances, they wandered toward the fire in the center of the encampment, their breath lagging like silver clouds behind them. The three Peri members gathered around Mia, smiling. It grew quiet. Closer to the fire, gray strands threaded the dark folds of Clin's hair and the firelight deepened the wrinkles on Sheyla's face, especially around her eyes and mouth. The woman's once bright-yellow hair had whitened to a quieter tone.

Mia nodded to the wound on Sheyla's arm. "Why don't you heal that up?"

Sheyla chuckled. "It is only a scratch. We use the healing hut for the worst of it and simply manage the rest."

Viv gave her a sideways hug, one Mia gratefully accepted. "So, it is just us four again, huh, Mi-mi? Nice contacts, by the way."

Mia slid past the comment. Let them believe her silver eyes were just a lie. "Has it really been ten cycles?"

"More! Ten and a half, at least." Clin thumped a hand on Mia's shoulder. She leaned into the hold. These people had helped her, left a soft spot on her soul.

"Too long." Sheyla's wide hazel eyes misted. "We are glad you have made it this far. We were worried about you, Mia."

Clin wrapped an arm around his wife's shoulders. "And not only us. After you left, everyone became concerned. You left under some questionable circumstances."

"I arrived under some questionable circumstances. I never would've survived that pirate attack if it weren't for you." Mia cringed at the memory, and at the necessity of continuing her lie. Pirates. Acedians, more lies. And the Acedians hadn't destroyed the *Scarlet*. She had. "I never would have gotten away from them if it weren't for you."

Guilt pressed in on her. She had already shaken the Acedians by the time she reached Fissure. It was the law Mia had to hide from. It was the law these smugglers helped her elude. Fitting.

Clin interrupted her thoughts. "The little shuttle you arrived in should still be in the crevasse, though in worse condition than when you first brought it to us."

The shuttle. Hope flared in Mia like a supernova, bursting to the tips of her fingers. Maybe they weren't stranded after all. "What happened to West?"

Clin's smile faded. "He died a few cycles back, a wash got him."

Mia didn't reply. Couldn't. The man had helped her smuggle onto the nutrition ship that got her off this rock. "When did they get so large?"

"The ones we let you see were only babies." Sheyla shifted closer, making the circle tighter, but Mia didn't mind. She welcomed their closeness. "We never let you near the adults."

Clin took a deep breath in before letting it go, seeming to think hard on something. He even scratched his chin, eyes shifting between Mia and his wife. "If you want, you can stay here for the time being."

Sheyla slapped her husband on the arm. "Of course, she will stay with us. Her friends, too. You can discuss the dilapidated shuttle in the morning. I will find a suitable dwelling for them to stay in. Viv, go see if we have anything left from dinner."

Viv nodded and scurried away, heading toward the outside of the encampment and vanishing inside one of the larger housing units. Clin cuffed Mia's back. "I will see you in the sunlight." He wandered off.

Sheyla smiled. "I will find you when I get a place ready, okay?"

Mia gave her a brief hug and a word of thanks and watched her walk away, in debt once again to the Peri family. Still, happiness spread within her like she had taken a heavy gulp of Paradousian tea. They had escaped the Acedians, Cassidy was being healed, and they had a place to stay the night, as well as a possible means of escape. She eyed the encampment, letting the memories flow into her. Clin had found her in the middle of the desert, beside a large crack in the dirt, a gash on her arm and tears in her eyes. He had brought her back to his home, to Sheyla and Viv, and taken care of her. Healed her. Folded her into their little family and taught her many things.

Clin taught her how to throw a spear. She was awful at it and got cut by a jagged edge that had not been properly wrapped. Viv cried at the sight, and Sheyla used the last of their gelion goo to keep infection away, even though the next shipment was a full month away. She'd always wondered where they were from originally, but Clin had never told her. She remembered discovering their formal speech patterns on another planet, Rhyada, and wondered if it was their home. A breeze chilled her skin, and the memories drifted away. Light glowed from each of the housing units, and snippets of quiet conversation filled the air. With the amount of people living here, they would be lucky to get a small living space. But a roof is a roof, regardless of the scraps it was made of, so Mia would be grateful either way. Harrison, Jeff, and Will stood next to a nearby fire, their expressions tense. She moved toward them.

"They have weapons and food and homes," Harrison spoke under his breath.

Will rubbed his neck and shifted slightly away from her. "I don't want to spend the rest of my life here."

Mia eyed the Dee brother. Will wasn't acting normal. Flashes of their fight on the Acedian ship darted through her. Of course he wouldn't act normal around her. She'd attacked him, punched him while under Donavin's control, and now her eyes had that Acedian glint. She'd have to stop this fear before it spread too far into the rest of the crew.

Jeff leaned closer to the flames, stretching his hands out to warm them. "We won't. I'm sure there's a way off this rock."

"Before the Acedians get us again?" Will looked at his brother, his dark profile stark against the flames. "Besides, I don't trust these people."

Mia drew up beside Jeff. "You shouldn't trust most of them. They're thieves and smugglers. This is a prison planet, after all. You can trust the Peris, though. They're good people. And Harrison even knows some folks here, too, apparently, though I don't know how."

Harrison sputtered and coughed. "Some of them are trustworthy. Still, I don't want to be here if the Acedians come."

"We'll be off this planet before that happens." Mia would make sure of it. She'd protect the Peri family like they had protected her so long ago. It struck her hard that she couldn't recognize Clin under all that dirt, that she had forgotten this planet. Even though she had only spent a short while here, they had connected quickly. Mia had only been fifteen. She had just lost Freya, just destroyed her second ship. She had been lost, and the Peri family had found her.

"How?" Jeff asked.

"I have a shuttle on this planet," she muttered, thinking back to the tiny shuttle she stole from the *Scarlet* in her getaway. "We might be able to use it to escape."

Harrison folded his arms across his chest, scoffing. "How do you know it's still there? What if someone else decided to use it?"

"Clin and Sheyla hid it for me. I told them they could escape if they wanted to, but at that time, they had Viv to think about. She was young. She didn't know what her parents had done. She didn't even know this rock was a prison-grade planet. They didn't want to tell her back then, wanted her to have a normal life and all. Or something of a normal life. Besides, people on this planet don't just get up and leave. So they stayed. The shuttle is probably in horrible condition." She looked at Jeff.

The flames deepened the shadows under his eyes. "Maybe I can fix it."

Mia hoped he could for all of their sakes. But even she was doubtful, it had been ten cycles after all. "Until then, we'll have a place to stay, reorganize, let Cassidy heal before jettisoning off again."

As if she had heard her name, Cassidy barged into the conversation, wrapping one arm around Mia's neck and flourishing the other over the fire. She beamed. "I don't need to heal anymore."

Mia had stumbled slightly under Cassidy's weight but held true and stared at the woman hanging off her. She pulled Cassidy's arm away from the flames. Not possible. Yet, as Mia searched her friend's arm for evidence of the injury, she found none. Cassidy's pale skin had some pink discoloration, but she could circle her wrist and flex her fingers without cringing. The fracture seemed entirely healed.

"The healing tech did all this?" Mia muttered, remembering the shiny surfaces. It was where Clin had removed her ID chip. Where Sheyla had healed her wounds.

"It did." Skyler moved into the fire's glow and glanced at Cassidy. "I healed most of her hurts, except the smaller ones. I didn't want to use up all their power supply. I didn't know about their tech, so I gave her some medication to ward off the pain at first. I might have overestimated how much she needed."

Mia inspected Cassidy. True to Skyler's word, most of the bigger wounds had been healed, but the one on Cassidy's cheek still had a thin layer of liquid atop the cut.

Cassidy's smile grew wider, her brown eyes brightened by the flames, apparent happiness, or drugs. "What's the plan now?"

Sheyla appeared beside Mia, placing a hand on her arm and eyeing Cassidy as well. "You will stay the night. I have made a place ready."

The slender woman motioned them to follow and ambled away from the fire. They passed a small group of housing units, a pen full of squat, scaled creatures Mia couldn't quite remember, and a large, open space fenced by stones. Many of the homes had gone dark, and conversation had died down. Mia's team were all responding differently to the encampment. The brothers stepped softly, Skyler seemed unimpressed, and Harrison strode around as if he knew the place by heart. Cassidy teetered this way and that, grinning at the people and peering intently at the animals. Waving at nothing. Finally, Mia wrapped a hand around her wrist, pulling her along with the rest of the group. They passed a few more pens before stopping at a moderately sized dwelling.

Sheyla pushed open the door, a scrap of metal emblazed with the Vespa crest. "It will be cramped. We have added extra beds, and there is food on the table." She looked at each of them in turn, stopping at Mia. "Make sure you remember the snakes, Mia, they are still as dangerous as ever. I will see you in the sunlight. Sleep well."

Sheyla smiled and disappeared into the darkness, much like her husband had done. Mia entered the one-room dwelling first, eyeing the glowing orb on the center of the table. She'd spent many nights up with a light like this one, haunted by nightmares. It gave off a dim white light, just enough for her to see. Mia barely walked four steps, before her boot hit the corner of the beds. Six simple cots had been set out for them. Each had a blanket set on one edge and a pillow at the other. Their heads were meant to be together, their feet, to the walls. Mia turned to call the others in, but her breath caught. For being such a meager resting place, they'd gone to the stars and back with the food. An entire spread—smoked meats, spiny green vegetables, and multicolored fruit, enough to feed ten people not six—had been set out. Next to it, an older-style water purifier boiled away, and a cup of mineral crystals sparkled next to it. It was common knowledge that the water on Fissure wasn't safe to drink until properly sanitized and mineralized. Even then, some folks had digestive issues. Metal cups and plates were piled on one side of the table.

She picked up a strip of meat. "Come see this."

The others crowded inside. Cassidy threw herself onto one of the cots and pulled the blanket around herself. Will did the same.

Harrison eyed the food. "Will it go bad if we don't eat it?"

Mia popped the piece of meat in her mouth and chewed. Spices and smoke hit her at once. "It doesn't taste bad, if that's what you're worried about."

The four of them tried out the different foods. Mia found she preferred the spiced meat over the hard spines of the vegetables, and the fruit over everything else. She remembered the sweet and sour tastes, so distant yet still familiar on her tongue. Most of the meal disappeared within moments. She poured them all cups of the heated water, dropping a mineral crystal in each one before handing them out. Taking a sip, the heat and metallic taste hit her at once. Mia smiled. Even this was just how she remembered it.

Jeff lingered by the door, munching on the last piece of smoked meat, and stared out into the darkness. "Do you think it's safe to sleep here?"

Even in the low light, Mia noticed the shadows under his eyes. "Yes," she said firmly. They had nothing to fear from these people, not with the Peri family here.

Jeff looked to Harrison. "You said only some were trustworthy, but are all of them trustworthy enough to not attack while we sleep?"

Harrison swallowed a mouthful of food. "They're smugglers. Yes, they've been known to knife people when threatened, but we're not much of a threat. Tired to the bone, clothes ripped to Helix. We probably wouldn't scare a Puruvian fly right now."

Mia chuckled. "The worst we'll have to worry about are silver snakes. If you see one, don't touch it."

Both Jeff and Skyler stared at her, although Harrison nodded vigorously.

"Are they poisonous or something?" Cassidy mumbled from her bed.

"No, they'll shock you to death," Mia replied.

At that, both Cassidy and Will sat up. Will shoved the blanket off the bed and shook his pillow out, eyes wide as saucers. "What kind of messed up planet has land-dwelling electric snakes?"

"They aren't natural." Harrison chuckled at Will's startled reaction, answering before Mia could. "They're mechanical. This is a prison planet, and those silver snakes are the way the government keeps track of the prisoners. Each encampment probably has about twenty or so."

"Shouldn't we worry that they'll see us?" Skyler asked.

Mia shook her head. "We found out a long time ago that the snakes only transmit once a month as this is a lower-level prison planet. On Helix or one of the other higher levels, they do daily and sometimes hourly transmissions. On Fissure they do it less so."

"How'd they figure that out?" Will asked, settling back down on his cot.

"One of the prisoners opened one up. They tried again soon after, but the government had equipped them with electricity. Shocked a man, named Orin, to death." Mia yawned, covering it with her hand. "The prisoners left them alone after that. And tomorrow, we'll be dressed like the others anyway, so it'll be harder for them to recognize newcomers."

Will looked like he wanted to say more but Skyler interjected, "Sleep the night. We'll see what we can do tomorrow."

Will frowned, wilting onto the cot next to his brother. With that settled, Mia ran a thumb over the orb's surface to turn it off, plucked a piece of violet fruit from the bowl, and plopped down next to Cassidy. Mia intended to give the sweet fruit to her, but Cassidy responded with a snore. Harrison yawned loudly and claimed the cot on Jeff's other side. Skyler curled up on the far one.

Mia sat on her bed, the one closest to the door and between Cassidy and Skyler. She unfolded the blanket and settled down. The bed sagged under her weight, probably filled with dirt, feathers, and anything else soft they could find. The housing units weren't that sophisticated. Weren't meant to be long term. After the day she'd just had, though, she could sleep anywhere. "Tomorrow you're going to tell me how you know these people, Harrison."

His reply came slowly and muffled. "And you'll do the same."

Just before sleep pulled her under, Mia thought she heard him say something else. She heard her name echo in her head.

Mia.

Chapter Four

THE NEXT MORNING DAWNED bright and hot. Their quarters provided little fresh air or relief from the stifling heat. The door, shoved wide open, didn't bring even the slightest breeze. Mia wiped her forehead and struggled to a sitting position. Already, the air shimmered with heat. Red dust caked one arm, probably from the travel here. She rubbed it off, remembering how everything seemed to stain red from the planet's dusty surface. She surveyed the others. Will snored in his corner, Jeff was sprawled on his back, and Cassidy still lay curled under the covers. Harrison had disappeared, but he seemed to know these people well enough so Mia tried not to worry, much. Skyler stirred. Footsteps crunching outside the door seemed to wake her. She sat up, her eyes narrowing at the doorway and the dual suns beyond.

A shadow appeared. "It would be best if you did not wear your 'tary uniforms." Sheyla's broad smile and sure posture—one hand on her hip, the other grasping a bundle of drab clothing—came into view. "I do not expect you to stay long, if you can help it, but you will not make any friends out here with those colors."

Mia stood and accepted the new clothes. "Thank you."

Sheyla patted her hand. "Breakfast is in the common area. As you remember, I hope."

"I do. I'll have to wake the rest of the crew," Mia murmured.

Sheyla gathered the empty dishes from the night before and left. Mia grinned, catching Sheyla's soft hum. Apparently, she couldn't turn off her mothering instinct. An ache threatened to form within Mia's heart, but she pushed it away. No time to dwell on impossible things. She dropped the bundle of red-stained clothes onto her cot and sifted through them, dividing them and chuckling at the color. Skyler got up and grabbed a new shirt, slipping out of the bloodied one she wore and into the fresh, short-sleeved attire.

Mia handed her the matching pants, and Skyler winked. "I know you'd love to watch, but my bottom's fine. Thanks, though." Cassidy stirred, stretching her arms and yawning as she rose. A smile spread across Skyler's face. "It looks like Cassidy has to change her entire outfit. Don't ogle too much, Captain."

Mia ignored the jibe and tossed clothes to Cassidy, as the nurse sashayed out. No need to get caught up in Skyler's games. Yet heat rose along Mia's neck, as Cassidy slipped out of her ruined pants. A familiar kick jarred Mia's stomach. Tightening her jaw, she willed herself to look away, changing her outfit as well. The rough material scratched her legs and arms.

"You can turn around now."

The laughter in Cassidy's voice resounded in Mia's ears. She turned back around, the blush spreading to her cheeks. "Was I that obvious?"

Cassidy gave her a soft smile, though it didn't entirely reach her eyes. "No, you are now, though." She attempted to smooth the rumpled fabric covering her shoulders. "Not the most comfortable thing, but it'll have to do."

Mia scratched her thigh. The fabric itched like crazy. "Shall we extend this lovely experience to the men?"

Cassidy gave a flourish with her hand. "Of course."

After the brothers woke, Mia and Cassidy joined Skyler outside. Cassidy went straight for Skyler, extending her healed arm to the nurse. Mia watched her go, a warm feeling spreading through her system. There was a good rapport between her and Cassidy just then. Familiar. Nice. And for a moment, Mia forgot why they had been off to begin with. Then the cold reminded her, resting under her skin, waiting to be used. The cold behind her eyes pulsed, and she blinked the pain away.

The brothers emerged moments later, Jeff still yawning and rubbing his eyes. Will glared at the dirt. It seemed his mood hadn't shifted from the night before. She made a note to talk to him in private. Sooner rather than later. Mia led the way to the common area. The place had grown since she last landed, but the food had always been easy to find. Following the steady chatter, they wound their way to the center of the encampment. The people they passed stared, gawking as if Mia and her crew were blue-skinned aliens. Mia straightened her shoulders and met each of them in the eye. It dawned on her later that perhaps that was a reason they stared.

The jumble of housing units opened into the large space from the night before. People pressed in on one another, forming a dense crowd, and the conversation droned, filling the space even more. It seemed as if the entire population inhabited the area. Makeshift benches of wood circled halved tree-trunk tables laid out on the dirt. Mia and her crew moved closer, winding their way through the crowded space.

"These people are resourceful," Jeff muttered, eyeing the wooden chairs. They could've used metal but that was better suited for houses and any makeshift tech they could create. Like the farming equipment used to plant and gather foods. Still, Mia remembered when a splinter had entered her skin in the most unfortunate of places and she winced, hoping the wood had smoothened over time.

Harrison came into view, dressed in similar attire. He chatted with Viv, laughing at something. When he saw them, he made his way over. Mia worked her way through the mob of people seizing hunks of dark bread, snatching purple fruit out from other's hands, and sloshing green juice onto the table. Smugglers and thieves didn't take food lightly or spare time on polite words. A water purifier billowed in between it all, dumping out clean, if terribly hot, water to any who wanted it. She pushed her way through the crowd to the disintegrator pouring out a grain mixture, scooped some of it into a bowl, and topped it with the closest fruit she could see—curved and bright pink in color. Tanti, if she remembered correctly, a fruit that grew wild here. Her crew barreled their way in behind her.

A stranger in ratty, unwashed clothing pushed her back, a too-friendly hand grazing her side and rear. She glared at the intruder with his unkempt beard, heavily tanned and wrinkled skin, and deep-set, pale-blue eyes. The man moved away. An overwhelming stench of sweat went with him.

Mia.

Mia looked around, scanning the faces of the crowd. Had someone called her name? Her crew seemed busy but one of them could've. Or the Acedians could be close. A tingle raced down her back. No, her hand felt fine, and only her own thoughts drifted in her mind. They couldn't have repaired their ship and found her already. She pushed her fear away.

Mia shoved her way out of the mass, ignoring the grumbles of the strangers she pushed past, and found a few spots at the edge of a table. She plunked her bowl down, sat, and dug into her meal. The grains had little taste, and the overripe, sweet tanti fell apart in her hands, but she scraped them both clean. Will slipped down next to her, still determinedly not looking in her direction. The treatment hurt, although Mia understood. After breakfast, she'd talk with him. Quietly, outside the other's reach. They had a good friendship, and she didn't want to lose that to Donavin too. She wouldn't.

Jeff tossed a chunk of bread onto Mia's plate and set down a metal cup of hot water, a mineral crystal sparkling and melting inside it. "Thought you might want some." He slapped his brother on the back. "Move over."

Will didn't move. He stared at his food, his hunk of bread uneaten. A large crack spidered on the edge of his metal plate. He kept his head down, eyes on the bread, thoughts obviously elsewhere.

Jeff shrugged and settled down. He gnawed on his piece of bread, crumbs and seeds falling onto his plate, but his gaze had left his brother and strayed to Harrison instead, who claimed the seat across from him. A tall, skinny man stopped by and clapped Harrison on the shoulder. Harrison grinned, shaking his hand, and opened his mouth to speak. Then, he clamped his mouth shut, simply nodded at the stranger, and turned back to the table in silence. He ducked his head, mixing some grains in his bowl, a blush coloring his cheeks.

Cassidy and Skyler joined them, both bringing plates heaped with fruit and greens, but when they sat down, they looked at Harrison. Curiosity sparked in Cassidy's eyes, and a smirk lingered on Skyler's lips. A fog of silence descended on the group, and Harrison seemed determined not to meet their eyes.

"How do you know these people, Harrison?" Mia asked, frowning. Blunt, sure. They all knew that now wasn't the time to be polite.

Harrison scratched his ear and popped a handful of green berries into his mouth. He chewed a bit before answering. "I wasn't the picture-perfect child growing up."

Jeff snorted. Cassidy shushed him.

Harrison took another mouthful of berries. "My parents were good people—strong, determined, loving. We had a good life and a good house and good values. But I'm an only child. The last to carry the family name and all that, and my father...he took it upon himself to make sure nothing ever happened to me, set down plenty of rules and curfews."

He gave his plate a goofy lopsided grin, and a lock of dark, curly hair brushed over his forehead. "I didn't like that much, so I acted out. I was young and idiotic. I thought it would be fun to steal things. At first it was just sweets from stores, but it escalated. The man who just stopped by, Oin, he and I became friends, kind of, and he introduced me to the rest of his gang. We smuggled wiring, engine parts, anything we could get our hands onto, really."

Mia's eyes widened at the story. She couldn't believe it. The admiral's lackey was a thief? In a million cycles, she would've never guessed it. Tearing off a piece of dark bread, she popped it into her mouth, listening.

Harrison shoved his plate away. "We actually tried to pinch an entire fuse cell out the back door of a local garage. They caught us, and we were thrown on Fissure. My dad bought me out and sent me to the military. Oin had to stay here."

Jeff sputtered, crumbs flying from his mouth. "Your dad forced you into the military? That's five cycles."

Harrison lifted his gaze and met Jeff's eyes, a smile still playing on his lips. "It was supposed to be punishment, but I ended up loving the military guard. I can never thank him enough for pushing me to join. That's why, when my military time was up, I became a Paradousian guard."

Rubbing a hand over his face, Jeff glanced at his brother. "The worst our old man ever made me do was clean latrines."

"But you had to do it often," Will muttered. He seemed to rouse himself from his thoughts to listen, eyes bright with interest.

Harrison chuckled and leaned forward, arms resting on the table. "Did you ever steal anything, though?"

Jeff laughed. "No, although I did talk back to Dad every once in a while. He'd smack me upside the head so hard my ears would ring for weeks."

With the story ended, Cassidy pushed a few pieces of greenery around on her plate, and Skyler tasted the juice, made a face, and set her cup back down. Mia stared at Harrison, still in shock that he had once been a thief. The admiral's lackey. Somehow, Mia was oddly inspired by him. He had a troubled past. He had made mistakes—not nearly as big as hers, but mistakes nonetheless—and he had changed his life for the better. Exactly what Mia wanted to do. Was striving to do. But Harrison, a thief? What was Jeff going to reveal, that he was a con man now? Did Will have a rocky past? Will. She pushed her plate away, intending on talking to him now that their meal had ended. A shadow fell over the table.

"If you want to go to your shuttle, come with me." Clin's voice hardened. "If we dawdle, the winds will be too heavy over the crevasse for us to manage."

After a few more quick bites, they stood. Cassidy gathered the used dishes, looking around for a place to put them, but Clin put a hand on hers. "Leave them on the table. We have a cleaning crew to take care of it."

Cleaning crew? That was different. They had done it themselves the last time Mia was here. He searched the crowd, signaled someone Mia couldn't see, and wound his way through the mass of people. She shrugged and went after him. Things had changed, and Mia wasn't quite sure how she felt about it yet.

They found Clin by the edge of camp, lacing his dark boots tighter around his ankles with something that didn't look like string. Intestines, if Mia remembered correctly. He swung a pack over his back, tightened the knots under his arms, and grabbed a red spear from the multicolored collection poking up from the dirt nearby. He tilted his head toward the weapons. "You should take one. It is prime hunting season out there."

Skyler and Jeff stepped forward, each one yanking the biggest spears from the dirt. Harrison and Cassidy chose smaller, narrower spikes. Will didn't select a weapon. Mia eyed the spears and chose the one nearest to her. The rusted, yellow metal felt heavy in her hand. Not a gun or a knife, but at least something. She offered it to Will. "You should take it."

Will didn't reply, moving away from her and toward Jeff instead.

"Your choice," she muttered, grimacing at his back. The rejection stung. She had to make him see that she didn't mean, or want, to attack them. She hadn't meant to hurt him. Not Will. Not any of them. Until they could talk one on one, maybe it was best to give him some distance.

Clin lifted his voice. "Anyone who wants to come to the crevasse is welcome. We leave now."

A few men joined them. They chose weapons and slung packs onto their backs before turning to Clin. He waited a few more moments before starting off toward the suns. The small group fell into step behind him, keeping their eyes shaded, flat ground providing little break to rest their gaze. Puffs of dirt rose up from beneath their trampling boots. Snippets of conversations floated toward Mia, but she tried to ignore them. Rumors about where she had come from didn't concern her. The constant humming from Jeff did, however. He never hummed back on the *Eclipse*. Now it seemed he had a tune stuck in his head. An annoying one, at that.

Harrison nudged her. "So, how about you, Mia? How do you know these folks?"

Her breath hitched. Of course he'd ask her. It was only fair after all. Should she be honest, though? It took her less than a heartbeat to realize, yes. Letting the rest of the group get a little farther away, she motioned her own crew closer. Even Will shuffled over, but he still didn't look at her. She whispered the story of landing on Fissure to escape the Acedians and how she had been able to smuggle off the planet, because the thieves didn't think she belonged anyway.

"Do you think it's weird that Clin asked others to join us where we'll find the shuttle?" Jeff asked, staring at the group ahead of them. "Wouldn't that mean others would know where it is?"

"It's common to go to the crevasse to hunt wash. The smaller ones are dumb and sometimes they fall in. Easy prey after that. Clin wouldn't have told the others about the shuttle," Mia said firmly.

In the midst of this conversation, an older man, Suli, she recognized him instantly as a man she had tricked trying to get away from the Acedians, leaned over and interrupted her. "How is the *Eclipse*? The old bird still flying?"

Mia.

She shuddered, as Suli leaned in closer. Of course he'd said her name. He wrapped an arm around her shoulders and a waft of oil engulfed her. She winced. Her group didn't know about the true origins of the *Eclipse*, but Suli waited for an answer. His black eyes glinted, and his thin, white hair stuck to his head, showing a patch of bald that hadn't been there before.

"The *Eclipse* is flying fine," she replied in a soft voice.

He laughed. Too loud. "Good, that old girl barely made it into atmo. We flew her right under her captain's nose and he didn't even recognize her, remember?"

Cassidy gasped, slapping a hand over her mouth to cover the noise. She kept her hand pressed there. Mia's ears burned, though she focused on Suli and not her crew. Yet another lie. Another thing to explain to them. "Yes, yes, I do remember."

"It's good seeing you." He squeezed her once more and let go. "Give the old bird a kiss for me, will ya?"

Mia nodded as Suli left and turned back to her crew. She expected them to be shocked, but they weren't. None of her crewmates seemed moved at all by the news of the *Eclipse*. Or the fact that she wasn't a true captain. Skyler shrugged, and Will rolled his eyes. Jeff stared at the skyline. Had they already known? And, if so, when had they found out? Then she looked at Cassidy. The hurt in her eyes was undeniable, shimmering in the light of two rising suns.

Cassidy moved past Mia, eyes to the dirt, and bumped into Suli, who had stopped only a few paces away. She muttered a sorry, but Suli didn't appear to hear her. It seemed no one heard. The group ahead of them had stopped and were busy staring at the skyline. No, not at the skyline, at the creature loping toward them, roaring. As big as the one by the lake, this wash was still squinting distance away. It came closer, hefting its thundering weight over the dirt, sending clouds of dust behind. The group didn't raise their weapons, though, or prepare in any way. They merely watched and waited. The wash disappeared, hissing and spitting. The sound could be heard for a few heartbeats, then nothing.

"Where'd it go?" Cassidy asked, looking back to Mia.

The men chuckled, and Clin answered. "Into the crevasse. It must have been old, forgetful. Come, we are close, as well."

We're coming for you.

Heart skittering, Mia grabbed Clin's arm. "Wait."

"Why?" He turned to her, signaling the others to stop.

"I thought I heard," Mia faltered. Thoughts had intruded in her head three times. Maybe four. But where were the other voices? Her thoughts felt too heavy to vocalize. It couldn't be them. Not him. Not Donavin. It just couldn't. Not so soon. She shook her head, let go of Clin's arm, and ignored the questioning looks of her crew.

Clin gave her a searching look. "Are you afraid of going back?"

"Afraid?" Mia tilted her head. *Why would I be afraid of the crevasse?*

"It was where I found you that night, after all. There is no shame in being scared," Clin said, his voice gentling to a quieter tone. He had incorrectly assumed why Mia had stopped, though she appreciated it all the same. Yes, he had found her next to the crevasse but he had saved her, and that's what she remembered most about this place. Not the pain. Not the fear. Rather the hope he and the entire Clin family had given her.

She gave him a smile. "I know. I'll be fine. Let's go."

They walked a few more paces, and the ground before them vanished into a steep decline. The crack spanned miles in either direction, gaping and wide. Rocks jutted from the walls and boulders lay on the bottom. The fallen wash lay on its back at the base.

Clin began his descent, picking his way across the rocks. Soon he touched the bottom. His men followed, as did Mia, but her crew took their time navigating the steep terrain. Relief swept through her when her boots hit level ground, and she breathed easily. The descent seemed far simpler than she'd expected. Climbing the cliff, wind and dirt whipping her face, and the warm hand of Clin floated to the surface of her mind. She lingered on them for a moment, allowed that warm memory to rest in her, before gently pushing it back. The rest of her crew appeared beside her, breathing hard.

Only Skyler seemed undeterred by the descent. She wiped some sweat off her brow. "Kind of warm down here, huh?"

Mia smiled, but she didn't think so at all. She shivered, cold dripping down her spine. A warning sign, of course. Something weighed down her attention. Made it hard to think. Still, she didn't want to bring it up. Not yet. She had to be sure before scaring the others.

Boulders rose high above them. The dirt here seemed wetter, the air fresher. Green plants sprinkled the base of the cliffs, ones Mia recalled tasted like pepper. She had helped to gather them once. Clin motioned for his men to take the south side, muttering to a few of them. His men nodded and wandered away, spears raised. Hunting something. Mia watched them for a little while, making sure none of them would go north to the shuttle, and she searched for Clin. He had vanished, probably assuming she'd remember where the shuttle landed. Thankfully, after all these cycles, she did. She motioned for Jeff to come along, and they wound their way deeper into the crevasse, heading north and into a more dangerous area that few, if any, dared to travel.

The rock walls narrowed. A section of the wall had caved in, forming a natural tunnel. The narrow walls opened again, and there lay the shuttle, still tucked behind a boulder where she'd left it. Vines grew around the engine coils, the narrowed bow jutted into the dirt, and rust covered the once-polished oval sides. Mia had always been fond of the shuttle, its metal red instead of the common silver or gray, its design simple, yet sturdy. Whatever hardships she had undergone on the *Scarlet*, nothing could compare to her shuttle. It had led her to safety, after all.

Clin stood beside the V-class shuttle and patted it. "I could not fix her. No one comes down this way far enough to see her either, so she has been safe as can be."

Mia turned to Jeff, but she moved slow, too slow, as if through a thick liquid rather than air. "Can you repair it?"

Jeff moved closer to the ship, leaning down to inspect it.

I've found you, Mia.

Mia jerked her head around, looking for the source. Nothing besides dirt, heat, and sky stared back, though Clin did tilt his head at her. The heaviness within her mind lifted, and she grabbed Jeff's arm, hauling him out of earshot of Clin. "We need to leave."

Jeff shook his arm loose. "What are you talking about? We came here to fix the shuttle."

"No, we need to leave." Mia lowered her voice. That last intrusion solidified her decision. She had to tell them. Right now. "They're coming."

Jeff rubbed his neck and gave her a look of disbelief, eyebrows arching to nearly his hairline. "Donavin's found us already?"

"I'm hearing their voices again." Mia tapped her forehead. She instantly regretted it, because even that light touch caused a spike of pain in her head.

"How's that possible? We just left them yesterday! They couldn't have rebuilt their ship so soon." Jeff words tumbled from him, stopping just as suddenly. He looked toward the tunnel then back at her. "Does Skyler hear them?"

Mia's chest tightened. Didn't he believe her? "I don't know."

"Well, ask her," Jeff replied. "I'll stay with this shuttle. It may be the best chance we have to get out of here."

Mia started to say more when a familiar scream shattered their conversation, coming from the south. Coming from where Mia had left the rest of her crew behind. Had left Cassidy behind.

Chapter Five

MIA GRASPED THE STONES, scrabbling for purchase as she raced through the tunnel. Jeff was close on her heels. Cold ebbed from her stomach, and she let it course through her body. Her breathing slowed. Her speed picked up. She burst out the other side. Cassidy stood, spear raised, tip pointing at the wash standing before her. The beast blocked the rest of the crevasse from view. It roared, but a javelin pierced its neck, finishing its cry. The creature tumbled to the ground. Mia followed the trajectory back to Skyler's outstretched hand only a few paces away.

Skyler narrowed her eyes at Mia, and her thoughts entered Mia's mind through their shared Acedian link. *You look paler than usual. Are you okay?*

Mia ignored the question, as the cold ebbed away. She trusted Clin's men would be more concerned with the fallen wash. "Have you heard the Acedians?"

"No," Skyler rushed up next to her and grabbed her arm, staring hard at Mia's face. "Have you?"

Clin's voice burst into their conversation. "That was quite a shot." He walked over to Skyler and cuffed her on the back. Cassidy had rushed over to them, too. Worry crinkled her forehead, and she drew her arm closer to her body as if on instinct, even though it was healed. Mia's heart cracked a little at the sight.

"Thanks," Skyler muttered, glancing at them before smiling at Clin.

He laughed. "You would be a marksman on this planet if you stayed long enough."

The men rounded on Skyler, pushing Clin away to shake her hand. She politely nodded to each of them in turn, clearly not wanting to be involved.

Jeff leaned onto Mia's shoulder, whispering, "I'd like to get started on the shuttle."

Both Jeff and Will started back down the tunnel, but Mia wanted her crew close. Her heart thudded against her chest. She grabbed onto Jeff's arm, holding him in place. Will stopped, glaring at the ground. The brothers frowned at her, shifting their gazes to Skyler. Cassidy stood next to the nurse and bit her lip, scuffing her boot on the dirt. It slowly dawned on Mia that none of them believed her.

I'm closer, Mia.

Sweat dripped down Mia's back, even though she felt colder than she had in days. Dizziness overtook her, her vision blurring. She struggled to shake it off and slowly, slowly, her sight cleared. It wasn't possible. She couldn't turn into one of them. Not now. A hand pressed on her arm. Skyler's hand.

"Mia and I need to go to the healing hut." Skyler looked at the rest of the crew and emphasized her next words. "It's probably just a false alarm, but we've been through a lot and I'd like to get her checked out. I'd like to get everyone checked out."

Clin tilted his head at Mia. "She does look a bit off. Even so, we need all the help we can get gathering supplies."

Off? Mia cringed. *Yeah, my eyes are silver. Clin didn't mention that, though.*

"I can stay," Cassidy said. "Will and Harrison can stay as well."

Mia wanted to say no. Wanted her crew to stick together. Wanted to do more. Couldn't. The heaviness returned.

Will stared at the wash. "As long as there're no more creatures waiting for us."

"It is astounding that the beast survived." Clin nodded to the creature and turned to Skyler. "Take her back."

"Thank you." She linked her arm through Mia's and started the ascent up the rock wall. They climbed, Skyler helping Mia more than Mia wanted. But each time she tried to shake Skyler's hand off her shoulder or back, the dizziness would return. Eventually, Mia accepted the help. They reached the top of the crevasse in record time.

"Be lucky I'm not carrying you out," Skyler muttered.

How are you feeling, Mia?

The thought, not her own and certainly not Skyler's, skittered across her mind. Mia couldn't concentrate. Her thoughts swarmed around the Acedians. What would she do on this rock if the Acedians found them? How would her crew survive? She glanced at Skyler. "You're sure you haven't heard them? At all?" Worry pitched her voice higher than its normal tone.

"Yes, Mia." Skyler smirked. "If I heard them, I would've said something. Now stop asking, try not to think about this planet or these people, and I'll help you as soon as we get to the hut, okay?"

Mia scoffed. How could she not think about her situation? She tried to calm her anxiety, breathing in and out, counting to five each time. Her muscles still tensed as they made their way over the flat ground and back to the encampment. They would be easy targets in such an open space. Skyler marched with confident footsteps through the camp, tilting her head in greeting when Sheyla waved. She opened the door to the healing hut for Mia, who shuffled inside trying desperately not to think.

Polished metal and clean surfaces dominated the small space. Tables lined one wall, cluttered with helioguns and white cloth. Cabinets spanned the three other walls, stretching from the floor to the ceiling. A hint of antiseptic floated in the air, stinging Mia's nose. Skyler motioned for her to sit on the gurney in the center, and she settled down on the small metal stool next to the bed. As soon as Mia sat, the dizziness slowly drifted away. She raised her hand to her forehead and pushed against the clammy skin, trying to banish it completely.

All business, Skyler turned to Mia. "What has Donavin been saying?"

I've found you. Donavin whispered.

Mia clasped her hands over her lap to stop herself from pushing them against her ears. "That he's coming to get me, that he's found me, found us, again."

Skyler nodded. "It's a way to spin you around. They haven't found us."

Mia's fists tightened. "How do you know?"

Skyler gave her a sad smile. "They would've already attacked if they knew where we were."

Her logic made sense, but Mia pushed further. "Why is he speaking to me?"

"He's not speaking to you exactly. It's a technique he uses to get under a runner's skin. Essentially, he sends a blanket message in the direction his intended target ran and hopes that they'll respond."

"Which I haven't," Mia quickly replied. Her stomach churned. If she led them here in any way, she'd never forgive herself.

Skyler leaned forward. "Or focus on where they are at the moment, delivering the necessary information back to him. That's why you shouldn't think too much about this planet or how we got here."

Impossible. Mia slumped forward. "How do I not think about this planet?"

"Focus on us instead," Skyler replied, gesturing to herself. "He'll keep on intruding. He already knows your so-called crew, so it won't help him. If you really need to, maybe think about how you stole the *Eclipse*. It's new information, though not something he can use."

Skyler's jibe didn't help Mia's attitude. But Skyler didn't seem terribly bothered that Mia wasn't a real captain. That just gave Mia more fuel to be annoyed. If only her other friends felt the same way.

Your crew no longer trusts you, Mia. They can't help you now.

Mia chewed her lip. "Is there any way to stop him?"

Skyler's attitude shifted. Her gaze drifted to the metal plating beneath them, and she took a deep breath before answering. "There is a way to block him. It's hard. Took me a few cycles to learn."

Don't get your hopes up.

"Show me."

"It's called containment." She flipped open her pocket and scattered some orange coins on the gurney. "Imagine yourself. Your thoughts are here." She pushed some coins outward. "Your memories are here." She slid a few coins to the other side. "You're spread out and looking at it through an enemy's eyes, a hunter's eyes, what do you see?"

Mia surveyed the coins. "Easy targets to pick off, one after the other."

"Yes. Donavin's the hunter. He wants to pick you apart, remove you, so he can make you into a drone. In order to stop it..." She gathered the coins together in a heap and traced her finger in a circle around the pile. "You contain yourself. And create a barrier to stop him. You can imagine a container or a pouch, anything to stop him from getting you. Personally, I put up walls. And I can show you how."

The next few hours passed quietly and quickly. Skyler tried to teach her how to block Donavin's attacks. Locking eyes with Mia, Skyler would concentrate on the link, forcing memory after memory to surface in her mind. Mia would try to stop Skyler by containing herself, pulling all her memories and thoughts into one location and imagining a wall to stop her. Skyler burrowed into Mia's head again and again. All of her walls fell. After ten, twenty, thirty failed attempts, Mia shook her head. Tiredness leeched her concentration. She tightened her grasp on the gurney until her hands shook.

Skyler put a hand on Mia's arm and gave it a reassuring squeeze. "It's frustrating, I know. But at least you feel frustrated."

"Why do you keep saying that?" Anger flared within her. Goosebumps raced up her skin, and she pulled away.

Skyler winced. "That's another technique Donavin uses."

"He turns off emotions," Mia said. "I know. He showed me. He's too far away to do it now, right?"

"He showed you?" Skyler's eyes widened.

"Yes, on the ship. Somehow he turned off…me. All my emotions, gone, my feelings for certain people, wiped away, even my anger disappeared." The air inside the healing hut became colder. Mia tightened her hold on the gurney. Pain flared in her fingers, but she wanted that. It helped her hold onto herself. "It would've been frightening had I been able to feel fear at the time."

Skyler leaned back. "He uses the bots to redirect the electrical system in the brain, shutting down the hippocampus, prefrontal cortex, amygdala—"

Mia released her hold and slammed her fist onto the surface instead. "I don't care how he does it. I just want to know how to stop it."

"He might be close enough to stop some emotions from processing," Skyler whispered.

Mia jumped up, pacing now. The hairs on the back of her neck rose. She pressed them down with a furious rub. "So, there's a chance I might just stop feeling all of a sudden?"

"Yes."

The simple answer made Mia angrier. "What else happens?"

"I don't know." Skyler sighed, speaking soft and clear. "It's never happened to me before. I've only seen it happen in others."

In the rational recesses of Mia's conscious, she knew she shouldn't be so livid. She knew Skyler was trying to help her. She knew it wasn't the nurse's fault, and yet Mia couldn't stop herself from being angry at the woman. Not just a normal annoyance, either, Mia was furious. She halted her pacing in front of Skyler and leaned down. "And if he succeeds, will I stop being me? Forever?"

"I don't know."

Mia wanted to punch her. Instead she said in a quick and low voice, "Tell the others, okay? Help them understand what's happening to me. I know they're scared of me right now, and they have good reason to be. Blast it all, I'm scared of myself. Maybe you can help them see it's not me attacking. It's Donavin. Maybe you telling them would be better, since you're a nurse and all."

She strode outside. Her anger consumed her, twisting the world around her into something ugly. The joyous shouts of smugglers, the brilliant sun beating down on her, the smiling face of Sheyla as she waved all swirled into a whirling mass of colors and sounds that hurt her eyes and ears. Mia gritted her teeth and lowered her gaze. Eyes on the ground, it was not long until she bumped into someone. She noticed the reddish shirt, sweaty collar, and strong jaw before she recognized Will. He tried to move around her, but Mia stood in his way.

"You're back early."

He averted his eyes. "Yes, I felt odd being in the sun for so long. I had to come back before the others."

She grasped his arm, fingers gripping his skin. "What's with you?"

"Nothing." Will tried to pull away.

Liar. Donavin's voice echoed.

Mia tightened her grip. Her palm tingled. "Don't lie, Will. You haven't spoken two words to me since we landed."

Will paled. "You can't order me around anymore."

"No, but we seem to be stuck in this mess, so we should at least try to work together."

Will met her gaze and fury flashed in his eyes. "Look, I tried to get over the fact that you lied. That you're not a captain and the *Eclipse* was never really yours. I even tried to work with you on the Acedian ship. I tried." Will's eyes grew dark. "Then you attacked us."

Mia skipped past the fact that her admission happened after they landed on the planet. She wanted to ask about it, but she couldn't concentrate. Not on that. "It's not like I wanted to."

Yes, you did.

Will glanced behind him, as if he worried someone else would hear. "You did attack us. How am I supposed to know you won't do it again?"

"I was being controlled," Mia spat out the words as if they were venom, tired of reiterating the same point. "Against my will."

Will's lips tightened into a thin line. He glanced at his arm. "Well, you aren't supposed to be controlled now, so let me go."

Such disrespect. Punch him.

Every fiber in Mia wanted to follow that command. Her other hand tightened into a fist before she could stop it, but the hurt look in Will's eyes made her pause. Wait, did she actually want to hurt him? No, she didn't. She released her hold. Will drew back, rubbing his arm.

"I need you to trust me," Mia said.

"Trust is something you earn." Will walked away, muttering, "You haven't earned anything yet."

Mia caught up with him, unwilling to let their conversation die with that on his lips. "Please, Will, stop and listen for a minute. Just give me a minute."

A horrible moment passed when Mia thought he wouldn't. Thought he'd keep moving. Thought the rift growing between them would never be healed. Eventually, though, he did stop and stare at her, eyes blazing. "What, Mia? What else do you have to say that'll make me believe you?"

"I..." Mia faltered. Not of her doing. The cold wove around her throat and tightened. She cleared her throat and tried again. Pushed through. "I'm sorry, Will, I'm sorry for lying to you. I'm sorry for dragging you and your brother into this. For bringing your family into this." Tears prickled in the back of Mia's eyes, heat rushed behind them, and when she blinked, her cheeks grew damp. "I'm sorry your sister died. I'm sorry your family has to rebuild everything, and I swear to you; if I live through this, I will help them rebuild. I will help them get their lives back. And I'm desperately sorry for attacking you, Will. You're my friend. We spent months together, and I know I lied about being a captain and how the *Eclipse* wasn't mine and how I wasn't a person with a horrible past, but the friendship we built, that wasn't a lie. It wasn't. It couldn't be."

She moved closer to Will and grabbed his hand. Lightly. She had to hold him, if only for a moment. If he would allow it. He didn't move. Didn't drop his hand. Didn't pull away. Instead, his cheeks grew damp as well. Her chest tightened, ached with the memories of those months on the *Eclipse*. She pushed through that.

"I tried to push you guys away, remember? I tried to distance myself but you and your stupid brother clawed your way back to me. You did that. So I'm sorry. For everything, I'm sorry." Mia dropped Will's hand and hugged herself, her anger flowing away. A knot that had been growing since that attack on Paradous untwisted from her stomach. "And I just wanted you to know that. You can leave now if you want to."

"And you won't attack us again?" Will asked, unmoving.

"I'll try my best not to. Even if that's what Donavin wants. As long as I have control over my body, I won't attack any of you. Ever again." Mia pressed her hands over her heart. She needed Will to believe her. Needed everyone to believe her. "Skyler will tell you more about it. Tell you what's happening. She understands, and please listen to her when she does."

He stood there, staring at her, cheeks shining with tears. Then, much to her surprise, he wrapped his arms around her and pulled her into a hug. One that started tense, as if his actions shocked even himself, then relaxed. One that lasted for more than a few heartbeats. One that filled her with such relief, such joy, she cried into his shoulder. They stood like that for a while before Will pulled back.

"So you're really not a robot, huh?"

Mia wiped at the corners of her eyes. "No. Not yet, anyway."

"Good. Not ever, okay?" He patted her arm, and when Mia nodded, he walked away.

Something had unraveled in Mia's soul at that confession. A knot unwound. Donavin didn't like that. Mia could tell. She could sense his anger, even though she wasn't angry, annoyance still tingled within her. Still wanted her to run. To move. To fight. And Mia couldn't deal with it any longer. She started off in the opposite direction, staring at the dirt but seeing nothing. Her and Will were on speaking terms now. What about the others? She needed her whole crew to trust her. With the Acedians on the loose, with Donavin able to control her like a puppet and this strange desire to fight everyone, how could she expect them to? Would she have trusted a woman who attacked them? A woman with silver eyes? Skyler drifted across her mind, and a flair of hope jarred the annoyance for a moment. They trusted Skyler. They could trust her. As long as she could hold on long enough. As long as she didn't attack them again.

Shouts pulled her from her thoughts. She looked up as a group of smugglers pointed and yelled at something outside of the encampment. Clin, his men, and the rest of Mia's crew were running across the flatlands, chased by a wash. Its growl rumbled in the distance. Some people shook spears as the group came closer, but Mia stepped out in front of them all. A strange sense of anger flowed back into her. Donavin's anger. Probably at the heart-to-heart she just had with Will. It was in that moment that Mia realized just how much Donavin was manipulating her. Did that mean he was close? And if this anger lingered, would she attack her crew again? She couldn't let that happen. Not again. Not ever. She could only think of one thing to dispel this building energy. Calling up the cold, she walked farther from the band of thieves.

Clin and his men rushed past, yelling that she should get back. Should get away. That this wash was dangerous. Her crew brushed past her, each of them laden with supplies, jugs of water, bags of berries and greenery, small carcasses of animals. Jeff grabbed Mia's arm, and for a terrifying moment, Mia wanted to trip him, to put him in danger. She pulled away. The only sounds she heard were the scraping of claws against the dirt as the wash charged closer, and the pounding of her own heart. She readied herself, dug her boots into the ground, tightened her hands into fists, as her fingernails cut grooves into her skin. The beast thumped closer, smaller than the last wash but just as fearsome.

I'm coming to get you, Mia. There's nothing you can do to stop me.

"Try it," she muttered to the dusty air. To Donavin.

Time seemed to slow. The wash lunged, leaping clear off the dirt, a cloud of dust rising behind it. The beast opened its mouth. Its stubbed white fangs reflected the light. Her core grew colder than she had ever felt, pulsing the sensation outward to her limbs. She reached her hands out. The wash slammed into her, and she didn't feel the pain. Couldn't feel it. They scooted backward a foot from the impact. She grasped the creature, one hand on its snout, the other on its neck. Her muscles pulsed and tightened, as she lifted the massive creature up over her head and slammed it onto the dirt. It landed on its back. Spears flew, piercing its exposed belly. The wash gargled, black blood spewing from its lips, and died. Mia fell to her knees, all energy and anger gone. Her vision blurred.

Chapter Six

THE NEXT THING MIA knew, the creature was gone, and she'd been moved to the center of the encampment again. The suns were going down, and a fire burned in front of her. Heat washed over her as she lay wrapped up in a blanket beside Sheyla. She didn't feel Donavin anymore. Didn't hear any more voices. Didn't have any weird anger inside her. Sheyla warmed a bowl of broth over the fire, stirring the tan liquid. Bits of green floated to the surface.

Sheyla smiled down at her. "It is about time you revived yourself, Mia. The sun is on its descent."

Desperately hot, Mia shrugged off the blanket and sat up, but Sheyla pushed the fabric back over Mia's shoulders.

"You were freezing, Mia, after that fight with the wash. If we could even call it that. Heat exhaustion. You pushed yourself too far, and this is what happened."

"I'm fine now," Mia grumbled. She wasn't used to people taking care of her like this, even Sheyla.

You don't belong with these people. The voice, not her own, echoed. Mia's grip tightened on the blanket.

Sheyla patted Mia's hand open and slipped the bowl into it. "You will be fine after I get some food in you."

The bowl radiated heat. It burned her fingers, but she sipped some anyway. The liquid scorched her tongue and throat and tasted wonderful, full of spice and herbs, just the way she remembered. She drank the rest.

"Thank you." Mia put the bowl down.

"It is not the first time I have had to deal with exhaustion. I gave you some medication, electrolyte pills mostly."

Mia shook her head in disbelief, a motion that had become all too common these days. "The government gave you those?"

Sheyla looked into the fire, the flames casting light and shadows onto her soft features. "Yes. A few cycles after you left. The Vespa government knows we are not terrible people. This is not Helix. We are not murderers."

Here Mia's guilt twisted a little. She tried to ignore it. Tried to listen.

"We do not have much power. A supply shuttle comes every few weeks or so. But it has kept us alive, especially since the wash population seems to be growing. Everything else we can handle, though the washes grow stronger every day." Sheyla gave her a searching look. "Although that is quite some strength you have, dear."

Mia shrugged. "It's...new."

"Do not abuse it."

Sheyla's whisper resounded inside Mia's heart. The image of Cassidy strapped to an Acedian table surfaced. She wouldn't abuse her strength, but when necessary, she would transform the Acedian weapon into a gift.

Sheyla patted her hand. "Stay here for a while, rest, and afterward, go be a captain."

"I'm not a captain," Mia murmured, the truth slipping out.

Sheyla gave her a knowing look. "To your crew, you are."

A few smugglers called out for Sheyla, and she waved at them, rising from her seat and giving Mia a pat on the shoulder before leaving. Mia frowned and let the blanket drop from her shoulders, watching Sheyla leave. The breakfast space had been altered, again. The seats were arranged in circles. Fires lit the centers. Glowing orbs burned on the outskirts of the encampment. The sun had descended, although the air was still hot. A rustling noise caught her attention, and she turned back to her fire.

Across the way in another fire ring, Harrison and Viv sat huddled together. They spoke in whispers, but when they laughed, and they did so often, it carried. Harrison fiddled with something in his hand. It glinted in the firelight. Curious and wanting to stretch her legs anyway, Mia went over to them.

"What're you working on, Harrison?" Mia didn't bother to sit down, indicating she would move away as soon as Harrison answered the question. No need to pry.

You belong with me. Again the voice whispered.

Viv waved, and Harrison spoke, "Glad to see you are okay, Mia, aside from your heat exhaustion, of course."

He lifted the metal object and brought it closer to the fire. Divots and grooves on the sphere deepened with shadows. "I found this on the ground when we landed."

The curved object didn't seem noteworthy, just a random piece of space junk probably, but she tilted her head and smiled anyway. "Well, whatever it is don't break it."

Harrison saluted her in the military manner, hand over heart. "Yes, ma'am."

She nodded and shuffled back to her own fire. It was a relief that Harrison didn't act oddly around her. To him, maybe it didn't matter that she wasn't a captain. Maybe it didn't matter that she had attacked them. Maybe he had forgiven her already. He seemed happy with Viv. The figure approaching didn't seem happy, though. The fires deepened Jeff's frown.

"Are you okay, Jeff?" Mia asked.

He stopped inches from Mia and folded his arms. "Will told me to come talk to you."

It was painfully clear that Jeff didn't want to talk about whatever Will had suggested. Mia kept still. "What…would you like to talk about?"

You belong to me.

"He said…" Jeff rubbed his throat a little, and sat down by the fire.

"Whatever it is, if it makes you uncomfortable, we don't need to talk about it." Mia sat down next to him.

"No, we should. He told me about the conversation you two had before you attacked that wash. About how you apologized."

Realization struck like a punch to the gut. How awkward was that conversation between the brothers? She should've apologized to both of them at the same time. "I wanted to tell you I'm sorry that—"

"Don't worry about it. I don't care that you weren't a real captain, and Cassidy's talked my ear off so I could understand your past and a part of me gets that. A darker part. And about the fight, I…I know what it's like." Jeff pushed his hands close to the fire, the flames nearly licking his skin.

Mia tilted her head. Jeff knew what it was like to have some evil madman controlling him? He continued before she could ask how.

"What you said about helping our parents rebuild, was that the truth?" He turned to her and seemed to grow more intense.

Mia nodded. "Of course. I'll do—"

"Will you shake on it?" He extended his hand. His fingers shook in the firelight.

"Of course." Mia took his hand into hers, his rough palm sliding against her smooth one. She squeezed tightly, and for a heartbeat worry struck her hard and fast. What if she couldn't do as she promised? But he relaxed, and she was glad for helping him in this small way. "Are you—"

Again he interrupted her, his words coming fast, like he was trying to speak before something cut him off. "Good. Because I felt helpless, you know? When my sister died. I couldn't do anything. I wasn't even there for it. We left, and I couldn't help them in the aftermath, either. That's why I was so angry all the time. When I feel helpless, I get angry."

"I know how that feels," Mia whispered. After her parents were killed, she had felt angry for a long time. "We—"

For a third time, Jeff cut her off. "I'm just happy that you'll be there. Helping them. In case I don't make it back."

"Why wouldn't you make it back?" Mia leaned closer and tightened her grip. Jeff was scaring her, talking the way he was.

"You never know." Jeff's chest rose and fell much too rapidly. His lips tilted into a frown. "And, Mia, I'm glad you and Will are doing better, and when you were out, Skyler told us how you can't control yourself...or control Donavin or whatever, but if you hurt my brother again, I will hurt you."

"That sounds fair."

"Good." He stood and looked down at her. The firelight washed over Jeff's face, and for a heartbeat, his eyes flashed silver. Mia jerked back, sure it was just her imagination. She'd been hearing their voices and she'd been running for so long, it was almost natural to see things. To have her head play tricks on her. He pushed his hands into his pockets and left, his back melting into the darkness beyond the fires.

I'm coming to take you, Mia.

She sighed. Somehow she thought that conversation with Jeff would've gone differently. That she could've said more. But Jeff cut her off at every opportunity. Maybe he just needed to speak his piece. To get it all out in the open in order to move past it. Maybe she would get her crew back together again. Whatever was left of it anyway. Jeff acted strangely, though. Too strangely. She far preferred this Jeff to the angry one from before. They hadn't had a real conversation without him yelling at her in a while, so maybe he was nervous?

A chill permeated her body, so she scooted closer to the fire. Its unwavering warmth felt good. Far too late, she remembered Skyler's advice to not give Donavin information he could use to find them. Had she given anything away? She pushed her hands against her forehead, willing herself to not think of the planet, to not think of anything that would help Donavin find them. If only he would just leave her alone.

Mia didn't know how long she spent curled up beside the fire, trying to think of nothing, but when she felt movement beside her and lifted her eyes, dusk had fallen completely. Deep purple lined with dark blue spread across the horizon.

Cassidy sat down next to her. "You were pretty intense dealing with that wash, Mia."

Emboldened by the conversations with Will and Jeff, Mia tossed herself out the airlock and confronted Cassidy as well. "And you're distant, Cassidy. Are you scared of me?"

Cassidy breathed deep. "No. You're still you. For now."

She'll be scared of you soon enough.

Cassidy put her chin onto her clasped hands. Her ring glinted in the firelight. Mia noticed, for the first time, an etching on Cassidy's band. From Kat, with love. Memories opened, one by one, as if she flipped through pages of a book. Of Cassidy twirling the ring when nerves hit. Of how she never took that ring off. Of how Donavin let her keep the ring, even after stripping her of everything else. Of Katarina, the girl with the high voice from Pargon. Why was she remembering these things now?

Cassidy sighed. "It's the fact that you lied that gets under my skin."

Mia shook her head, trying to ignore the inscription even though it annoyed her. She knew exactly what lie Cassidy referred to. "It seemed like everyone already knew the *Eclipse* was a stolen ship."

Cassidy nodded. "Yeah, you talked about it before, on the *Eclipse*, actually."

"When?" Mia asked, the warmth of the fire not entirely reaching her anymore.

Cassidy looked at the flames. "When Jeff asked you to tell your whole story."

Mia winced. The incident came back in glaring detail, strapped down to her own infirmary table, by her own crew, Jeff bending over her, shouting at her to tell the truth. She didn't remember everything she had said, but apparently she had told them everything. She took a deep breath before speaking. "If you knew about it and you're not scared of me now, what's with the cold shoulder?"

"I didn't think." Cassidy paused, as if gathering her thoughts. Her lower lip trembled. "I was upset about the *Eclipse* being stolen, but in the grand scheme of things you've done, it's not that...horrible."

Mia grimaced. In the grand scheme of things? Stacking up next to destroying ships and taking lives, apparently theft wasn't so bad. Nevertheless, it pained her to realize Cassidy still thought of her like that. Judged her caliber by those actions. The rest of her crew maybe, but not Cassidy.

Cassidy's words tumbled from her. "I didn't realize at the time that having a stolen ship meant that you're not really a captain. That even with that detail, that huge facet of your life, that from the very beginning you lied to me. And you kept up the charade even after we...even after Paradous. I thought you'd told me the whole truth." She paused again, twining her fingers together and biting her lower lip.

"So," Mia muttered, glancing into the shifting red and yellow flames. Sadness and guilt twisted her stomach. She should've told Cassidy the truth on that blasted planet. Should've told her about the *Eclipse* then. Should've said everything. "What now?"

Cassidy faced her, tears shimmering in her eyes. "If this is ever going to work, Mia, if we are ever going to work, we need to tell each other the truth. The whole truth. Every time."

Tired as Mia was, and as thoughtful as Cassidy's words had been, annoyance sparked in her. The memory of the morning when Cassidy made everyone breakfast and mentioned of an intruder in her cabin surfaced, clear as day. Of how awkwardly Cassidy had been acting. Mia's chest tightened, and she clenched her jaw. Her memories shifted to the conversation on Pargon between Cassidy and Katarina, that random woman who seemed to know Cassidy so well. How they fought and Katarina stormed off in tears. How Cassidy never mentioned the intruder again and when asked, diverted the questions. The ring on Cassidy's finger glinted. A sudden intense jealousy that couldn't have been her own, and yet could be, tightened Mia's hands into fists.

"Have you told me everything about your life? How about the Katarina woman? You did sleep with her, didn't you?"

Cassidy drew back, shaking her head. "She...she has nothing to do with anything."

Liar.

The word crashed into Mia's mind and, even though it was not her own, she agreed with the statement.

"Liar! You wear her ring. You twirl it when you're nervous. It's etched 'From Kat, with love.' How do you think that makes me feel?"

Cassidy cringed. "That was ages ago. She doesn't mean anything to me."

Mia narrowed her eyes. "She means more to you than you think."

Slipping the ring off, Cassidy dropped it into the fire, the action so smooth Mia gasped. "No, she doesn't, Mia. I would have thrown it away the second I knew it bothered you."

The band flashed a brilliant sapphire within the crimson flames. Mia pushed her forehead into her hands. How did they even get on this topic? It didn't make sense. Then she felt it, the soft probing into her thoughts, how memories she wouldn't have thought of otherwise flashed through her mind. Her whirling emotions made sense now. Donavin attempting to control her again. She swallowed the lump forming in her throat and caught Cassidy's gaze. The sight of Cassidy's brown eyes calmed Mia's pounding heart.

"Honestly, I just saw the etching now. It shouldn't bother me, but..."How could she tell Cassidy that soon she might not be able to feel jealousy or love or passion, that soon Cassidy might be just another stranger tucked away in her memories?

Cassidy nudged Mia with her shoulder. "And to think, you were once an eagle-eyed thief. Shocking what time can do."

That harmless touch spread warmth through Mia's body. Donavin's presence melted away. "Shocking, yes." And finally, the words Cassidy had uttered before hit Mia. She should tell the truth, no matter the consequences. Even though Jeff had said Skyler had talked to them, Mia needed to say it, too. She needed Cassidy to hear it from her. "Donavin's trying to control me, Cassidy. He's trying to steal my emotions. I don't know how, but it's scaring the Helix out of me."

Cassidy nodded. The flames threw shadows on one side of her face, and the side Mia could see suddenly tightened. Hardened, almost. She leaned forward. An intensity Mia hadn't seen before shone in Cassidy's eyes. "Thank you for telling me, Mia. We'll figure out a way to stop him. I promise. He won't take you away." She laced their fingers together, pushing her palm onto Mia's scar. At one time, Mia would've drawn away. Such direct contact to her old wound would've scared her. And whomever she was with, probably. This time, she didn't. This time, she allowed Cassidy to draw the scarred hand into her lap. "Tonight, let's just rest while we can, okay?"

The night passed quietly, the purples and blues ebbing away to black. She sat with Cassidy in silence, enjoying her company. The conversations with her crew replayed again and again in Mia's head. Will, Jeff, Cassidy, even Harrison. It seemed they understood. Or were trying to, anyway. She'd have to thank Skyler again in the morning. For explaining everything to them. Cassidy leaned into her. Mia allowed herself a small smile. There was no other place she'd rather be than right here with Cassidy.

"Just what do you lovebirds think you're doing, eh?"

Mia started at the sound of Jeff's jovial voice. She eyed him, wondering why he was so happy all of a sudden.

He grinned at her, raising his voice. "If you two nestle any closer, you should just get a housing unit."

In the blink of an eye, Mia's happiness dissipated. The warmth faded.

Remember what I said, Mia? Love makes you weak. I can save you from it.

Laughter rippled around them, from Viv and Harrison and the others sitting about their fires. Even Cassidy chuckled. Mia didn't find the remark, or Jeff's sudden shift in attitude, funny. Or her own, for that matter.

"Don't be so serious. It's an old joke." Cassidy nudged her. When Mia didn't respond, Cassidy's smile fell. "Are you okay?"

You don't have time to run anymore.

Mia frowned, searching the sky. A smattering of stars blinked through the darkness. The scar on her palm pulsed. In a flash of aqua swirling light, the first Acedian blast hit the encampment.

Chapter Seven

THE ACEDIAN SHOT GLEAMED overhead, slamming into the animal pens. Shards of wood and metal flew in every direction. Cobalt sparks danced over the ground. The few creatures that survived bolted away from the flashes, squealing.

Mia kicked dirt on to her fire. "Put the fires out! Put them out!" She yelled at the people around her. "They're easy targets."

One by one, the flames around them disappeared, smothered by tossed dirt or boots. But the orbs still lit up the camp, casting their white glow far brightly for Mia's liking. How could she turn them all off though? Hordes of prisoners ran away from the huts, ran away from the encampment. Cassidy rose from her seat. Harrison pulled Viv closer to them. Even Jeff moved next to Mia. She grimaced as another missile darted through the air and exploded over the ground, close to a group heading south. Where were Skyler and Will?

"We need to find the others," Cassidy shouted, grabbing Mia's arm.

Mia nodded. Skyler would only go to one place in a crisis like this. She motioned for the others to follow and dashed to the medical unit. Prisoners, in their haste to get away, crushed her group together. Pounding footfalls ceased every time an Acedian weapon hit the ground and started up again when the shock faded. It seemed no one knew where to go.

Clin made it easy for her to find him, his voice rising over the cacophony. "Everyone gather around the medical unit. The field will protect us from harm."

The field? Mia had no time to question as the crowd fled in that direction. Two bursts of aqua light flashed, and the huts in the far corner of the encampment exploded. Shards of metal spiraled away. A third smoldered ahead of her, metal blackened by the impact though still intact. Sensing another shot, she dropped to the dirt, pulling Cassidy beneath her. Cassidy squeezed her eyes shut, and Mia put her arms around Cassidy's head, touching their foreheads together. Even through the fear, a small smile lifted Cassidy's lips. The shot connected, sparks curved, bathing the area in an ethereal light. The lightning collided around them, warming the air, missing them by mere inches. Dust billowed upward from the impact. When the lightning died down and the dust settled, Mia struggled to her feet, pulling Cassidy up with her.

Mia felt nothing this time when he did it. She felt fine. Then, just as suddenly, she didn't. She couldn't do anything to stop him. Couldn't control her actions. And before her eyes, her worst fear came true. The last thing she heard was his voice whispering in her head.

Time to try again.

She shivered. Goosebumps rose on her arms and legs. Hair rose on the back of her neck. Her gaze swept the camp. Enemies surrounded her. The brunette woman—Mia accessed her data banks—whose name was Cassidy Gates, tightened their handhold. No longer broken, the female target proved to be more of a threat this time around. Mia briefly wondered where her Acedian ally, Skyler Jones, had disappeared to. But she did notice the eldest Dee brother—Jeffery—shoving a younger woman behind him. Mia scrutinized this skinny, blond-haired girl. Juvenile, scared, no military background, no criminal history, no records of any kind on this new target, Mia turned away. The girl was a nobody. Not worth her time.

Next to the other Dee brother stood her next target, Jer M. Harrison, the military man. Data on their last encounter filled her mind. He was the one to grab her from William. He was the one to stop her from finishing the job. He was the one to pay. She let go of Cassidy's hand and grabbed hold of Jer Harrison's shirt instead, yanking him toward her. Her punch landed squarely on his nose. The others mouthed words, but Mia didn't care. She had to finish her target. The man curled up in a ball on the ground, hands over his face. Mia narrowed her eyes, forcing them to see through the darkness. Her vision sharpened. Blood seeped through his fingers. She smiled. Pathetic. The younger female lunged, trying to stop her. Mia grabbed hold of her. Mia's fingernails tore a red line in the youth's flesh, and the girl whimpered, backing off. Dropping down next to Jer Harrison, Mia shoved a knee onto his chest to hold him in place and threw back her fist, ready to punch him again.

Before she could, the brunette, designation Cassidy Gates, grabbed and pulled her off Jer Harrison. Mia landed on her back. The woman straddled her, grasping her hands and pushing them into the dirt. This one was not weak anymore. Gates tried to say something, the words lost in the space between them. Nothing this woman could say would stop Mia from finishing her duty. She kicked and flailed. The woman hung on. Moved closer, in fact, mere inches from her now, her whole weight pressing down on Mia. Elder Dee brother knelt beside her and leaned his full weight on her legs. She felt no pain, only pressure. He mouthed something. Jer Harrison stared at her.

She threw out a link to the ally ship. *I'm here.*

We know.

The sky lit up as another shot tore through the air, exploding against the ground with a shower of aqua sparks. Jeffery threw himself to the side as a bolt flew past his shoulder. Jer Harrison dropped to the ground, curling into a ball to protect himself. Cassidy flattened herself, covering Mia with her body. Mia could just see past the waves of brown hair that now covered her face. Sparks flew over them. One split and forked into smaller currents. A spark hit Cassidy in the back. The idiot woman—no, she wasn't an idiot, Cassidy never was—jerked upward, bending back as the shock ran through her. Her muscles tensed. Recognition flashed through Mia. Cassidy was afraid. Cassidy was hurt. The sparks died down.

Hands appeared on Cassidy's shoulders, as Jeffery pulled her off. Mia was up on her feet in an instant, and she backed away, head aching. Cassidy was her enemy. They all were. Instead of engaging the Dee brother, Mia turned her attention on the swarms of people, throwing out an arm to stop one, kicking the legs out of another, punching a third one in the neck. They went down. So easy. These people made it so easy to be dominating. Jer Harrison now rose to his feet, his face contorted in anger. He lunged for her. Mia grabbed hold of his neck and threw him to the ground. He lay still. Strangers pushed against her in their haste to get away, in their hurry to get somewhere, in their fear of the Acedians. Mia smiled. They should be afraid. Jeffery tried to grab her from behind, but she ducked under the assault. She elbowed him in the stomach, and he doubled over.

Mia ignored them now. Her enemy was taken care of for the moment. She searched the camp for what she needed. There. The embers from the fires glowed but not nearly bright enough. She ran to them, picking up a shard of wood along the way. She plunged the wood into the embers and waited for it to catch. It did. She tore to the center of the camp, lighting the seats, burning the tables.

Jeffery reached her side, saying something she could not hear. Or something Donavin didn't want her to hear. She tilted her head. He didn't know these people. He shouldn't care about these people. And yet it appeared that he did. The torch threw light onto his features, the balled hands and tense shoulders, the twitching muscles in his jaw, the silver gleam in his eye. Mia blinked. The man's—no, Jeff's—hazel eyes narrowed at her.

Jeffery shouted again, but she didn't understand. Her body trembled from the cold now. Finally, the Dee brother attacked. Mia ducked under his first blow and came around to return the favor. The man was fast. Too fast. He spun around and threw another punch before she could get her hands up. This fist connected with her shoulder and threw her off her feet. She hurtled to the ground, landing hard but feeling nothing. Her head cracked against something. She saw stars. Jeffery came closer. Then she saw nothing at all.

Mia opened her eyes, blinking into the brightness until her vision cleared. Sheyla and Will sat huddled by the corner. People crammed around the edges, pushed back against the gleaming metal cabinets. They were in the medical unit. Skyler leaned over her, putting a cold compress on Mia's head. She tried to move. The pain bursting from her shoulder made her yell instead. She grabbed it and moaned. Her head pounded just behind her left ear. Be strong, she ordered herself. Strong. Now, move. Taking a few deep breaths, she forced herself to a sitting position.

Jeff stood by the open door, folding his arms across his chest. "Are you sure he's not controlling her anymore?"

Skyler nodded. "If he were still controlling her, she wouldn't be in so much pain right now." As if to prove her point, Skyler poked Mia's shoulder. The jab made Mia yelp, and she scooted away from the nurse.

The last thing she remembered clearly was the Acedian shots. Her head pulsed again, and she grabbed it. Snippets came back. Running to the medical unit. Hearing Donavin. The sudden change within her. The fight with Jeff. She stared at him. "I attacked you, didn't I? I didn't mean to."

"Yes, and we know," Jeff replied. "Harrison's sporting a bloodied nose, Cassidy got shocked by one of those weapons, and Viv has a gash on her arm." Sheyla's sudden intake of breath made him pause and look at her. "You're daughter's fine. It's just a surface wound." He cocked an eyebrow at Mia. "Plus, you banged your head pretty hard. It's a wonder you're not in a coma."

She got to her feet, swayed, and grabbed hold of the first person she could to catch herself before she fell. *Cassidy.* Cassidy straightened, wrapping her arms around Mia for added support. After a moment, she eased Mia back into a sitting position.

"You'll be okay," Cassidy whispered.

Mia winced, holding onto the table now, glancing in Jeff's direction just in time to see him nod to whoever stood outside. He lingered between her and the rest of the group. Harrison stumbled in, clasping Viv's hand as she followed. Viv didn't look in Mia's direction, and Mia's heart panged. Another tie severed. Guilt clung to her like a shadow, threatening to swallow her. She tightened her grip on the table.

Will pulled his brother into a hug. "I would've gone out to find you, but Sheyla said this was the safest place to be, that everyone would come here."

Viv rushed over to her mother. Blood dripped from a cut on Viv's forearm, and Harrison grabbed a foam gun to mend the wound. He tilted her chin up. "It won't be long now."

She smiled. "Thanks."

"We will be safe in here." Sheyla hugged her daughter close.

An explosion boomed outside, followed by the unmistakable sound of something heavy thudding in the dirt. Shouts rang out.

"How will this be safe?" Cassidy looked around at the small space. "Not everyone can fit in here."

"They do not have to." Clin pushed through the mass of people crowding at the door. His gaze slid over Mia and Cassidy, as he went to his family and wrapped his arms around them. "The field will protect us all."

Mia shook her head, trying to get the pounding to stop. "How? What field?"

"Go see for yourself." Clin gestured to the door.

Using Cassidy's help, she limped outside. It seemed as if every smuggler in the encampment had made it here. They hugged close to the unit but didn't appear frightened. Another shot hit nearby, the cobalt sparks arcing to their direction. No one moved. Mia held her breath, fear closing her throat. The spark smashed onto an invisible barrier, flaring azure before fading away. Sparks scattered this way and that over the domed field before disappearing.

"We might actually survive this," Cassidy whispered.

An explosion glowed, bigger than the others, taking half the huts with it as it disappeared. They could see clear across the encampment on almost every side.

"If this keeps up, the only place left will be here," Mia muttered. "They can just come down and take us by force if they want to."

Harrison appeared next to her. "They won't."

"How do you know that?" Cassidy's voice lowered.

He pointed into the darkness. A glimmering white light appeared, slicing a path through the sky. Another white light shot out opposite the first.

"Because we're not alone," he replied.

The lights halted and blossomed. The Acedian ship exploded in a fiery blaze then went dark. The smugglers cheered, but Mia stared hard at the dark sky, certain another attack would come. It didn't. With those two hits, the assault on the encampment had been stopped. How was that possible? She turned to Harrison. He fished around in his pocket for a moment and pulled out the metal object Mia had noticed before.

He spoke into it. "Target eliminated."

"Copy that, ready to be shifted?"

Shifted? Like on Pargon?

Harrison glanced over his shoulder. Viv stood nearby, just as awed as everyone else. He grabbed her hand, pushed something into it, and said into the communicator. "Yes."

Mia couldn't believe her eyes. One moment Harrison stood next to her, and the next he glowed and faded from view. The dirt beneath him shimmered slightly, as if the ground itself had some internal light.

"Captain," Will yelped.

She glanced at him and at Skyler standing next to him. The nurse disappeared.

"What's going on?" Jeff looked around.

Cassidy's hand jerked from Mia's shoulder. She turned in time to see Cassidy dim. Mia reached out but met only air. She swiveled back to Jeff and Will, intending on ordering them inside, hoping she could figure out a way to block whatever was happening to her crew. They disappeared as well. The smugglers had backed away. Movement caught her attention. Clin waved her over. No, he waved at her. Then he, too, disappeared from sight.

Chapter Eight

MIA BLINKED. CLIN HAD disappeared. So had everything else. Enclosed in a smooth, opaque cylinder, she couldn't see anything outside. She pressed her palms to the cool surface, and the glowing white dome beneath her dimmed. With a quiet hiss, the glass surrounding her lifted. She tensed in the cool, clean air. Was this an Acedian ship?

As soon as the glass rose above her head, the words *MS Escambia* etched over the square hatch told her no. And the fact that her scar didn't hurt. The circular cabin spanned out around her, empty save six women in military garb standing a few paces away and five glass cylinders lined up beside her. Straight-backed and not a single hair out of place, the women scowled at her. The other cylinders rose, revealing the rest of her crew, and the military women stepped forward, grabbing them all. The one who latched onto Mia's arm seemed determined to break it, squeezing until Mia's skin whitened. The woman's dull, brown eyes challenged Mia to speak, but she didn't.

The soldier pulled Mia over to the hatch and waved it open, yanking her out into the narrow, unlit corridor. Light from the open hatch spilled into the corridor. The bulkhead seemed smooth, no other hatches or even viewports marred its surface. One solid sheet of metal surrounded them, a military-grade, detonation corridor. Mia grimaced.

Her soldier made little noise as she moved down the corridor. Mia lengthened her stride to match the soldier's, but the woman always moved one step ahead. Her crew and their escorts followed. Once the hatch sealed shut, only a faint glow could be seen from the other end of the tube.

Mia cleared her throat. "Where are you taking us?"

The soldier didn't reply, and by then they had reached the end of the corridor. The soldier keyed opened the hatch and pushed Mia through. She stumbled across the threshold and turned back, trying to get another question in. Her escort had already stepped aside. Her crew staggered in behind her, giving her questioning looks, but Mia only shook her head. She didn't know what was happening any more than they did. Only Harrison and Skyler seemed calm, their faces serious, though not worried. The hatch slid shut, leaving the soldiers outside. A square cabin stretched out before her, lit with bulbs drifting near the ceiling. Hatches lined the bulkhead. Not something Mia would expect on a military warship. They usually liked keeping things simple, one route in or out. It was warmer in here, if only by a little bit. Skyler pushed out of the group and stood in the center of the cabin.

Mia moved to join her. "What is this?"

Skyler didn't answer. Instead, she watched the far hatch. It hissed open, and another group of people shuffled out, wearing skintight white outfits that covered them from head to toe, accompanied by hoods that covered their heads and glowing face shields that flickered periodically. They stood at attention in front of Skyler. One extended a bright-yellow glove and took hold of Mia's arm. Behind the glow of the face shield, the man's eyes widened, though Mia didn't know why. Her eyes, maybe. The scent of disinfectant and singed hair wafted over her. She wrinkled her nose and tried to pull out of the man's grasp, but Skyler's hand on her shoulder made her pause.

"Don't struggle," she muttered. "We will be separated for a few moments. These are the good guys."

Reluctantly, Mia allowed the man to guide her over to the hatch. The man punched a button and the doors slid open, revealing another dark chamber. Mia's hair tingled on the back of her neck. She didn't want to be separated from her crew, not on a spaceship she knew nothing about. Not while the Acedians could be close by. Still, she would trust Skyler.

Swallowing a bubble of fear rising in her throat, Mia glanced over her shoulder at her crew. The other white-suited soldiers had reached for them. Before she could see more, her soldier shoved her into the darkness. The hatch slid shut, but not before Cassidy's yelp of, "Where are you taking us?" slipped through.

Darkness pressed in on Mia, suffocating her. Not her idea of a welcoming party. Despite Skyler's reassurance, Mia's heart skittered in her chest, and her palms grew sweaty. She focused, pushing the fear away. Cold seeped into her head, tracing a thin line across her temple before leaking into her eyes. Another snaked around her neck and pooled by her ears. The chamber became clearer. Four bare walls surrounded her, one hatch in front and one behind. She picked up a faint clicking noise and moved to the wall, trailing a finger down the metal. A thin layer of dust coated the surface, and a soft hum came from the bulkhead.

A sudden blue light burst from the metal. It wavered for a moment before changing to a deep crimson. Mia shaded her eyes. The hum grew louder, the red light, brighter. A wave of hot air crashed into her from above. Were they burning her alive? She balled her hands into fists. Should she try to get out? A nagging in the back of her mind whispered *no.* Skyler said these were good people. They'd saved her and her crew from the Acedians. Maybe they could save her friends from her, too. She relaxed and released the power from the Acedian curse. The cold faded inside her.

The red light dimmed. The heat dissipated. The dust on the deck panels had disappeared, and she suspected any dust on her would be gone as well. The hatch slid open in front of her and blue light spilled in. She hesitated.

A voice filtered through a comm system by the hatch. "Enter Chamber 2, remove clothing. Liquid decon starting in fifteen…fourteen…"

Mia stepped into the next cabin. Moist air engulfed her, and the hatch slid shut behind. Great, another small chamber with two hatches and just enough room to strip. A trickle of clear liquid started from the ceiling panels. Frowning, she undressed. The liquid splashed onto her head, streaming down her shoulders, cold liquid without a scent. A dual set of sprays burst from walls beside her. Mia pursed her lips against the onslaught, anxious to get back to her crew. She needed answers. Finally, the sprays misted and stopped. Gusts of cool air whooshed around her, drying her completely, and a section by the exit hatch opened, clean clothes folded inside. She slipped into the layers of soft, black fabric and straightened the silver trim on her shoulders. Then she waited by the exit hatch, glaring at the metal as if that would make the time pass faster.

After a few more moments it slid open, revealing a large circular cabin. A thick glass hatch on the opposite end broke up the monotonous metal walls. Her crew sat on the benches that lined the cabin, clearly expecting her. Cassidy gave a halfhearted wave.

"Always exciting, huh?" Jeff mumbled as she entered.

Mia took a seat next to Cassidy. "Where did our escorts go?"

Jeff nodded to the glass hatch. "Out that door."

Chamber 2b was etched into opaque, white glass. Chilled, Mia tucked her feet underneath her. Skyler rummaged around beneath her seat for a moment and produced a pair of boots.

She handed them over. "Told you we'd be okay."

Mia accepted them with a nod. But they weren't okay. She eyed Harrison, who averted his gaze. It was after she laced the boots up that she noticed the different uniforms of her crew. Her original crew wore long-sleeved, black shirts and matching pants. Jeff and Will wore vests. Harrison and Skyler wore shirts with one black strip down the same arm and leg, and a diagonal stripe across Harrison's chest. Skyler's clothing was blue, Harrison's red. The glass door slid open, and a straight-backed, familiar figure loomed in its frame. Admiral Boreas.

Harrison snapped to attention, rising to his feet and putting a hand over his heart. "Sir."

Admiral Boreas responded with a curt nod. "Good work, Harrison."

Good work? In doing what, getting back onto a military ship? Mia tilted her head.

Skyler jumped to her feet, her shout ringing through the small cabin. "What about me? I risked my ass out there."

Admiral Boreas' eyebrows twitched, his lips pulling up in a small grin. "You did good, Jones."

Mia rose, words tumbling from her mouth. "'You did good, Jones?' What's going on here? Where's the Acedian ship? What happened to the people back on Fissure?"

Admiral Boreas held up his hand and glanced at Skyler. She nodded. Admiral Boreas turned back to Mia. "Miss Foley, come with me."

His gaze swept the cabin and the rest of Mia's crew, before he spun on a heel and marched down the corridor. Skyler and Harrison fell in step behind him. Jeff squeezed his way past Mia, meeting her gaze and frowning. He motioned for Will, who came forward. The brothers followed behind Skyler and Harrison, matching their strides with this crew almost too perfectly. The brothers had joined the military in order to leave Paradous, and the first thing the Vespa military taught was how to march.

Mia took one questioning look at Cassidy before trailing after them. Cassidy lingered close, her gaze never leaving Jeff's back. Mia, on the other hand, drank in the details of this warship. The corridors were wide, but no space was left unused. Glowing screens lined the bulkheads, lights lit up the deck and ceiling panels. They passed a wide viewport and a blue tint caught her eye. The entire viewport could become a monitor if necessary. A high-tech ship for sure. Soldiers streamed down the corridors then stepped to the side, saluting when the admiral strode past. The pomp and circumstance made Mia feel like she was in a parade or a funeral. Either way, she didn't like it.

Admiral Boreas stepped into an open hatch, followed by the rest of her crew. Mia gaped at the giant space. The cabin contained a single table and chairs, yet would've held at least eleven bunks back on the *Eclipse*. A pitcher of water and glasses sat on the table. Two guards stood on either side of the hatch, armed with massive, twin-barrel, energy guns.

Admiral Boreas motioned to the chairs. "Please, sit down."

Skyler and Harrison did so, with Jeff and Will not far behind. Across from them, Mia pulled a chair out for Cassidy and settled into one beside her. Admiral Boreas eased himself at the head of the table and laced his fingers together. He didn't speak, and neither did her crew.

So Mia did. "Are the Acedians gone?"

"For now." Admiral Boreas leaned across the table and poured himself a glass of water.

"And what will happen to the camp on Fissure?"

Admiral Boreas took a drink before answering, his steady gaze locking on hers. "I've contacted the guards. A supply shuttle will arrive by daybreak, and some of my men will stay behind to help rebuild. They will not be bothered by the Acedians again."

Mia nodded and waited a heartbeat. "Why did you say those things to Skyler?"

A thin man with black hair and an even darker expression entered the room and sat across from Admiral Boreas. He straightened his uniform. Two bars on his shoulder, one thick, one thin, marked him as a commodore. *Bay* was stitched beneath the bars. He trained his eyes on Mia, giving her a curious piercing stare. "She's a spy."

A collective gasp rose from the table, and Mia's eyes widened. A blasted spy? She tore her gaze from Commodore Bay and turned to Skyler instead. Did everyone have a double life?

Jeff coughed and thumped on his chest. "A spy?"

Skyler smirked. "I prefer to be called a double agent, sir, I—"

Admiral Boreas interjected, "Before we get into that, we must discuss how it all started." His gaze landed on Mia. "Do you know who the Acedians are?"

"They're a band of murderers bent on destroying people's lives," Mia replied evenly, though anger bubbled in her stomach at the thought of them.

"That's what they do, but that's not who they are." Admiral Boreas gestured to Mia's left hand and tapped the table. The cabin lights dimmed, and her scar flashed in the center of the cabin. A holoimage. Everyone leaned forward, Jeff more suddenly than anyone. Mia glowered at it, tightening her hand into a fist and shoving it into her lap.

Admiral Boreas grimaced. "That scar on your palm is the symbol of a rebellion led by one Charles Donavin. He had a falling out with us and decided to fight back. No one wanted to join him. With the bounty of the Vespa government at everyone's fingertips, who would? So Donavin decided to create his own followers, calling them Acedians. They gunned for the government, capturing people, killing them. Turning them against us. We had to stop them, but we didn't know how. They were everywhere and nowhere."

"It's because they look like us," Jeff muttered. "They can blend in and attack."

Commodore Bay sighed. "Like on Paradous, yes. Like on Pargon. Like on any planet of any one of the five solars. Everywhere and nowhere. We had no way of knowing how they turned our best soldiers against us or how to stop them. We couldn't even find them."

Admiral Boreas tapped his index fingers together. "When a transport shuttle was taken, it was another blip on our radar. There was nothing we could do to stop it. We would never get there in time to save the people onboard, and the Acedians would be long gone by then anyway. Then you arrived on our deck, claiming to be tortured by these people, claiming to have seen horrible things. Waving your palm around like it was proof. I didn't understand it at the time. You were just a bumbling child, wailing about an explosion. I thought you were lost, to be honest. I didn't look close enough. I sent you to our nurse ward and thought nothing of it. I had much bigger issues to worry about."

"That was you?" Mia narrowed her eyes. Memories flooded back to her. She had been on a military ship before. She had tried to tell them about the Acedians. About the bad people who killed her parents. They hadn't listened. She'd escaped those nurses, fearful of strangers and angry at the world. Irritation at the memory tensed her body. Mia nodded toward Skyler. "What about her?"

The admiral smiled. "We found Jones a few cycles after you. Her bots were activated and turning her too fast. The scar on her shoulder was obvious. We had learned more by then. More, but not much. She was on the precipice of becoming one of them. We took her to the one scientist we thought could stop it. He managed, after multiple tries. We had helped her before realizing what an asset having an Acedian could be."

They'd helped Skyler. The thought slowly sank in. Maybe they could help her. She leaned back in her chair, hands still pressed against her lap.

Skyler pursed her lips. "I didn't think it was too soon."

Admiral Boreas tilted his head, smiling. "We realized afterward she could still infiltrate their system, still gain knowledge, still imitate them. It helped, but we don't know enough. The scientist we hired could turn the bots off, though the person in question had to go to the planet where the scientist lives. He would not come to us. And it would work only if the participant was willing. With the power becoming an Acedian gives the victim, the chance of finding those willing would be slim."

Mia scoffed. Finding willing participants would be easy. Something didn't sit right with his story. Her crew felt it. Cassidy fidgeted. Jeff's eyes narrowed. Will kept glancing at the exit. Skyler bit her lip. Even Harrison stood and paced. The guards tracked his movements, as did she. "You know how to deactivate the picobots?"

Admiral Boreas took another sip of water. "No. The scientist didn't share the technique of how. Or even how the picobots worked in the first place. His world, his rules, he said."

Mia narrowed her eyes at the admiral. She didn't like where this conversation was going. Fear wormed its way into her heart, making it hard to breathe. Still, she cleared her throat and said, "So, you needed some way of getting that information."

"Yes," Admiral Boreas said. "Skyler could only learn so much without being detected. Donavin had to think she was on his side. We needed more. We needed someone who was hunted by them, someone they wanted. Only then could we discern their methods and their attack patterns. We needed someone who was still turning. Then I remembered you, the little lost girl. I realized you had been a victim of the Acedians. I knew from that moment, we had our way of finding out how he turned our own against us."

Mia's head started to pound. She clenched the fabric of her pants with shaking fingers. The government didn't help when she was younger, maybe they wouldn't help her now either. Should she leave? Cassidy slipped a hand under the table, relaxing Mia's grasp and twining their fingers together. Her first mate sat straight in her chair and stared at the admiral, but as if she knew, she flicked her gaze to Mia and gave her a subtle nod. Whatever Mia's decision, Cassidy would be with her. That thought calmed her, if only a little. She forced herself to listen, even as the beating of her heart filled her ears.

Admiral Boreas took another sip of his water, and Mia wanted to knock that stupid glass from his fingers. "Tracking you down was hard, but your way of life was too unique not to stand out eventually. A young girl would board a ship looking for work, and that ship would mysteriously disappear. It had to be you. We did manage to save a few, the ones you aided in getting away."

Shock rippled through Mia and her skin tingled. Those precious seconds pulling the alarms, letting people leave on the escape pods. Relief swept through her after all these cycles. She had been able to save a few lives.

Admiral Boreas continued, "Some of them are even on this ship. After all, where do you think we got Jones from?"

Mia's eyes widened. Skyler was on one of her ships? She whipped her head around to stare at the nurse. "You were an Acedian. You didn't get away. I didn't save you. How did you get here? What ship were you on? I don't remember you."

Skyler gave her a sad smile. "You wouldn't remember me. I was on the *Scarlet*. We didn't work together and that ship was huge. You blathered a lot to Freya, and she was my best friend. You didn't save me while I was on that ship, but you did give me hope that I could get away from them."

Freya. Mia's stomach tightened. "But I didn't get away. They let me go."

Skyler chuckled. "And how was I supposed to know that? I only knew what Freya did."

"How come you never told me this before?" Mia leaned forward. After all the time they had spent together. After Paradous, or on Fissure surely, she could have told her this. The shared connection, to the *Scarlet* and especially to Freya, shocked Mia to her core.

"You never asked." Skyler shrugged. "And quite frankly, I thought it would be too painful a memory...for both of us."

Admiral Boreas broke the conversation with a cough. "Didn't you ever wonder why we never caught you, Mia?"

"Or did you think you were just that good?" Commodore Bay grinned, a grin that made Mia's skin crawl.

After a few moments of silence, Mia realized they wanted her to respond. She breathed, calming herself. "I thought if the government or military knew I was being hunted then someone would help me."

She knew how weak that sounded, how childlike. She couldn't help it. The holoimage brightened then disappeared, but she couldn't tear her eyes from the space in front of her. After cycles of forced solitude, of shoving everyone away just to escape, of killing to stay alive, it burned deeply that the government had known about her all this time. That they could've helped. Even though Donavin had torn up her list, those names still sat heavy in her heart. Now, more than ever. The ships she wouldn't have destroyed, the lives she wouldn't have ended. How could they have done this? Didn't they care about the people she killed trying to get away? Tears prickled her eyes. A squeeze from Cassidy brought Mia back to the present.

Commodore Bay cleared his throat. "We couldn't help you without risk of Donavin knowing you were being followed. The most we could do was not imprison you."

Mia jerked as if hit, the statement slapping her across the face. "Not imprison me? That's your idea of helping?"

"Of keeping you as safe as we could, yes," Commodore Bay said. "When you landed on Paradous and started acting Acedian, we knew it was simply a matter of time. Skyler could become a part of your crew and deliver you to Donavin, securing her place in his eyes, and she could also help you escape. Harrison could call for backup once you were off the ship."

Admiral Boreas' eyes brightened, urgency in his voice now. "We needed facts, Miss Foley. And you became the catalyst for just that. The only way we could get that information was through the willing participation of Jones, and the unknowing participation of you."

Enough. Mia pushed her chair back and got to her feet. Skyler stood as well. The guards raised their guns and pointed them at her, the power cells charged and humming, as a steady, blue light glowed from both barrels. Cassidy stood and shifted her weight to block Mia from their threat.

Mia asked, "Am I a prisoner here?"

Commodore Bay's smile faded. "Actually, yes."

Skyler made a guttural noise, glancing between her two commanding officers. Will and Jeff got up, the scrape of their chairs echoing through the cavernous space.

The commodore relaxed in his seat. "We saved Skyler too soon. We didn't learn enough. We can only discover how a person changes and how to counteract Donavin's devices by observing that change ourselves."

Mia stepped back. Her breath hitched. No. She had to say it aloud to believe it. "You're saying...you want me to turn into an Acedian?"

The two guards stepped forward, guns at the ready.

"Yes, Miss Foley," Commodore Bay said. "That's exactly what we want."

.

Chapter Nine

COMMODORE BAY GUIDED MIA and her crew to a cabin quite different from the rest of the ship. A cot took up one side, blue sheets tucked in at the corners. A holoimager glowed to life on the opposite wall, throwing images of nebulas and constellations onto the bulkhead. A viewport dominated the cabin, and a real, miniature, darkwood tree sat in the corner. Here, at least, they tried for some personality. Here, in the ship's brig. Mia rolled her eyes.

"This is where you'll be staying. Ask the regenerator for drinks." Commodore Bay motioned to the small white table surrounded by chairs in the center of the room. "Food will be brought to you at each mealtime."

He ushered them inside, including Skyler. Harrison, however, stayed next to Commodore Bay. Mia twisted to speak to the commodore, but the hatch hissed shut. She placed a hand on the cool surface. The metal vibrated slightly, and the gentle whir of the locking mechanism sealed her and her friends inside. How could they get off a military ship? Mia leaned her pounding head on the metal then turned to face the cabin.

Will went over to the regenerator. "Water, cold."

The table thrummed, the center glowed, and a glass of liquid materialized.

He arched an eyebrow at the glass, picked it up, and took a sip. "It's good."

"If we had one of those on the *Eclipse,* we wouldn't have fought so hard for that last cup of coffee." Jeff grabbed the glass from his brother, poking him in the side.

"Now's not the time, Jeff," Cassidy said.

A muscle in Jeff's jaw twitched. "We can talk about whatever we want, Cassidy."

Will backed away from his brother and roamed the cabin instead. He kept glancing in Mia's direction. Pain needled into her head.

Skyler scooted close, the faint scent of disinfectant lingering around her. Mia wrinkled her nose. "Why are you even in here, Skyler? You're part of this military."

"They probably...they probably want me to keep an eye on you and your crew."

The confusion in Skyler's voice was obvious, but Mia didn't acknowledge it. She kept her gaze trained on the viewport and the blackness beyond. Rubbing her head, she tried to make the pounding stop. Tried to find some semblance of peace. At least, in this blasted military ship, she didn't hear Donavin. She took comfort in that.

After a moment, Skyler cleared her throat. "I didn't know. Please, you have to believe me, I didn't know. I thought they were going to help you like they helped me."

"If you didn't complete your part of the mission, we wouldn't be here right now." Mia sighed. "It was Harrison who contacted this ship." She eyed Skyler. "Did he realize this was what they wanted?"

Skyler shook her head. "I don't know. Commander Harrison and I never really spoke before this mission."

"Commander Harrison?" Cassidy moved next to them, her voice rising in surprise.

Jeff's eyes widened. "Harrison is a commander? Of what ship?"

"The sister ship to this one, the *MS Bell*," Skyler replied. "He was just stationed at Paradous to gather information if the Acedians attacked. They did, and well, you know what happened next."

Mia couldn't believe it. Harrison was a thief and a commander of a spaceship. So he'd been lying this whole time, too. He'd played the admiral's lackey part quite well indeed.

Will flopped into a chair, clearly unimpressed. "The *Bell*. That was the other warship in the firefight."

"Yes." Skyler rested against the bulkhead, running her fingers through her hair.

"And now we're here," Mia said. "In a plush prison on a warship traveling to who knows where." She shivered and rubbed her arms, struggling to make sense of all this. The constant pounding over her left eye didn't help. Or the sudden sense of apathy dulling her thoughts, eating away at her emotions like acid. She frowned. Maybe Donavin could affect her here after all. That blanket messaging technique Skyler talked about on Fissure. If Mia didn't quite know where she was at the moment—on a ship she'd never heard of before going who knows where—maybe Donavin wouldn't know either?

"Maybe I can figure that out." Skyler positioned herself in front of the holoimager and started flipping through the stars.

Cassidy fidgeted, and stalked around the regenerator "We have to get off this ship."

Mia shoved herself off the bulkhead. A wave of nausea washed over her, but she put a hand out to stop Cassidy's pacing, desperate to think of something other than her own condition. "Any suggestions how?"

Cassidy's eyes flashed. "Maybe there's a crack in their codes. Or maybe we can surprise whoever gives us the food. Or maybe..."

Anger suddenly spiked in Mia. Cassidy's suggestions weren't good enough. They were never good enough! A sweat broke over Mia's body, and she moved to the nearest bulkhead. "Or maybe I can just punch my way out."

She called up the cold, pooling it in her right fist. Pain traveled up her arm and neck and ended at her temple. She jerked her head to the side, wincing, but her concentration remained firm on the power within the picobots. She tensed and threw a fist against the bulkhead. The metal screamed in protest, bending around her hand.

My little Mia, are you trying to break free of something? Try again.

Mia gritted her teeth. She withdrew her hand and pounded the metal again. Confusion fogged her senses. The metal was tough, heavy, thicker than what Donavin—no, what she originally thought.

Again.

The cold pooled in her other hand. She pounded the metal with both hands, throwing one punch right after the other.

Much thicker.

The impacts jarred her arms, nearly cracked her fingers, still she hit the metal.

Faster.

She complied. The bulkhead bent, didn't snap. She glared at the opposite wall, but Cassidy stepped in front of her and put a hand on her shoulder. Donavin's whispers ceased.

"At least this one doesn't melt back together again." Cassidy nodded to the dented metal.

Mia shook her hand off and backed away. Will, Jeff, Skyler, Cassidy. Donavin. Too close. And her friends were still coming closer. They crowded around her. She crossed the cabin and pushed her back against the viewport, trembling. Her breathing was ragged. Her legs trembled. The space felt too cold. Her hands didn't hurt at all, even though they were bright red. She dug her nails into her arm but felt no pain. Where was the pain? What was happening to her? Only her head twinged, now, throbbing with each breath she took.

"Stay back, I'll handle her." Cassidy waved at the rest of the crew to back off.

"Cassidy, she might turn violent again," Skyler whispered.

Cassidy frowned at her. "Just stay back."

Even with the space between them, Mia still felt trapped. "I'm not going to be a prisoner on this ship. I'm not going to be someone's lab rat. I'm not going to turn into an Acedian. I'm not going to help them—"

Cassidy cut her off. "I know."

You don't have a choice, Mia. You never did.

Mia's chest tightened. "This is a military-grade warship, Cassidy. A warship. How are we ever going to find a way out? They want me to turn, Cassidy."

Cassidy moved closer. "We'll find a way, we always do."

Her quiet voice calmed Mia, though not enough. The walls still closed in on her. "I can't be an Acedian. I hurt people when he controls me. I don't want to hurt anyone anymore. I can't become like them." Pushing her hands against her throbbing head, Mia squeezed her eyes shut.

If only the pounding would stop. If only the cold would go away. If only everyone would leave her the blasted well alone. A warm hand gently pulled at hers. She opened her eyes. Everything seemed sharper now, the slight hint of green flecks in Cassidy's brown eyes, the smattering of freckles on one side of her nose, the lines in her lips. Mia's hands shook.

Cassidy drew her into a hug. "We'll figure it out. The admiral spoke of a scientist who can stop this. We can find him. But you need to calm down."

Mia took a deep breath and let it out. The sharp scent of disinfectant still clung to Cassidy's skin. Mia tensed and tugged away. A strand of Cassidy's hair caught in Mia's clothes and drifted to the deck, curling on the panels. "I can't turn into one of them."

"I'm here for you," Cassidy breathed. She lifted Mia's hands and kissed one of her knuckles. "I promise."

The spot she kissed tingled. The cold in her hand dissipated, and a pang started there instead. Mia breathed easier. Finally, her hands stilled.

"Good," Cassidy murmured, laying her forehead against Mia's. "Good."

Donavin's voice broke into Mia. *You don't need love.*

A needle of pain jabbed her temple. She pulled back. Who was this woman before her? She searched her memory. The brunette didn't conjure up anyone specific.

The woman knitted her brows. "Are you okay?"

"I'm fine," Mia replied. She had to.

The brunette tilted her head. "I can tell when something's wrong, Mia."

"I'm okay…" Mia searched for the brunette's name but none came to mind. She glanced around for clues. Skyler Jones stopped working on the holoimager.

"Cassidy," Skyler finished for her. "Her name's Cassidy."

Cassidy gasped, hands tightening around Mia's. "She forgot my name? How?"

Skyler paled, then broke them apart and placed herself in front of Mia. Mia frowned. She had no reason to hurt the brunette. To hurt Cassidy. Skyler's gaze flicked over her face. "Donavin's pulling her away."

Mia shrugged. "I'm fine, Skyler."

Skyler grabbed Mia by the shoulders. "One second you're all gooey-eyed with Cassidy and the next you're stoic? No." Skyler's voice dropped an octave lower, her forehead creased. "This isn't a blanket effect. Donavin knows where we are. What you're doing. He has to. He's going through the final stages."

Will stepped toward them. "What's happening to her?"

Before Skyler could reply, Mia turned toward the hatch. Its locking mechanism activated, creating a soft hum, and it hissed open. Though a group of guards waited outside, a single soldier, gun slung over his shoulder, entered the cabin. Brown hair receded on his wrinkled forehead. Piercing blue eyes narrowed at Mia. He jutted his chin in her direction. "You're needed."

"No," Skyler's shout rang through the cabin.

Mia backed away, but the soldier grabbed her by the arm.

"Commodore Bay figured we might as well start as soon as possible," he muttered, dragging her toward the hatch. Worry pierced through her confusion like a fork of lightning. She had to stay with her crew. Had to! She thrashed, dragging her boots against the deck. Both Skyler and Cassidy moved to help, and the solider swiveled his gun their direction. "Don't even think about it, ladies, you're staying right here. We'll bring her back when we're done."

I know where you are, Mia, a little birdy told me. You don't need to worry.

Almost instantly, Mia stopped struggling. Her eyes unfocused, blurring the world. Why was she struggling in the first place? Cassidy yelled for her, but Mia didn't care.

Somehow, Skyler got past the guard and grabbed Mia's hand. "Contain yourself, Mia."

The soldier punched Skyler, who landed in a heap on the deck, and shoved Mia through the hatch in front of him out the hatch. She went without a fight.

"Glad to see you've given in," he said.

Five armed soldiers greeted them outside. They formed a tight circle around Mia and ushered her down the corridor. Now outside, away from her crew, her feelings returned, crashing over her, worry clenching her muscles. Still, she was Mia Foley, Captain of the *Eclipse*. And it made her a bit proud to have so many guards around her. Even if they weren't actually for her.

Mia smirked, eyeing the guards. "Don't you think this is overkill for one woman?"

"Commodore Bay doesn't take any chances," a soldier replied.

They stopped by a hatch marked *Laboratory Zone 1*.

"Apparently not," Mia replied. "Think your lab is close enough?"

The balding soldier sneered. "We don't want our rats scurrying far, now do we, silver?"

Mia clenched her jaw, knowing full well she could knock his lights out if she wanted to. Now wasn't the time for that. Not yet. She scowled at the man.

He laughed and punched in the code to open the hatch. Bright light washed over Mia, brighter than she could see through. He shoved her inside. A needle jabbed her shoulder, the metal piercing deep. A salty taste invaded her mouth. Her muscles relaxed, but before she fell, someone caught her and carried her to a table. They tied her wrists and ankles down and placed a wide strip of fabric across her stomach. A sliver of tape sealed her mouth. She blinked the brightness away. A medic covered in white leaned over and placed a mask on her mouth and nose. Brown eyes peered at her. Familiar eyes, almost. She held her breath, as a steady stream of air whooshed over her face.

"This will help calm you." The medic's voice was muffled by her face shield. Yet her voice was familiar. Leaning closer, the medic whispered, "Try not to struggle, Mia, it won't help. Not here. Not yet."

The sudden concern from the medic seemed off. And how did the medic know her name? Did everyone around here? Or was this someone she had saved?

"She won't need that, soldier."

Mia recognized that voice. Commodore Bay lurked somewhere in the cabin. She glanced around but could only see white curtains surrounding her.

The medic pulled the mask away and gently squeezed her arm. A click resounded in the small space and a green holoimage mimicking Mia's face appeared above her, pulling her attention. Her flesh and bones drew away, leaving her muscles behind until most of them disappeared. Soon, only an image of her brain remained. Mia shuddered at the sight. The image zoomed in, showing a jumble of pathways and pinpricks.

Another soldier leaned into her view, eyeing the holoimage of the brain. "The picobots are small enough to go between the neurons. They fill up the synaptic clefts. Occipital, parietal, temporal, frontal lobes, the entire brain is being compromised." The man looked over his shoulder. "Do you think the others are like her?"

"No," Commodore Bay replied.

We don't need anyone else.

The holoimage version of her muscles rematerialized. She twitched, pushing against the hard table. The holoimage moved with her, its hand twitching.

"Look how perfect her musculature is. He must have altered her over time, cycles even, that's why he took so long to activate her." The soldier almost seemed in awe. As if this was a good thing.

The holoimage glowed. "Something's happening."

I can do this with just you.

"Fascinating. Her limbic system just activated. Her amygdalae are being stimulated. Her primary auditory cortex is—"

Mia didn't hear any more of their conversation. Her body quivered. Anger overwhelmed her once more. She snapped free of her bonds and ripped the tape off her lips. The soldier tried to back away, but wasn't fast enough. No one was faster than her. She punched him in the throat. He crumpled. Sliding off the table, she tore through the white curtains. The medic had vanished, gone to do some other task. A bare cabin lay beyond. Commodore Bay wasn't in there after all. Three guards aimed guns at her. One soldier's gaze flicked to the ceiling panels. She followed. A little black bulb swiveled to face her.

So he wants a show does he? Give him one for me.

Mia grabbed the guard and elbowed him in the face, grappling for his gun. Winning, she threw the weapon and smashed the bulb. A shower of sparks brightened the cabin.

Not here.

Mia stopped fighting. The other guards reacted quickly. One punched her in the stomach while another wrapped his arm around her neck. A third slapped bindings on her wrists and shoved her through the hatch. More waited on the other side. Donavin's control ebbed. Pain blossomed in her abdomen. Her elbow ached. She groaned, hazy and sluggish. Fear pounded in her heart. Had she hurt the medic? Mia had recognized the woman, though from which ship she didn't know. Donavin was winning. She was losing herself.

The corridor seemed to sway. Blur. Her head throbbed again. The soldiers kept a firm grip on her arms, and two more followed. Skyler had showed her the containing technique, how to pull together and protect herself. Mia tried imagining walls, but nothing formed in her mind's eye. She imagined one of the *Eclipse*'s storage containers. A simple metal box with a lid. Solid, sturdy, familiar. How would she put herself inside it? A blue light glowed within the container. She snapped the top shut. Was that light her? She felt no different. Her boots made an odd scraping sound on the deck, distracting her. It was only after she looked down that she realized she was being dragged. Idiot. She should've been trying to escape. She thrashed and kicked, and the men stopped. They arrived at the brig's hatch and righted her. One of the soldiers entered the code.

The hatch slid open. Her crew rose from their seats and stared at her, while the guards shoved her inside. The hatch shut behind Mia with a slight hiss. Pain needled in the back of her skull. A little black bulb was tucked into the corner of this cabin.

You don't need to feel anything anymore, Mia.

Mia turned to her friends, to Will stepping forward, to Jeff smirking, to Cassidy stopping just an arm's length away, and finally to Skyler who grabbed hold of Cassidy and shoved her aside. Mia focused on the silver eyes of the woman now in front of her. Her vision blurred.

"Skyler, help," she pleaded.

Pain spiked once more in her head.

Chapter Ten

IT FELT LIKE SHE was falling, darkness clouding her vision, cottonflower muffling her hearing, cold numbing her limbs. Then the world brightened again, her vision cleared, her hearing sharpened. She focused on the ex-Acedian, on the nurse, on the friend standing in front of her.

Skyler reached for her, pressing against her arm, shoving the sleeve up her skin, shouting, "You can fight this. You have to fight."

But it all seemed distant, as though Mia was just a passenger tucked away in the corner of her own mind. She tried to move. Couldn't. Something blocked her. So, she was just a passenger. At least she was still here, still present. Still whole. At least for now. Mia hung onto that hope. Donavin controlled her now, leafing through her memories, invading her with his thoughts.

Jones is a spy? She helped you escape? Traitor.

Mia didn't want to fight her friends, but he did. Her gaze swept over Skyler's military uniform, and without warning, she punched Skyler in the gut. Skyler groaned, falling to the deck. Mia dropped to her knees and landed astride the woman.

"I will kill you, traitor." The words weren't her own.

Blood dribbled out the corner of Skyler's mouth. "You'll have to try harder than that, Donavin."

Mia punched her again. Blood spurted from Skyler's nose. She groaned. Her eyes fluttered shut.

Even though it was the furthest action from her true self, Mia smiled. "Trust me, with this body it won't be that hard."

She got to her feet and searched the cabin. Will and Jeff stood by the regenerator. Cassidy backed away. No weapons. No armor. No guards. Perfect. She started for Cassidy.

No. Mia's thought ripped through Donavin's barrier.

Ah, you're still here? Allow me to welcome you to my world, Mia. It's a lovely place. Keep your eyes peeled, though.

Mia's eyesight sharpened. Fear wrinkled Cassidy's face, webbed into the corners of her eyes, the barely perceptible tremble of her chin, the vein pulsing in her neck. In the slight shaking of her brown eyes as she backed away. Things Mia never would have noticed before now captivated her.

Mia frantically pushed her thoughts out. *Don't you dare hurt her, you quasar!*

The corners of her own lips twitched up as Donavin responded. *Why, Mia, I would never do such a thing. You might though.*

Cassidy raised her hands in front of her. "I know you don't want to hurt me."

Mia moved faster than even she could imagine, pushing her arm into Cassidy's neck in an instant. "I'm not her any longer, fool."

Cassidy tore at Mia's hold, gasping for breath. Her fingers scraped uselessly against Mia's arm. She changed tactics and shoved an elbow hard into Mia's stomach. Doubling over, Mia let go. She righted quickly and grabbed Cassidy's shoulder. She jerked down, ripping the sleeve off and scratching a deep red line across Cassidy's skin. Cassidy yelled, pushing her other hand over the wound.

No, Mia shouted, but her thought was swept away.

Cassidy clenched her teeth. "I don't want to do this, Mia. I don't want to fight you. I know it's not you." Tears welled in the corners of her eyes. "I won't."

"I will."

Mia turned to the speaker. Jeff stepped forward. Donavin brought up images of him in Mia's head. Memories she couldn't have, memories that weren't hers. Hauling him from the *Eclipse*, torturing done by electrocution, the sizzling of burnt flesh. Their gaze met, Jeff's green eyes flashed silver for only a moment and for only her.

Donavin linked with Jeff, his voice echoing. *Jeffery, how are you?*

Jeff's thoughts spiraled over their link, answering Donavin's query. *Leave me alone! Skyler will hear you. She'll know what you're trying to do. She'll know.*

Donavin snapped their link apart but realization sank in. Jeff was turning into an Acedian. Mia's gaze flitted to the deck panels where Skyler lay motionless. *She won't be an issue now.* Donavin linked with Jeff again. *I'm afraid this will hurt though.*

Mia lunged, latching onto Jeff's arm with one hand and his throat with the other. Caught off balance, Jeff stumbled back onto the regenerator. He swung his fist around, connecting with her side. She squeezed his throat tighter in response. Jeff swung from above, knocking her arm away and shoving her backward. She regained her footing, but Jeff moved fast. Too fast. Acedian fast. He knocked her to the deck, grabbing both hands in one of his and forcing them down. Then he slapped her. Hard. Mia didn't feel it, and this time she was thankful. But why only a slap?

"Snap out of it!" He shook her. "Stop fighting us, Mia. We're trying to help."

Mia grabbed his arm, locked a leg with his and bucked, rolling Jeff over her shoulder and standing in one fluid motion. He regained his footing, a flash of pain creasing his features together. They circled each other. His green eyes burned into hers.

Donavin shoved his thoughts out. *Good.*

Jeff barreled into her, slamming her back against the bulkhead. She kneed him in the groin, and he doubled over, wincing, and when their gazes locked, his green eyes flashed silver. His face smoothed, and his thoughts reverberated in Mia. *Am I convincing enough?*

Mia shoved him away. He tumbled to the deck, groaning. She stepped closer to him but a hand pulled her back. Will's blow landed square on her jaw and sent her sprawling.

"Don't touch him again." He pulled her upright and socked her in the eye. She crumpled, although Donavin's mirth caused her body to shake with laughter. Her lips pulled back into a grin.

He's a strong one, but he won't be after Jeffery becomes mine. Poor man, the pain will be too much. Maybe he'll follow his brother along like he's been doing for the rest of his life.

Mia pushed out her thoughts over the link, anger surging them through. *He won't.*

Will righted her again. This time, Mia didn't struggle. Donavin didn't want to anymore. Will shoved her into a chair beside the regenerator and called to Cassidy. "Find something to bind her with. Anything."

Cassidy moved from her spot by the hatch and glanced around. Fear still creased her forehead. "We don't have anything strong enough to hold her."

"I have something that will," a voice came from the hatch.

Mia didn't need to see the man to recognize the voice. Commodore Bay had finally come to play. She smiled but didn't attack. Donavin didn't want to. Bay stepped through the open hatch and walked to the side, reaching up for the little black bulb. It detached, and he placed an identical one in its spot. Cassidy stepped in between the commodore and Mia. Even Will moved closer, keeping a firm hand on her shoulder. The commodore tossed a rope to Cassidy. A flimsy, threaded rope.

Cassidy threw it away. "You know that wouldn't hold a Jihhasian mole."

Commodore Bay nodded, meandering through the cabin. He lingered by Skyler and Jeff, then he turned to Mia. He started clapping. A slow, annoying sound. "I'm impressed with the speed you've acquired."

He tilted his head and met her gaze. *And you too, Donavin. Well done. I figured you'd want to take out Jones. Mia's a fine specimen, though. You molded her perfectly. And the Dee brother will be an asset to your ranks.*

No. Mia wanted to back away. Wanted to scream. She couldn't. It couldn't be possible. Commodore Bay was an Acedian? What about his eyes? They weren't silver!

Donavin answered her question. *Lenses.*

The simplicity infuriated her.

"Leave her alone," Cassidy said, her voice lowering.

Mia rallied around Cassidy's threat. Could Cassidy possibly confront him? This was his ship with his rules and, to top it off, he was a covert Acedian. Mia sat, as if rooted to the spot. Donavin wanted to wait, so she did.

Commodore Bay walked back to the hatch, stepping over Skyler as he went. "Don't worry, Miss Gates. I have everything I need from her at the moment." He produced a vial from his breast pocket. The vial contained a dark red liquid that looked like blood. "It's hers. I intend to test it to see how the bots work in the bloodstream." The commodore flicked his gaze to Mia. *We're almost ready with the accelerated picobots. This should give me enough to work with and disseminate.*

Donavin pushed through the link a warning. *Careful. This one's still active. A fighter.*

Bay arched an eyebrow. *Really?*

"Fascinating," he said, out loud this time.

Cassidy moved back, even closer to Mia now. "What's fascinating?"

Bay nodded to Mia. "That she's so docile, when just moments before she wanted to kill you."

When Cassidy remained silent, Bay motioned to a guard standing outside the hatch. The guard's dark eyes met Mia's for a heartbeat, and he tapped the tray twice before handing it to Bay. An odd motion. Mia didn't understand what it meant, and Donavin didn't seem to care. He focused her hearing on Bay. "This is your evening meal. From the look of your companions, you'll need it."

He shoved the tray toward her. After a moment's hesitation, Cassidy took the tray. Mia could see blood seeping from Cassidy's wound and the red handprint she'd left behind on her arm. The crimson stain contrasted with the paleness of her skin. A strand of her dark clothing caught in the cut. Mia wanted to brush it away, but Donavin didn't, so she remained still.

Commodore Bay put a hand to his heart in a military salute and backed out of the cabin. The hatch sealed shut, locking the rest of her crew with not one, but two Acedians. Donavin forced her to look at Cassidy. At her brown hair streaming down her shoulders. At the wound still weeping blood. Would they survive a night together? Would she?

Chapter Eleven

BLEMISHES MARRED ONE SIDE of the nearest crimson berry. Its sweet scent wafted over to Mia. Fresh baked bread, fruit, and speckled cheese sat haphazardly on the tray, waiting for someone to take a bite. It had been sitting out for an hour. No one touched it.

Will sighed. "It's probably poisoned."

Cassidy shrugged. "Seems like a lame attempt to kill us off." She picked up one of the berries and thumbed it between her fingers.

Struggling against Donavin's hold, Mia wanted to shout. *Don't eat it!*

Cassidy popped the red berry into her mouth. "If I die in a few hours, we'll know."

It wasn't fair. What if Cassidy did die from such a simple act, such a simple stupid little thing?

***

The hour had passed slowly, and they had taken turns tending to Skyler. Will had carried her to the cot, where Cassidy wiped the blood from her face and covered her to keep her warm. They had helped Jeff up, propping him into a seat. Throughout all of this, though, they had not let Mia sit unhindered by a hand or a watchful eye.

Even now, Will's palm rested on her shoulder. "Should we knock her out or something?"

Jeff, who sat across from her, shook his head then winced. "No, she's not showing signs of aggression right now. Who knows? Knocking her out might actually let Donavin in further."

Cassidy sat next to him. "Do you think they're fighting right now?"

"I don't know." Jeff ran a hand through his hair. "I wouldn't want to help him."

"I wish Skyler was awake," Cassidy murmured. "She knows more about the Acedians than any of us."

Will shifted his weight, his palm growing heavier. "She's working with the military, though. How can we trust her?"

"Why would they shove her into this prison with us otherwise?" Cassidy glanced over at the cot where Skyler rested. "She didn't know."

After a moment of silence, Will asked, "So, what do we do now?"

Cassidy chewed on her lip. "Break out. Find a way to help Mia. Go into hiding, maybe, after we do."

She grabbed a piece of cheese and took a bite of it. There, under the cheese, something glinted. It caught Cassidy's attention, and she plucked it from the tray.

"What's this?" She held it to the others. About the size of a thumb and wire thin, the metal object glinted green and blue.

Jeff moved closer. "It's a memory chip. You put it into a ship or shuttle's comm device, and it shows whatever's inside." He looked around at the cabin. "We can't use it in here, though."

"Are there more?" Will dug into the food, shifting it this way and that, spilling some onto the deck, but found no other memory chips. "No. Who gave it to us, anyway? Harrison, maybe?"

No one answered, because her crew didn't know. Mia knew who had given it to them. The dark-eyed guard. That's why he had tapped the tray. They couldn't use it in here, though, why give it to them? Mia worried that Donavin would do something, attack, if the memory chip was something useful to her crew. He didn't. And that concerned Mia even more.

Cassidy rubbed the back of her neck and sighed. "Well, keep it hidden, for now, okay? Whoever gave it to us might be trying to help us. Help Mia."

Will nodded and slipped the chip into his pants pocket, while Cassidy looked at Mia, forehead creased with worry. Mia stared back. Donavin wanted to listen, to observe, to remain still and unobtrusive. Mia didn't. She willed her arm to move. Her muscles didn't even twitch. She tried moving her foot. Not even a shift. Maybe something small would work. She tried to blink. Nothing.

Stop trying, Mia. You don't control anything anymore.

Donavin's thoughts infuriated her. As did his constant manipulations of her senses. One moment she'd hear everything in the cabin—Will's quick breathing, Cassidy's heartbeat, the gentle hum of the regenerator—the next she'd hear nothing. Her eyes would focus on the smallest detail like the stitching on the blanket only to blur as she looked out the viewport. He was test-driving her, seeing if he liked his new drone.

A heavy weight pressed down on her, calling her to sleep, while Donavin tugged at her resolve. She slipped away for a moment, his picobots taking a deeper hold. The blue light in her mind's eye dimmed. She stared at William and Jeffery Dee: brothers, one an ally, one a threat. The picobots in Jeffery's system would take over in less than a week. One week and a new drone would be theirs. Her gaze turned to Cassidy Gates, another threat but not a physical one. At the stupid female who—

No. Mia roused herself. She pushed, fueling her energy into that blue glow, locking it deeper away. Somehow Donavin hadn't found it yet. Hadn't gotten all of her. *Cassidy is not stupid.*

"I wonder what's happening to her," Cassidy said.

"Something we need to stop," Skyler muttered from the corner of the cabin.

Mia's head jerked sideways. Donavin apparently wanted to look at Skyler, the ex-Acedian. The nurse sat up, pushing a hand to her forehead. She groaned, her eyes landing squarely on Mia. "Has she attacked anyone else?"

"No," Cassidy whispered.

A frown wrinkled Jeff's face. "Aside from me, and Will, and almost you."

"She didn't mean to," Cassidy replied.

Skyler scooted her legs off the bed to rest her boots on the deck. "No, Mia doesn't want to, Donavin does."

Donavin's anger thundered. *The traitor better stay seated or I'll force her to.*

Skyler stood, her face paling. She wavered for a moment and sat back down again.

Mia's lips pulled into a smirk, Donavin was happy about Skyler's pain.

"What happened while I was out?" Skyler asked.

Will related the commodore's comings and goings to Skyler. She grimaced. "He clapped? And gave us food? What the breach is that about?"

"No idea," Will said. "We still need to find a way out of here before Mia goes berserk on us again."

Cassidy stepped forward. "It's Donavin doing these things, not Mia." Her voice took on a defensive edge.

"I know, Cassidy. I know." Will raised his hands.

Skyler frowned. "You might need to stop thinking of her as Mia.

Once Donavin goes through the final stage there's not much of the original person left."

Instinctually, Cassidy shifted closer to Mia. "But there is some left, some part of her, right?"

"Maybe, but that's a breaching tiny maybe." Skyler hesitated. "I showed her a way to contain herself back on Fissure. There's no telling if she could do it. She might be just a drone, now."

Cassidy's hand drifted across Mia's forehead before coming to a rest on her shoulder. "There is a chance?"

Skyler rubbed her cheek, the skin still red and slightly puffy from Mia's punch. "Yes, a slight chance."

"Then that's enough," Cassidy whispered.

The weight of Cassidy's hand comforted Mia, but in one swift motion, faster than anything before, Donavin forced Mia to act. She jerked from Will's grasp and twisted. The clear shot became apparent moments before Donavin took it.

No! Mia willed herself to stop. Willed her muscles to freeze.

They didn't and in the end, her fist slammed into Cassidy's side. The attack wasn't hard, but Cassidy stumbled back. She rubbed her side, and her eyes filled with fear. Doubt.

Will yanked Mia back into the chair. "She could probably kill us all. Why doesn't she?"

"Donavin's playing with us," Skyler said. "There really might be nothing left of her."

I'm here, Mia thought. *I'm still here.* But no one could hear her. No one except Donavin. She had never felt so helpless.

Jeff scoffed, staring not at Mia, rather at Skyler, a hard glint in his eyes. "Can't you just connect with her to find out?"

"No." Skyler's lips tightened into a thin line.

Before she could explain herself, Donavin pulled Mia's focus elsewhere. Liquid ice seeped into her eardrum, sharpening her hearing. The hatch's locking mechanism whirred. A heartbeat later, the hatch opened and someone stepped inside. Harrison made a show of going over to the recording bulb and taking it down, just like Commodore Bay had done, and then slipped back over to the hatch. He closed it.

Will's grasp tightened on Mia's shoulder. "What do you want?"

Harrison fidgeted, staring at the empty space where a replacement bulb should be. It seemed he was trying to make a decision and hadn't quite come to it yet. Cold descended in the back of Mia's eyes. Her vision focused on Harrison's neck. A tiny red puncture blemished his skin above his collar.

Donavin's joy came out in a rush, filling her like a cool breeze. *Perfect.*

Confused about why such an insignificant thing would be perfect, Mia ignored him and tried to listen to the conversation instead. Donavin complied and pulled her focus back once more.

"They'll get suspicious if I stay here too long," Harrison said. "We'll have to do this fast. You have to reach the scientist before she's gone completely."

Cassidy folded her arms across her chest and tilted her head, giving him a sneer Mia hadn't seen on her first mate's face before. "Why should we trust you?"

Harrison ignored her and looked at Mia instead, giving Mia an apologetic smile. "I knew it was protocol to contain you. I didn't realize they were going to turn you into one of them."

Skyler let out a disbelieving laugh from her place by the cot. "You didn't get thrown in here with us."

Harrison grinned and spread his hands. "Of course not. Commodore Bay can't throw me into the brig. Not without Admiral Boreas' authorization at least. Without *Bell*, this ship wouldn't have had a chance against that Acedian warship." His gaze shifted to the rest of the group. "I've seen the things they do to their enemies. I've heard even worse stories in here about what happens. I don't want that to happen to any of you. Besides, I'm probably the only chance you have at getting out of here."

The boy makes a valid point, Donavin mused.

Cassidy placed a hand on Mia's shoulder, though hers was much gentler and softer than Will's. "Won't your superiors know?" she asked. Anger still crystalized her voice, all hard edges and sharp points.

"Not if you knock me out. Take my gun. Cause a huge scene in here. This'll make it easier." He threw Cassidy a small package, which she caught one-handed. "Inside's a comp-tact we confiscated from Sheryl Stargazer, the woman on Pargon. I can use it to tell you where to go."

"How do we know you're actually helping us?" Disbelief infused Will's tone, and even though Donavin didn't look at him directly, Mia could picture the frown on his face perfectly.

Harrison walked closer to them before passing by them completely, moving out of Mia's and Donavin's view. There was a slight rustle, and Will's hand lifted from Mia's shoulder. Donavin forced Mia's head to the side, staring at Will as he turned away from her. They glared at Will's back.

"Twist it," Harrison said.

Twist what? Mia hadn't a clue.

"What is it?" Skyler asked.

Before Donavin could make her move, Will turned around once more and wove something around Mia's wrists. A halved orb connected by a thin strand of pulsing light. The strange light instantly affected her. Numbed, her arms hung heavy. Donavin tried to move them, flooding ice down her arms to her fingertips. Nothing happened. She still couldn't move her limbs, but neither could Donavin. It was a small, if odd, comfort.

"You don't think we would have Acedians onboard without a way to contain them, did you?" Harrison replied.

"It emits a high-energy pulse wave that immobilizes the bots," Harrison explained, moving back into view. "It's temporary. It's all we have now to combat them."

"Why didn't you give that technology to me?" Skyler yelped.

He waved the question away. "You'll take one of the shuttles. They're small and fast, and I can scramble your trail." He tapped the side of his face. His left eye glowed bright orange. "There's no one in the corridor. Now's your time."

Was he serious? Mia couldn't tell, but she didn't see any other way of getting off the ship. Her gaze shifted to Skyler.

Skyler tried to stand and fell back onto the cot with a grunt. She shoved strands of dark hair out of her eyes, frowning at the group. "I'm going to need help here."

"Okay," Cassidy said, giving Mia's shoulder a slight squeeze before letting go. "Jeff, you help Skyler. Will and I can handle Mia. I'll take the gun."

Jeff tapped a finger on the regenerator to a beat only he could hear. A nervous habit, just like his brother. Mia locked eyes with him.

Donavin linked to him. *Stay on the ship, Jeff. Help here.*

He shoved away from the table. "No."

"What?" Will's voice pitched.

Donavin pressed harder. *Stay on board the ship, Jeffery. You can help them here.*

"I think I can do better work here. I can figure out who the scientist is and transmit it to you." Jeff stepped back, shaking his head. "But I want to go with you."

Stay with the military. Donavin insisted. Mia could only listen to his strange request. Confusion swirled in her mind. Stay with the military. Why? What was the point? Then it dawned on her. It was a test, like so many others she had encountered. A test to see what he would do.

Jeff jerked his head to the side as if he'd been hit. His hands clenched into fists.

Mia knew the struggle he was going through. Knew the push and pull of Donavin's picobots. Knew the oddity of having two minds in your own body. Didn't her crew notice how odd Jeff acted? No. No, they wouldn't. After all, she hadn't. Not really. Not until it was too late.

Will brushed against her arm as he moved closer to his brother. "You have to come with us, Jeff. We might be able to help Mia, and maybe we can get closer to saving our friends on Paradous, too."

"I want to..." Jeff glanced at Mia.

Stay on board.

"Stay with the crew," Jeff finished.

Mia's gaze flitted to Will. The scowl marring his features gave her a bit of hope. Surely his own brother would think something was off. "Of course you do," he said, slapping his brother on the shoulder.

Donavin swiveled her gaze back to Jeff's, his anger pounding. *You will pay for that.*

I have to stay with my brother, Donavin.

Jeff broke the link, went over to Skyler, and picked her up. Skyler protested, but Jeff merely held her tighter. "It'll be faster if I carry you."

Skyler sighed and rolled her eyes in a reluctant consent.

"Good," Cassidy said. Mia's gaze swung to her. All business, Cassidy put in the comp-tact and blinked a few times before tapping her temple. The comp-tact glowed bright orange. It wouldn't be easy to hide the device, and of course, Cassidy would be the one to risk it for Mia's sake at least. She pulled Mia to her feet and led the way to the hatch, then looked at Harrison. "Do you want us to actually hit you?"

He lifted his chin and smiled. "A solid punch to the jaw will do."

Cassidy motioned to Will, who, after a slight hesitation and a wince, punched Harrison. Rocking back, Harrison clutched his face and let out a moan.

"Sorry," Will said, helping him steady.

When Harrison finally lowered his hands, a red bruise spread from his cheek. Blood dripped from his nose. He sniffed and said, "No, that was good." He paused for a moment, orange eye focused on the bulkhead behind Will. "It's still clear. Go."

At that signal, Cassidy opened the hatch and slipped out, leading with the gun and pulling Mia behind.

Quietly, Mia, no sudden movements or noises.

Mia pushed her thoughts toward him. *Why do you want to leave, Donavin? You have an ally onboard.*

I have an ally on your crew, Mia.

Not yet.

True, not completely. Soon, I will. The contentment in his thoughts concerned her.

Cassidy tapped her temple once, searching the winding corridor before them. It was empty, but the comp-tact could use all of the recording bulbs to see farther than just around the corner. They crept past an oblong hatch with a spiral design etched into one corner. The symbol didn't hold any significance to Mia, though Donavin's hesitation was obvious.

You don't need to see any more.

He focused on Cassidy, until Mia could distinguish each individual strand of her swaying hair, each thread of fabric running through her clothes, until the trickle of blood from her arm wound seemed like a waterfall, until the veins running through her arm became blue mountain peaks. Because of such focus, Mia couldn't tell where they were going, but the halting route took many turns. They stopped often and whispered around her.

"This way," Cassidy murmured.

A hand gripped Mia's arm. Will's voice came quietly. "I think I hear footsteps in that direction. He could be leading us into a trap."

Donavin sharpened her hearing. The distinct clunk of boots hitting the deck came from directly ahead. *What will you do? It's the quickest way to the shuttle bay.*

"He's not," Cassidy snapped. "We're essentially there, anyway."

They continued forward a little while longer then turned and stopped.

"See?" she said.

She's a little nervous, isn't she? Donavin chuckled.

Shut up, Mia snapped, already growing tired of his commentary.

Why don't we aid her in this dilemma?

Donavin withdrew the intense focus, and Mia's vision cleared. Her crew stood inside a dimly lit corridor. A large circular hatch loomed on her left, and Cassidy stood by her right, prying open a control panel. Mia jerked away from Will's grasp. She twisted and slammed her boot against the hatch. The kick created a satisfying, and horrifying, clang.

"Here, you fools, we're down h—" Mia shouted before Will grabbed her from behind and muffled her voice with his hand. Cassidy dropped the wiring she had been working on with a quiet gasp and spun to her, one eye going wide, the other still glowing. Skyler gave a few short motions for them to continue working and didn't notice the small smile on Jeff's face. Mia did, however, and somewhere inside her Donavin smiled in return. Will tightened his hold, and Cassidy continued to work. But those sounds were enough. The distant steady tread started running.

"Hey!" A voice came from their side.

Mia's gaze darted to the sound. She smiled. A tall, thin soldier stepped into view and pointed a gun in their direction. The man looked each one over in turn, but once he got to Mia, his mouth fell slack. "No way."

The soldier wavered for a moment before he rushed to their side, knocking Cassidy away from the panel and opening it up. "Saving Mia Foley. My sister would get a kick out of this."

They watched, as the man pushed his fingers into the wiring and fiddled around a little. The hatch to the shuttle bay spiraled open. Without waiting, Jeff barreled through, carrying Skyler with him. Will followed close behind, tugging on Mia and Cassidy as he did. Cassidy didn't move.

"Are you the one who gave us the memory chip?" she asked.

The man gave her a broad, toothy smile, and now Mia recognized him. He was just a kid on the *Oasis*, a bumbling little boy clutching onto his mother. The ones who had been in the escape shuttle with her. The ones who had pulled her aboard.

"No, one of the others did that." His gaze shifted to Mia, bright-green eyes glimmering. "We didn't want you to turn into an Acedian, Mia. The admiral was wrong to try to do that to you. You saved us from the Acedian attack, now we're saving you."

Mia couldn't respond, Donavin didn't want to, so Cassidy muttered a quick thanks and pulled her toward the shuttle with Will. Donavin flipped through Mia's mind, trying to figure out who else had helped her, who else had seemed familiar. The sanitation guard was from the *Scarlet*, one of the healers on that ship; the dark-eyed man was from the *Luminaria;* and the medic, she was from the *Jubilee*. Amazing any of them lived. She remembered them all. A rush of relief flowed through her before Donavin shut it down.

Why would they go through so much trouble to save a drone? The thought reverberated in Mia. Donavin didn't know. Didn't understand. The thought crashed through Mia even after the man shut the hatch, even after they darted across the nearly empty shuttle bay, even after they clambered inside the only shuttle left.

Mia caught glimpses of the shuttle, as Will and Cassidy yanked her inside. Jeff placed Skyler in the command chair and slid into the other. The others sat on benches that lined the hull. Pods probably filled with supplies took up the rest of the space. It was a tight squeeze, even for their small crew. Will shoved her onto one of the benches and flicked a switch by her head. Metal straps flapped across her chest and locked her in. An unneeded safety measure, though, Donavin didn't seem to want to escape any longer. This concerned Mia. Donavin seemed all too calm for a prisoner.

Harrison's voice shot through the comm system. "I'm opening the bay hatch. According to everyone else, this is just a routine flight to scan the area. Go slowly. I'll tell you when you can hit the MP Drive propulsion. And Cassidy, take out the comp-tact. These things don't hold much energy. Put it back in when you reach the scientist. I'll be able to show him you're one of us."

Cassidy placed the device back in its container and onto the seat next to her. The engine hummed to life. The deck rumbled. The cabin dimmed, and the shuttle rose, as Skyler maneuvered out of the bay. They flew around the *Escambia* for a while, scanning the streamlined military ship and the darkness beyond. Skyler transmitted the necessary information back to Harrison. A map appeared on the starboard side of the viewport. Blue stars formed, a line connecting them together and ended at a tiny, darker blue dot.

Harrison's voice came through the comm again. "These are coordinates to the scientist. Follow them and you'll find him. Follow them and you may be able to help Mia. Hit the Drive in five...four...three...two...one."

The blast rocked Mia back into her seat.

Chapter Twelve

MIA STUDIED THE BASIC map. A simple map, with only a few points of light leading to the scientist. Without looking at the shuttle's internal sensors, Donavin would never know. And with the bonds proving stronger than anything else he'd encountered, he couldn't break Mia free and command those screens. Donavin had become a passenger, just like her. He seemed fine with it, though, and that concerned Mia. Apart from inspecting the only hatch in the shuttle and the various buttons around that hatch, he didn't shift Mia's body or twist her into his weapon.

He did seem annoyed though. His musings echoed. *Bay claimed that soldier was on our side. He was supposed to kill her.* Donavin fabricated an image of Cassidy lying on the deck, a puncture wound through her neck. *I wonder if he's wrong about other things.*

Even a fake death scared Mia. She willed it away, and to her surprise, the image shattered. Drifted into darkness. The shuttle came back into view. Had she done that? No, probably not. Probably just a test like when Donavin challenged Jeff's resolve back on the *Escambia*. A good designer always tested his new drones.

Donavin forced her eyes down and to the side, inspecting the straps holding her in place. The straps cut into her skin, whitening the flesh around it, but Mia didn't feel their pinch. She didn't feel pain anymore. Except the psychological pain of wondering what she would do next and to whom she would do it. Her focus wavered, yet Donavin seemed content in his control over her as well. He didn't try to suppress her this time.

When she pushed back, he answered. *You can come along for the ride. It won't be long now, anyway.*

A rustle of movement caught her attention. Donavin shifted her sight forward. Cassidy sat across from her and opened one of the pods etched with an ellipse engraved with the letter M. Medical supplies. She lifted a bubble gun from the other items and placed it next to her on the bench. She also retrieved a bottle of clear liquid and a foam gun.

Unbuttoning her shirt, she pulled dirty black fabric from her shoulder.

Donavin forced Mia to look away, narrowing her vision to the screens out of reach. Mia tried to turn back, to see the scratch on Cassidy's shoulder. A muscle in her neck twitched, but her head didn't turn. If she could claw at the man holding her captive, she would. She could only sit. Sit and stare at the useless, stupid glow coming from the screens.

She loves you, you know. Donavin's opinion filtered through her in a derisive tone. *Love makes you weak. Without her you are halved, just like without you, she will never be whole. You'd be surprised how compromised that makes people.*

Mia pushed her thoughts out. *You will never hurt her again.*

A feeling of happiness came over their link. Mia tried her best to ignore it. When Donavin allowed her vision to broaden, Cassidy had already covered the wound with a bandage, and Will stared at the comp-tact.

Donavin forced Mia to glance downward, looking at the orange comp-tact that sat next to Cassidy. He wanted that device. He lifted their gaze.

"No." Cassidy's voice was firm.

"No, what?" Will asked a little too innocently.

She frowned. "You can't use the comp-tact."

Will broke out into a grin. "Not even for a little bit? I heard it's like being connected to every single device on the planet and can be activated just by the person's thoughts and can—"

"It's not all that grand," Cassidy interrupted, putting a hand over the comp-tact, shielding it from Will and Donavin's hungry gazes.

"Can you at least tell me how it feels?" Will leaned closer to Cassidy.

"Well, it's—"

Donavin muffled Mia's hearing, but she didn't care. Will looked so happy. It reminded her of the day they'd spent on Pargon, when Will first saw a comp-tact and babbled like an idiot about it all the way to the Tin Roof. So much had changed since. Both Will and Cassidy laughed, pulling her out of her memories. If Mia could smile, she would. It comforted Mia that some things hadn't changed. Her stare drifted to Skyler.

Jeff was mumbling something to Skyler. Cold leaked into her ears and his mumbles became clear. "How long will it take to get to this scientist?"

"Tomorrow night if we push it."

Jeff's frown deepened. "Do you think she'll last that long?"

Skyler waited a moment before answering. "If she's in there, she's fighting."

Aside from Skyler tapping the controls and shifting their course to stay on track, the crew stilled now, each person lost in their own thoughts. The steady hum of the engines lulled Mia into a stupor. Donavin's thoughts didn't intrude. The quiet seemed unnerving, but she welcomed it. She tried to move her eyes, shift them even slightly to the side, couldn't. As she sat there quietly, she realized that time with just herself felt nice, immobilized as she may be. Her thoughts wandered to Cassidy, as they always seemed to do. At least she had taken good control of the crew. A surge of pride raced through Mia at that thought. If only Cassidy could see how oddly Jeff acted. They traveled to a place far away from the military ship. But they also traveled with another Acedian, one no one seemed to notice, not even Skyler.

Jeff yawned, breaking the silence, and curling up like a technopet.

Will started to nod off, then jerked up, gaze flitting to Mia. "Should someone watch her?"

"I will." Skyler volunteered.

"Wake us up if anything goes awry." He settled back again, snoring within seconds.

Jeff grumbled about his uncomfortable navigation chair for a moment, then he, too, settled. Even though she ached for sleep, Mia couldn't rest. She dared not. What if that's how Donavin took full control of her? Her head seemed full of cottonflower, but she couldn't settle her thoughts. What was on that memory chip? Her crew hadn't mentioned it yet. And they got off the ship so easily. Was Donavin's only plan now to turn Jeff and use him to attack? Surely he could figure out a way to get out of these bonds. Maybe he didn't want to escape at all.

Cassidy must've been thinking the same, for her quiet voice floated through the shuttle. "Should we even be going to the scientist?"

Skyler swiveled around in her chair, arching an eyebrow. "Why not?"

Cassidy tilted her head to Mia. "We could be leading Donavin to him."

"It's either this, or Donavin figures out a way to override the Mia we know completely." Skyler scowled.

"What if he's already done that?" Cassidy leaned forward, closer to the nurse.

Skyler stared back at the control panel, refusing to meet Cassidy's eyes. She seemed to gather herself, straightening her back and tilting her chin up. "Then deactivating the bots would take one more drone away from him."

Cassidy's voice quieted even more. "Do you think he has full control of her now?"

"Honestly?" Skyler replied, more to the control panel than to Cassidy. "Yes."

Mia wanted to scream. Her throat tightened, and no sound came. If only she could connect with Skyler one more time. Just for one second, to let her know she still existed.

Cassidy shook her head. "But you said—"

"I know what I said," Skyler snapped. She glared at the panel and sighed. "I can't go into her mind any longer. We're all drones to him. We're all connected by him. We should all be able to link with any one of us and speak with him. He blocked me, because he knows I'm a spy. He blocked me, because he doesn't want me knowing any more of his plans."

"So, she's gone?" Cassidy's voice wavered, and she pushed her hand to her heart.

"Probably, yes." Skyler stopped, as if only now realizing the implication. Finally, she met Cassidy's gaze. "I'm sorry."

Cassidy's back stiffened for a heartbeat before hunching forward, head in her hands, mumbling something. Mia's heart cracked right down the middle at the sight of it. She desperately wanted to hear those words. She strained, but Donavin didn't care. Skyler rubbed Cassidy's back, and after a moment, Cassidy lifted her head. Instead of looking at Skyler, she faced Mia.

"No," she said.

Mia wished she could signal her somehow. Tell her she still existed within this body. But Donavin didn't. So, in the end, Mia stared dispassionately.

Cassidy took a deep steadying breath. "No, I can't believe that. I need her." Cassidy's voice cracked. She took another breath. "She can't be erased so easily."

"Believe me, she wouldn't go down easily, but he's one tough quasar." Skyler leaned over and looked into Mia's eyes, as if wanting to peer into her very soul and see if Donavin truly rested there.

But I'm tougher! Mia shot the thought out, concentrating with all her might on that familiar silver tint.

Skyler's eyes widened. She stayed locked with Mia. Mia tried to push her thoughts out again. No links formed. Had Skyler heard her?

Donavin crashed back into her, leashing his hold tight around Mia. Ice flooded her system. She'd never felt so cold. Sadness leaked into her as well. Donavin laughed at Mia's misery. *Let's not communicate with the traitor, okay?*

Cassidy grabbed Skyler's arm. "What is it?"

Skyler waved a hand at her. "I...I thought I heard something."

"From Mia?" Cassidy scooted closer, darting back and forth between the pair.

Skyler winced. "Maybe."

"Was it her or Donavin?" Cassidy's voice quickened.

"I don't know. I couldn't tell." Skyler leaned back in her chair and rubbed her forehead.

"But...but I thought Donavin blocked you."

"He did and is doing so right now." Sympathy creased her brow. She blinked a bit too rapidly and faced Cassidy. "That doesn't mean he can't communicate with me. He's toying with us."

Tucking her knees up to her chin and wrapping her arms around them, Cassidy seemed to consider Skyler's explanation. She hugged her knees tighter. "I'll watch Mia tonight. You get some sleep."

Skyler reached out and rested a hand on Cassidy's knee. "You sure?"

"The woman I love might've just died today." Cassidy's features tightened. "I couldn't sleep after that."

Love? Mia locked onto that word. The blue glow inside her grew brighter. Could Donavin see it?

See what, my pet?

No, it seemed he couldn't. Mia vowed to do everything possible to make sure he'd never see that part of her. Donavin didn't seem to care. He sharpened Mia's hearing instead.

Skyler nodded. "Can I stay in the command chair though?"

"Of course, even in your condition, you'd know how to pilot this thing better than I would."

"It's a lot more comfortable," Skyler teased gently.

Cassidy smiled in return, but it wasn't real. She kept her back rigid. Skyler curled up in her chair and soon fell asleep. Wiping a hand across her eyes, Cassidy stared out the viewport, then at the map. She touched a blue dot at the end of many others. Their destination. Swallowing, she turned away from it and moved closer to Mia. She reached out a wavering hand. Stopped. A slight lift on Mia's part would have made them touch. Of course, she couldn't.

Cassidy sighed, rose and kissed Mia's forehead. The simple contact burned like a hot raindrop on a sculpture of ice. Cassidy smelled like blood and sweat, but Mia didn't mind. She didn't deserve this woman's love or hope, but she welcomed it all the same. Cassidy claimed the seat across from Mia and merely stared, drifting over Mia's features.

Mia usually disliked scrutiny, and she dreaded it now. Cassidy shouldn't be so close, not within striking distance, not within a star system from Mia in her current state.

Then Cassidy moved closer still and took one of Mia's hands in her own. "I don't believe it, Mia. You're still in there somewhere. I know you are. I'll find you and bring you back."

Cassidy kissed Mia's forehead once more and settled back on the bench.

Donavin forced Mia to meet Cassidy's intense gaze. *Look closely, Mia. This might be the last time you ever see her. I will break you. Then I will break her.*

Mia ignored the man who controlled her body, focusing instead on the warmth of Cassidy's eyes. The earlier conversation between Cassidy and Skyler lingered on Mia's mind. Then something clicked. If he could push into her memories, perhaps she could push into his. They were connected, after all. She tried accessing the link by concentrating on the coldest part of her mind and envisioning a strand there. A silver line appeared. She readied herself and pushed across it.

Chapter Thirteen

THE SILVER LINE FADED and a light bloomed in front of Mia's eyes. She tried to blink but couldn't. Impatiently, she waited for the light to clear. She wasn't in control. Some part of her thought she might be if she crossed over the link. No, Donavin still commanded her. Still wanted her body to sit patiently on the shuttle. Something seemed different, colder than ever before, like she'd submerged herself entirely in a frozen lake rather than just her arm or her leg or her heart. The light cleared, and she found her gaze focused on a pale-green screen. The screen muddied and a map appeared, the exact same map found hovering over their shuttle's control panel. A hand reached out and poked one of the blue dots. The dot shimmered for a moment then lay still.

A female voice came from beside her. "We know nothing of that planet, sir. Without a more detailed map, we won't be able to get there."

The hand lingered over the map then slid a finger across the screen, blackening it. A reflection appeared in the screen's glass, her reflection. A reflection not her own. Charles Donavin gazed back. Mia currently inhabited the man who was actively trying to take her life away. Who had killed her parents. Killed Will and Jeff's sister. And she still couldn't do anything about it. But maybe she could find some information to help the others. She had no idea how to even find someone else's memories, though, much less open them. Still a passenger, she listened to the conversation unfolding around her.

"What do you want us to do?" the female voice asked.

Donavin didn't look away from the blank screen. "Leave me."

After a brief rustle of movement and the whoosh of a hatch opening and closing, Donavin frowned. He punched the controls on the panel, bringing it back to life. A military ship appeared. The *Escambia*. Donavin brought up its schematics, searching for something. The corridors glowed brighter. The veins of the ship itself. Finally, he paused, one finger hovering over a particularly large empty space. A cabin perhaps. Donavin took a deep breath. Mia could feel the air being sucked in and let out of his lungs as if she was Donavin himself. He closed his eyes and darkness overcame them.

Thoughts immediately bombarded Donavin's mind, disjointed, hectic, muddled. Images flashed by—specs of a shuttlecraft, a plate laden with meat, black cloth—they scattered like Fissurian dirt between her fingers. More images bombarded her. Images of many different people, of different planets. She couldn't make sense of it. Donavin must have, though, because soon only one image remained. A photo of a couple dressed in white tuxes rested inside a simple black frame. Their hands were held up, wedding bands displayed. One man smiled broadly, but the other's gaze lingered on his lover's face. Commodore Bay. A silver thread curled from the photo. The frame grew bigger, taking up Donavin's entire vision. Donavin pushed himself into Commodore Bay's consciousness and unknowingly pulled Mia along.

Light seared forth. Commodore Bay blinked. The light came from a single candle burning in the center of a table. Donavin's laughter filled this new head.

You're becoming sentimental, Bay.

I wasn't expecting you for some time, Donavin. And don't play the sentimental card on me. You have your own memories.

True. Donavin stilled his laughter. *They don't hold a candle to yours.*

I was celebrating my anniversary, but you already knew that, didn't you?

I know everything about you, Bay. How could I miss someone as special as Isi?

Commodore Bay looked away, his gaze now resting on an open notebook. The pages seemed creased and worn, sections smudged. The flickering candle provided just enough light to see the markings scrawled upon them. A simple spiral had been drawn on the corner of one page, only to be drawn again in expanded form, and again a third time with spokes spearing from it, like thorns on a vine. Notes had been scribbled around this spiral, spanning to the other. A series of tiny numbers ran along the bottom. Bay picked up a pen and wrote the current date, his hand jerking and smudging ink. He slammed the pen down. *Useless idiotic utensil. Why can't I make notes on my monitor?*

Donavin projected a haughty air. *Because, you fool, this way of writing ensures this information will not be seen by unwanted eyes. What have you discovered?*

The new bots mixed well with the older generation found in Mia's blood. Commodore Bay traced the design on the page. *Their spiral form allowed the bots to connect with and override the older generation's mechanics.*

Good. And in others?

I injected five soldiers with the new version. It is my understanding that one of those soldiers helped you escape. The new design enhances their effectiveness tri-fold. The soldiers will be yours within a week, maybe less. The rest of the accelerated picobots are almost ready. We may not even need to get to the scientist.

One of the soldiers who helped them escape? Fear clutched her, almost made her withdraw. The toothy grin of the young male soldier came to her, the one who had helped them open the shuttle bay. Was he one of theirs?

Donavin projected anger. *No, he's still a threat, but the map is incomplete. You should have this information, Bay.*

Commodore Bay fingered the page, crinkling one corner. *Admiral Boreas never gave me that authorization. If I try to obtain it, I'll be caught.*

Fool, I'll have my ship take care of this meddlesome crew and the scientist. Spread the accelerated bots to your crew as soon as they're ready. Admiral Boreas should be among the first.

Bay stopped fidgeting and smoothed the page. *He should be completely yours within two days. The rest will follow. Soon the entire armada will be under your control.*

Good. Did you find Harrison?

I will. He can't have gone far.

Find him.

Donavin withdrew from the commodore before he could form a reply. Following his example, Mia withdrew as well, pulling herself back into her own mind over the strand. She waited for Donavin to come crashing back, furious she had invaded him. He never did.

Harrison might be in trouble, the entire military force on the *Escambia* could be compromised in a little more than two weeks, and her crew barreled toward a planet Donavin hunted. She couldn't even warn them. Will shifted on the bench directly across from Mia, distracting her from her thoughts when he cleared his throat. Curled on the bench next to him with one leg dangling off the side, her first mate gave a soft snore. When had he and Cassidy changed shifts? It concerned Mia that she didn't recall their doing so.

He met her gaze and leaned in close. "Listen, Mia, Skyler mentioned that there's a small chance you've survived...whatever it is you're going through. I still don't understand it completely, and probably never will, but that doesn't matter."

Donavin crept into Mia again. *What's this? He's actually catching on? Amazing.*

Breathing steadily, Will leaned closer still. "I think you've been fooling us all along, Donavin, ever since the Acedians captured us from the *Eclipse*. The Mia I know wouldn't hurt us. Lie to us, yes, but not try to kill us. That's not who she is. I have to admit that speech you did on Fissure was pretty convincing, but if there was even the slightest sliver of her in you, there's no way she would hurt Cassidy. So this message is for you, Donavin. I swear, on my parents' lives, on my brother's life, on everything I hold dear, I will get revenge for my sister's death. We will get revenge."

With that, Will sat back on the bench, glaring at her. Sorrow squeezed Mia's heart at his words. Yes, it was good that Will didn't trust her...but he thought their conversation back on Fissure was a lie, too? How could she make him believe it wasn't once Donavin was removed? If Donavin was ever removed. And if Mia was still herself when they tried it.

Stirring, Skyler stretched her arms. Donavin forced Mia's gaze in her direction. Jeff kept his position, curled up in the navigation chair. How much time had passed by? Mia didn't care where she looked anymore. If she could yawn, she would. The heavy fog of sleep encroached on her. Cassidy awoke, nearly slipping off the bench. A good deal of time must've passed. Four or five hours at least. Donavin shifted Mia's gaze to her, watching Cassidy shove the pods around, withdraw one marked with F, and open it. A pile of little white pouches spilled out.

"Ugh, protein bags?" Her lips pulled back in disgust.

Will grimaced. "Couldn't you work your magic and fix it up a bit?"

"No spice in the galaxy could save these." Cassidy handed one to Will, who ripped it open and gulped it down despite his complaints. A smear of white liquid stained the corner of his lips.

Will shuddered. "Tastes like cold gruel with a hint a tang of metal."

"Be grateful we have something." Cassidy threw a pouch to Skyler, who caught it.

"Should we..." Will motioned to Mia and to Jeff.

A heavy wheat scent filled the shuttle, and Mia's stomach growled. She wanted food. Even a protein bag would do. However Donavin didn't seem to need it, so she remained still. Her mind drifted into the fog, wanting to sleep.

Skyler shook her head. "There's no way I'm trying to feed Mia in her state, and Jeff can eat when he wakes up." She paused for a moment as if considering something. Finally she moved from her pilot chair to sit in between Cassidy and Will. "While he's out, though, can we discuss something?"

Will nodded, wiping the goo from his lips.

"We might have another problem. Have you noticed anything off about..." Skyler waved her hand in Jeff's direction.

Yes! A surge of optimism pulsed in Mia. Of course Skyler knew. Of course she would recognize the signs. Mia expected Donavin to be worried, but he gave no reaction, at least not within her mind.

Will shrugged. "He's just taking the death of Sarah hard, that's all."

Skyler pulled her lip between her teeth, clearly uncomfortable. She glanced at Cassidy and whispered, "I don't think that's the issue here."

"And you're suggesting, what? That Jeff might be an Acedian or something?" His jovial tone gave away just how absurd he thought the notion.

"Maybe," Skyler replied.

A calmness suddenly spread through Mia. Donavin's calm. *Have they figured it out?*

Why would Donavin be fine with this? Mia didn't have the strength to care. The push into Donavin must've weakened her more than she realized. She just wanted to sleep, but he kept her focused on the conversation.

Will's smile faded. He kept his voice quiet, yet the words exploded with such vehemence even Cassidy shrunk back. "How could you even think that?"

Skyler's lips tightened into a thin line. "He's been acting strange lately. That bit on the *Escambia*?"

"People change their mind, Skyler. It's not against the law." Will folded his arms across his chest and raised his chin.

They stared at each other.

Cassidy broke their intense silence. "Can you hear Jeff, Skyler? Can you push into his mind like you used to do with Mia?"

Sighing, Skyler shook her head. "I've been trying, but I can't seem to get a link with him."

Will narrowed his eyes. "So he's not Acedian. If you can't push into him, he can't have those robots in his system."

"I think—"

Will waved his hand at her in dismissal. "You're just becoming paranoid. You're seeing Acedians everywhere."

Skyler stood, looming over them now, silver eyes flashing dangerously. "Because they are everywhere."

"My brother's not one of them." Will grabbed another protein pouch and heaved it at Jeff. It smacked him in the face and woke him, effectively ending the conversation.

Donavin laughed. *Good boy. Anger solves everything, you know.*

Jeff stared at the pouch as it landed in his lap. "What the blast?"

"Breakfast time." Will gave him a smile.

Jeff yawned as he opened the pouch. "What are we talking about?"

"How delicious this food is. Try it, you'll be surprised," Will answered, jumping in before the others could. With the way both women stared at Will, doubt and worry crinkling their features, Mia doubted they would've said anything though.

Jeff downed the contents of the bag and made a face. "Oh yes. Delicious."

Will slid into the now-empty command chair next to his brother. "Told you."

After a bit more roughhousing, the crew settled into a pensive silence. Skyler shoved Will aside so she could control the shuttle. He shuffled to the bench behind his brother. Jeff stared at the map and gulped down three more pouches of protein before declaring himself full. Cassidy took inventory of the supplies. Mia wanted to sleep. She needed sleep. She couldn't. Wouldn't. She had to do something. Anything! She had to stay awake. Forcing herself to concentrate, she again tried pushing herself across the link. The light blurred her vision for a moment.

Donavin's gaze still rested on the schematics of the *Escambia*. He flicked the image away and closed his eyes, concentrating on a strange, dark-blue dot. The image grew wider, and soon they inhabited another person. Their focus pulled out, now resting on a holoimage. It looked familiar, too familiar. The dots hanging in the air could only mean one thing. Jeff. Donavin was in his mind.

How are you doing, Jeffery?

Jeff didn't reply.

Donavin laughed. *You're right. There's no need to talk.*

Jeff's hand glided over the controls as he pulled up a more intricate map. He looked at it for a second before staring at the hull instead. The image flashed away.

Look at the map, Jeffery, Donavin insisted.

No, Jeff replied. *You can't be really in my head.* He shifted away from the map and curled into a tight ball, closing his eyes.

Open your eyes, Jeffery, Donavin said.

His eyes opened, but he shoved an arm over them. The dark skin of his biceps dominated their vision.

Good. Now remove your arm.

Jeff's arm started to shake. Beads of sweat formed on his skin, as he strained against Donavin's control. Donavin shoved anger over the link, opening Jeff's memories like a book. He searched through until he found the one he wanted, the one of Sarah being killed. Donavin pushed the memory forward, gathering the pain and the guilt that went with it, replaying it over and over in Jeff's head. Punishing him. Then Donavin drew back into himself, taking Mia with him.

Donavin opened his eyes. The screen before him now lay dark, reflecting his own face back at him. He focused on something Mia hadn't noticed before. Just beside his collar, and smaller than a coin, sat a pin shaped like a blue bow edged with silver.

Suddenly, the scenery changed. Bright light dominated their view. As it faded, two suns hung in the sky. Bright-green grass spread out before them. Gentle rolling hills. A sweet berry scent filled the air. A blue stream trickled by in the distance. A young girl chased a yellow hornbug across the hill nearest them. A bright-blue bow held back her fiery hair. The girl turned and rushed toward them, her face breaking into a grin, freckles spattering over her pale skin. Hands reached out and grabbed the child, spinning her around and around before setting her back down again. Her cherry-red dress swirled as she ran off, laughter filling the air, mingling with the cool breeze and drifting away.

A memory. Donavin's memory.

He had a daughter once. Mia recalled him saying so on his ship. She hadn't believed him, hadn't wanted to think that such an evil person could spawn a child. But there the girl ran, whole, happy, and undeniably his. A cloud rolled over the suns, shadowing them and the little girl. She fell hard onto the grass, rolling out of sight down the other side of the hill. The child's laughter morphed into screams.

They rushed toward her and dropped to their knees by her side. The girl doubled over, hugging herself. Donavin's hands gently pried the girl's arms away, and the girl started coughing. Not a simple cough, a dry heaving one that shook her body. Blood spurted from her lips, foam following soon after. The grass transformed into a table, and they stood.

The child kept coughing, rubbing her limbs then stretching them as far as she could. Her entire body started to shake. The fever.

Cassidy's parents had that radiation sickness, Mia thought. The one contracted from the new technology, the new weapons. It afflicted the girl. They blinked. Men in government issued outfits appeared around Donavin's daughter. Then blurred.

Cassidy's parents? He asked.

The scene shattered, pieces fading into darkness, as the black screen returned only to brighten into a white, glaring light. Donavin sharpened Mia's vision, and Cassidy, not the black screen, not the field of grass, came into view.

Donavin screamed inside her head. *How much did you see? How much did you hear? Never mind, I'll find out soon enough.*

He sifted through her recent memory, finding the conversation between him and Commodore Bay. Stunned, Mia couldn't stop him.

His fury projected across the link. *Nothing of pressing interest.*

He severed the link, and Mia seemed alone in her body. Tiredness leeched her anxiety. She didn't try to move this time. There would be no point. A command filtered through her—*gather information*—and she knew her body would accomplish the task. For now, though, she stared straight ahead.

Her crew sat huddled together, chatting. They stared at her. A buzzing noise filled the shuttle and clouded her hearing. Will slapped his hand on the control panel and the buzzing stopped. He slipped something Mia couldn't quite make out from the panel. They kept looking at her, talking. Were they talking to her? With her? No. Cassidy glanced at Will and took the item from the control panel. The thing glinted green and blue, and finally, Mia recognized it. The memory chip. She concentrated on her crew until she could focus and distinguish each one.

"We have to assume the Acedians are following us," Cassidy said.

"And the military," added Will.

Disappointment crashed through her. Why didn't they talk about the memory chip? What was on the blasted thing?

"We don't know for sure if Harrison can be trusted," Jeff said. "He hasn't given us much over the comp-tact."

Cassidy glared at him. "To be fair, Harrison said we would connect again planetside, not along the way. He did lead us to this planet. And get us off the military ship."

Only then did Mia realize Cassidy had put the comp-tact back in.

Her left eye glowed steadily, but not as bright as on the *Escambia*. How much time had passed?

"According to this calculation, we're here." Skyler pulled up an image of the scientist's planet on the viewport. White clouds covered most of the sky, but underneath it patches of blue and green could be seen.

They'd reached the planet already? Mia had only spent moments in Donavin's mind, how could so much time have gone by?

"It looks like a nice enough place to live," Jeff mused.

Skyler faced him. "Scan for the scientist's home."

"Scanning. There's not much life on this rock, some animal biosigns and vegetation. There's one, more prominent, biosignature coming from the northern face, next to that jagged peak." He pointed to the only mountain range on the planet. "Everywhere else is water or flatlands. Seems like that would be the place to build."

"Then that's where we'll go." Skyler maneuvered the shuttle into the upper atmosphere. "Let's hope the guy doesn't have defense systems."

The shuttle lurched sideways. Mia's stomach lurched as well, and she felt pressure on her arms as the bonds pushed against her skin. Holding her steady.

Cassidy yelped. "Should I try to contact him?"

"Sorry, no, that was just us breaking atmo," Skyler replied. "It should be pretty clear sailing from here."

Skyler's prediction rang true, and moments later the shuttle settled down on the planet's surface. She powered down the main systems and turned to Cassidy. "You're up."

Cassidy nodded, then tapped her temple twice and stared off into the distance.

"You're sure we can trust this guy?" Will glanced at the aft hatch as if he could see the scenery through the metal and didn't like what he saw.

"Well, he saved my life." Skyler got up and retrieved the gun Harrison had given them. They had apparently stashed it away under the bench. "I was young when he performed the procedure. He worked frantically to do it. He seemed scared, but then again, there were a bunch of military with me, too, so maybe he was uncomfortable with that."

Cassidy stirred beside them. "Apparently we need to wear the comp-tact. That's it."

She rose, motioning for the crew to follow. Skyler opened the aft hatch and a blast of warm air swept over them. Dust traveled inside with it, along with the crisp scent of nearby water and something oddly tangy Mia couldn't quite place. New planet, new smells. Before she had been attacked, she had always liked the discovery of it all. The bonds clicked by her side and retracted, freeing her. She stood, and Cassidy led the way out. Both Will and Jeff grabbed Mia's arms below the shoulder. The barrel of Harrison's gun jabbed her in the back.

"Don't do anything stupid, or I'll be forced to use this." Skyler pushed the gun harder into her back.

Mia didn't reply. Even if she wanted to, she couldn't. Donavin had returned. His laughter filled her ears. Something was happening to her. Something different. She weakened. Unbearably, uncontrollably weakened. Things became so clear. Simple. Gathering information was all she needed to do. Donavin didn't need to force her gaze left or right anymore, she automatically followed his commands and analyzed her surroundings. The face of the mountain towered over her, blocking the sun. Drab brown dirt and rock stretched out in front of her, behind it lay a field of emerald-colored grass. The distinct lapping of water onto rocks could be heard over Donavin's chuckling.

A faint flickering came from the base of the mountain. Her sight sharpened. The scientist's house lay before her. Tucked inside a cave, the entrance looked like the rest of the mountain. Washed brown and tan, she would've missed it were it not for the Acedian's gift. The air around his house shimmered, and Mia pulled up data about force fields. The field around the house moved constantly, like water skittering over a hot surface, but to the untrained eye it would seem motionless. Mia stilled. Donavin seemed unsure of this new blockade, so she analyzed it further. Not a Helian design, not military grade either. Mia clenched her hands and looked over her shoulder at Skyler. Of course, the only Acedian ever to come into contact with it would have to be the traitor. This time she didn't mind calling her friend a traitor. That's what Skyler was after all.

Cassidy stopped before the shimmering field. "This seems too easy."

Skyler stepped up beside her. "There's a force field surrounding his house."

"His house?" Cassidy peered around, gaze drifting to the base of the mountain and up it, clearly not seeing the entrance to the scientist's home.

"Straight ahead." Skyler pointed at the doorway.

"A force field?" Will's voice came from beside Mia, but she didn't look at him, keeping her eyes trained on the force field, looking for signs of weakness. She found none.

"I don't think it's meant to hurt us," Skyler replied. "Come on."

The traitor stepped through the field and, because her bots weren't activated, because she chose a life of weakness, it didn't hurt her. Cassidy went through next. Panic nudged Mia's apathy away. What would happen to Cassidy? What if the field wasn't safe? The field flowed around Cassidy as if part of her, and the apathy washed back over Mia. Jeff and Will tried to push her through. The field hardened the moment she touched it, like a plane of smooth glass. No matter how hard they tried, how much they pushed, Mia couldn't pass.

A man approached them. "If she is Acedian she won't come through."

The voice startled her crew, but Mia had noticed him as soon as he exited his clever door. Short, wrinkled, and entirely bald, the man wore only a pair of rough gray pants. Mia accessed her databanks and came up empty. Donavin's fury lashed out over the link.

The old man meandered up to Skyler and hugged her, the top of his head barely reaching her shoulder. "Skyler Jones. How have you been?"

"Well," Skyler replied. "Very well. We're—"

Cassidy interrupted them, stepping forward and addressing the old man. "She's not Acedian. Mia isn't. Not yet. I have a message from Commander Harrison. He said you might be able to help us." She took the device from her eye and handed it to him.

The man put the comp-tact in his eye and stared hard at the packed dirt beneath his bare feet. He nodded then stuck his hand in his pocket and revealed a small clear triangle. He gestured to the Dee brothers. "You two come through first."

Will stepped forward without hesitation and went through easily. Jeff straightened his shoulders and walked through as well, but he shuddered while doing so. The others didn't seem to notice, although the old man narrowed his eyes. He sidled up to the field, tapping the triangle onto the defense system. A sparkling archway appeared next to the triangle. Mia doubted if anyone else could see it. No one had the eyesight she did. She stepped inside the force field. The old man tapped the defense system again and the field melted back into place.

Mia tensed. Trapped. Donavin pulled her lips into a frown and forced the feeling aside. The old man smiled, his dark eyes shining, and led the way to his home. He swung the wooden door wide and allowed everyone to file in before clicking it shut. How could a wooden door click? Fear now pulsed from Donavin. Trapped couldn't even begin to describe his response to the sight that lay before Mia's Acedian eyes.

Chapter Fourteen

THE ENTRYWAY OPENED TO a lab. Dust floated in the ray of light pouring into the room through a shattered window. Metal cabinets lined the walls, their doors swung wide open. The contents of the shelves lay smashed on the gray floor. Broken monitor screens stood in the corners. Shards of glass sparkled. A single table, with a rusted dome hiding the top portion, sat in the center. Empty bags hung from bars on either side, wilted and dry though they seemed to have held vibrant pink liquid at one time. Tubes coiled around the bags, and wires splayed from them as well. A cracked spherical light hung from the ceiling.

The little man led the way around the wreckage to one of the screens. He stepped in front of it, and the metal cabinet beside the screen opened to another room. This lab looked like its predecessor, though cleaner than before. Another spike of fear came from Donavin over the link. Curiosity, too. Skyler had escaped here. Fled with the military to this destination.

Mia grimaced. Her head jerked to the side, looking for the window like the previous room. With no window in sight, the bare wall seemed to laugh at her, and Donavin's intrigue heightened. So this space was different. Multiple lights brightened the space, the metal table glinted, the cabinets were closed. This must be the real workplace. Her muscles tightened. A chill pooled around her eyes. Donavin forced her to focus on the bags hanging beside the table. These contained yellow liquid. Voices swirled around her.

"My name is Nin."

"My name's Cassidy, and this is Will and Jeff. That's Mia."

Mia moved closer to the bags. Donavin wanted her to rip one open and analyze the contents. She raised a hand, but before she could touch one, a spark ran through her body, freezing her in place. Another spike of fear pulsed through the link. Donavin tried to sever their connection. He couldn't. Something forced him to stay. The force field. Aggravated, Donavin pulled the cold back as far as he could.

Wait. Why was she staring at some weird yellow liquid? Mia tried to move. Couldn't. Donavin attempted to force her eyes left, toward Nin. They wouldn't budge. She didn't have control of her own body but neither did Donavin, and he couldn't leave, couldn't run away. A trickle of fire dripped through her, her own joy. That knowledge comforted her. If only a little. Mia tried to remember the heat from Cassidy's eyes. From her kiss.

"Will you set her down on the table for me?" Nin's voice sounded strange to her. Distant almost. Hands grabbed her. Jeff and Cassidy lifted and eased her onto the cold, hard surface. Her muscles relaxed so she could settle and froze once more. She stared straight up, looking at the impossibly smooth ceiling, eyes watering from the white light above her. Anger surged over the link. Donavin seemed mad he couldn't move his drone. Annoyed that he couldn't leave. If Mia could smile, she would.

"Good." Nin approached the table and leaned over her. His dark gaze raked down her body then back up to her face. "Her eyes have changed color. Are you sure she has not turned?"

"Yes," Cassidy said, and Mia warmed a little more. Cassidy still pulled for her.

"No," Skyler muttered. "We're not sure."

Nin maneuvered himself around the table. He disappeared then reappeared by her other side clutching a square device in his hands. The table started swiveling upward. For half a heartbeat, Mia wondered if she would fall. Something clicked beside her ear, and a band slid over her arms, legs, and stomach. A thinner one hooked around her forehead, strapping her into place. Mia's view changed from the glowing bulb on the ceiling to the tops of the cabinetry then rested on her crew.

The table stopped rotating. Nin went over to the cabinetry directly in front of her and opened it. Needles of various sizes hung from hooks, tubes resting carefully beneath them. Nin plucked one from its holder, bringing it over to Mia's side. He shoved up her sleeve and took a sample of her blood, injecting it into his strange little device. The device shuddered, melting into a tiny replica of the scar on her palm. Nin nodded before it morphed back into its original form.

Fury pounded through her as Donavin screamed. *Picobots! He's using picobots against me?*

Nin tapped the corner of his square device and snapped it into two pieces. He twisted the top portion entirely around and popped it back on. The hood above her emitted a yellow light. As if alive, the wires and tubes next to her uncoiled, snaking onto her body. The cable traveled down her stomach and wrapped around her left arm. The strands seemed to solidify into one thin wire, piercing her wrist. No pain from the wires reached her though. The tubes wrapped gently around her other arm, stopping in the crook of her elbow. Something, maybe apprehension, passed through the link. A strange, wavering emotion.

Nin set the device down on a rolling table next to him. He winced, as if something hurt him. "You know, she can leave it all behind if I don't do this."

"What?" Cassidy moved forward.

"Whatever she has done because of him, she can stop caring about it. And not just because of him, even before him. Whatever horrors she's witnessed or committed...she can leave it all behind."

Cassidy set her hand on the table next to his device, pulling his attention. "What are you talking about?"

"The transformation," Skyler replied. "He's talking about turning into a drone."

"We don't want Mia to turn," Cassidy said roughly.

Donavin's sudden fear infused Mia. *She has to.*

Nin grabbed Cassidy's arm. "I've never had it done myself, but I've seen it. In people. In lab experiments. It is life altering. She won't forget about what happened in her past. He can only do that for short periods of time. She'll merely forget how to feel about it."

"Just do the procedure," Cassidy said, pulling from his grasp.

Nin appeared not to have heard. He eyed Cassidy as he motioned to the screens around him. They winked on, displaying a lush blue sphere. Old Earth. Nin walked over to them and pressed his hand onto the monitor. "It's not his fault, you know. Charles? He just wanted to dull the pain. He couldn't save her, his Elanora, his little girl. The government killed her to keep the fear of the radiation poisoning from Old Earth from spreading. If the people feared the new technology, how would the government make money?"

If Mia could roll her eyes she would have. Surely, the government would find another way to make money. Surely. And yet, this man seemed intent on rambling.

Nin dropped his hand from the monitor. "Her death almost killed him, and I created the picobots to help. Their first design was mine. It dulled his pain, made him forget about his daughter for a little while, but did so much more. More than I ever imagined. He left our home world a happier man. I had moved on and thought he had as well. I traveled here, to this deserted planet, to work. It was only after Skyler was brought to me that I realized my mistake. Of course, he would use them to avenge his daughter against the government that would not save her."

Stop. Stop reminding me! Donavin lashed out. Finally, memories of Nin came back and flashed across Mia's mind. Memories of their time together, of Donavin and Nin, the endless late nights Nin worked to help Donavin. The thousand failed experiments. How the picobots took a cycle to develop and how broken Donavin was during that cycle. *You can't leave me!*

Cassidy stalked over to the man and grabbed him by the shoulders. "I don't care about him. Just get the blasted bots out of her system. Save her!"

But Donavin's sorrow flooded Mia's system and, for the first time, he seemed crazed. An icy sensation spread across her body, blanketing her. She didn't care. She wanted Donavin to disappear. Above all, she wanted to sleep. She felt tired, so very tired. And cold. It seeped through her, washing the warmth away. Donavin's satisfaction filled her. The warmth ebbed. She slipped further back and allowed Donavin to spear his frozen tendrils further into her. Welcoming it, she fell deep into a cold embrace. If only her eyes would close, she could sleep.

I won't allow you to leave me again, Donavin said.

Skyler gently pried Cassidy's hands off Nin. Cassidy turned away, tucking her hands under her arms, shaking. Tears ran down her cheeks. When had she started crying? But Mia didn't care. She just wanted to sleep. So she let herself drift away. The room blurred. Voices whispered around her. Why couldn't the voices leave her the blasted well alone?

Nin spoke, "It would be marvelous to have the serenity she must be feeling."

"It's not serenity. It's a prison. He doesn't have the right to kill people." Skyler's voice seemed louder. "The Acedians could be hovering over this mountain right now and if not them, the military."

"Even if they are, it'll take time, hours at least, to find me." Nin's voice grew louder.

Skyler slapped something, a table perhaps, rattling its contents. "Just do it."

The sound startled Mia enough to refocus her attention. Nin loomed over her. Placing a hand on the hood, he glanced at Cassidy. "If I do this and she is a full drone, she will die."

"I know," Cassidy whispered, moving closer to Mia and placing a gentle hand on her arm. Tear tracks stained her face. "Do it."

Nin tilted his head. His steady gaze lingered on Cassidy for more than a heartbeat. Finally, he sighed. "Very well. Step away."

She leaned down and kissed Mia on the cheek, though the heat barely came through this time. "Come back to me, Mia. Please, come back."

Nin nudged Cassidy away, lowering the hood over Mia's face. It stopped just short of her upper body. The yellow light from the hood shone like the sun, burning her eyes. Finally, it dimmed to black. The wiring lit up in violet, aqua, and crimson strands. Beautiful. Deadly. Cold.

"If you're in there, this will hurt." Nin tapped the hood.

Her final transformation began.

Chapter Fifteen

A STEADY HUMMING CAME from the hood. The wiring grew bright, brighter than she had ever seen, bright enough she thought she'd go blind. The colors blurred to blue. The same blue she'd locked away. The light seemed to warm, then burn. The machine might've stripped the flesh from her bones for all the pain it caused. Her pulse pounded in her ears. The process must've broken her entire body, shattered every bone. The humming changed to thrums, each wave ripping through her muscles. Streams of light burst from the wires, shocking her each time they landed. If Mia could've screamed she would.

If I can't have you, Elanora, no one can.

In one last attempt at control, Donavin flooded her. Liquid ice spiked her mind, chest, abdomen. The pain disappeared. Everywhere seemed frozen. A sculpture chipped from ice.

I will make you forget. I will make you forget everything.

All of Mia's thoughts, all of her memories, all of her vanished. The warmth vanished. But the kiss still lingered. Cassidy's plea still drifted in her head. *'Please, come back.'* Slowly, ever so slowly, Mia did. Pushing against the cold, the emptiness, she grasped onto those words. *'Please, come back.'*

The warmth spread across her cheek and raced down her body. Nausea came in waves, alternating chills and heat traveled over her skin. She blinked, trying to clear the pounding in her head. The wiring dimmed. The blue faded. Sorrow, guilt, fear—her own true emotions—swamped her. Her body ached with each breath, but at least she breathed on her own accord. At least she felt the aches and soreness. Mia smiled. Donavin's presence was no longer in her mind. She knew he had left her for good. Driven out by Nin's machine.

"I'm in control," she murmured, knowing no one could hear her over the steady thrumming. The nausea slowly faded away. She blinked a few times to be sure. Flexed her fingers. Yes, she had control.

The machine wound down, and Nin lifted the hood. "Now, we don't know if she's here. Please, don't get your hopes up. We don't know if your love survived."

The hood snapped back into place, revealing her crew. She smiled so wide it hurt. "Of course I survived," Mia replied. "What the blast do you think I've been doing in here?"

Her crew stood by the cabinetry, far away from her and Nin. When Mia replied with such enthusiasm, Cassidy rushed over. Her smile could calm a thousand meteor showers, and Mia found it calmed her just as easily.

Skyler stopped her. "Wait."

"Why?" Cassidy tried to break free from Skyler's hold, eyes never leaving Mia.

"We can't be sure it's her yet," Nin replied.

Cassidy bit her lip and nodded, waiting by Skyler's side. He took a sample of Mia's blood. After being painless for so long, she winced from even that tiny prick. He lifted the square device and injected the new blood sample. The square melted in his palm then morphed back into a square.

Nin turned to Skyler. "Let her go. Mia is clean."

Cassidy tried to move, but Skyler still held her back, frowning at Nin. "Her eyes are still silver."

Sighing, he seemed to gather himself before replying. "Her eyes always will be, like yours. I can't fix that."

"I don't care," Cassidy said.

He fiddled with the table. The straps retracted. Mia fell from the metal prison and into Cassidy's waiting arms. The warmth of the embrace surrounded Mia, comforted her more than anything else in the universe could, and Mia nuzzled into Cassidy's shoulder, inhaling her familiar scent. They hadn't been able to wash for days, and Mia still loved the way Cassidy smelled.

"Mia, are you okay?" Cassidy asked, pulling back.

"Yeah, a little dizzy, but I'm here." Mia kissed her on the cheek and tucked a strand of brown hair out of her eyes. "Thanks."

Cassidy tilted her head. "For what?"

"For helping me find my way back."

Mia wiped the tears from Cassidy's cheeks and kissed her, this time on the lips. Cassidy leaned into her. The kiss became deeper, hungrier. Mia threaded her fingers through Cassidy's hair, the softness running through her hands like water. In full control once more, Mia focused entirely on Cassidy, on the sweetness of her. She wanted to be closer—no, needed to be closer. Cassidy bit softly on Mia's lower lip, and she felt her knees buckle, but she held on, held up by Cassidy's strong embrace. Someone coughed, once, twice, the third time breaking them apart.

Skyler smirked and lowered her hand. "Maybe your reunion should wait for a little while."

Cassidy tried to move away, but Mia kept an arm wrapped around her waist. Nothing could make her let go. Not yet. She pulled Cassidy along, shaking each of her crewmember's hands in turn. Skyler gave her a wide smile. Jeff stiffened when Mia offered her hand but gave in.

Surprising her, Will yanked her in for a hug. "I'm glad you're back, Captain."

"I'm not a captain, idiot," Mia muttered.

He shrugged and grinned. A blush crept up his ears. "Technicalities. I'm just glad you're you. Fully you, I mean."

Nin stepped forward. One eye glowed orange, the other, a normal if incredibly dark brown. Before he could say anything, Mia grabbed his hand and shook it. "Thank you for saving me. For bringing me back. I'll never be able to repay you."

Nin accepted the thanks with a smile. "As I had a hand at creating your destruction, I had a hand in ending it. It all evens out. I need to ask you a few questions, if you don't mind." With Mia's nod, Nin continued, "Do you feel any dizziness or nausea?"

Amazingly, she felt fine now. "I did when I first woke. Not anymore."

"What do you remember from your encounter with him?"

Mia opened her mouth to speak then closed it. What did she remember? Donavin was gone, though fog still clouded her. "Snippets here and there, not much. I remember seeing my crew in the *Escambia* brig, somehow we got onto an escape shuttle. How long did we travel?"

Will cleared his throat. "A day and a half."

Mia gasped. "A day and a..." Everything she remembered from her time under Donavin's control could fit into a few hours. Tops. She sighed. "I remember hearing voices. You introducing yourself, Nin, and Cassidy. Then I was here."

Jeff spoke up, scratching his head and giving her a strange look. "You don't remember anything else? How we escaped the *Escambia*? The conversations we had on the ship? Getting here?"

Mia shook her head. Cassidy rested a hand on the one Mia had settled on her hip, twining their fingers together. Still, Mia shuddered. Disconcerting, how easily Donavin could snatch something away. "Will I ever remember?"

"Of course." Nin's dark eyes glinted. "After some time, his

influence will wear off. You'll remember everything."

Jeff shifted under her steady gaze. She couldn't blame him for acting oddly around her, but the hairs on her neck tingled. Something was off about him. What about the real threat? She had almost forgotten about—

"The Acedians," she said aloud. "Blast, the military. Are they coming after us? We should leave. Is the shuttle still in working condition?"

"Slow down, love," Cassidy interjected, giving her hand a squeeze. "Nin has a shield around this place to protect himself from the Acedians, and Harrison wiped out our trail from the military."

It took a heartbeat to register, Cassidy had called her *love*. She tried to keep her voice at a decent level. Her throat still constricted. "So we're safe?"

"My technology will keep the Acedians at bay," Nin replied. "For now."

With that reassurance, Mia became keenly aware of how close Cassidy stood beside her. Of how one hand still grasped Mia's, folding together on top of Cassidy's hip. Of how her other had mirrored Mia's movement and slipped around Mia's waist. Arm still wrapped around Cassidy's waist, Mia wished they could be closer, and from the way Cassidy had captured her, it seemed like she wanted it, too. Mia struggled to push the feeling away and concentrate on Nin. He shoved the table sideways. It gave with little effort despite its size and weight. Under the table lay a circular design. Nin tapped the floor with his foot and the circle spiraled open. A steady yellow glow came from within, and he gestured them in.

Mia stepped away from the hole, tugging Cassidy with her. "Where are we going?"

Nin chuckled. "I have more comfortable rooms below this lab. You could stay up here if you would prefer, of course."

Letting go of Cassidy, Mia lowered herself through the horizontal door, feeling with her boot to find the steps built into the wall. She reached the bottom and moved out of the way, surveying this new space. A white, circular room stared back. Empty, save for the single computer monitor bracketed on one side and a blue light that hung from the ceiling. Cassidy stepped down beside her. Mia claimed her hand and pulled her close once more.

"I remember this room," Skyler exclaimed as soon as she reached the bottom.

"It seems…nice." Will glanced around, arching an eyebrow.

"Yes, positively charming," Jeff muttered. He gave the place a cursory glance.

Nin chuckled. "Just wait, it'll be nicer than you could imagine."

He closed the spiral door above them. Vibrations shook the entire space. The room began to change, shift, sections of the room melting. Eyes widening with shock, Mia tightened her hold on Cassidy's hand. They watched as the whole room changed.

"You don't need to worry," Nin assured them.

One section of the room became a desk for the computer monitor to sit on. A chair blossomed from the floor, the back of it twisting together from bands of white and stiffening in place. Another section punched upward into a couch and low table. The wall beside the couch shimmered, melting into an archway.

"The alignment is complete." Nin gestured to the archway. "You're free to wander my home."

No one moved, simply taking in the new room. Mia gaped at the fresh surroundings, blinking at the glaring whiteness of it all. Then it hit her.

"This room is made with picobots," Mia muttered. "Like the Acedian ship."

Nin nodded. "Where do you think Donavin got the idea?"

"This is their tech?" Will paled and looked up at the circular door.

"No, it's my technology. Donavin may have abused it, but I assure you it is safe in my home." Nin put a gentle hand on Will's shoulder.

Jeff punched Will's arm before walking through the archway. His voice drifted back to them. "Yeah, I'm sure we'll be fine here. Let's look around."

Will sighed, trailing behind his older brother.

Nin strolled to his desk and plopped down in the chair. "There is one more thing I would like to discuss. I've developed the ability to erase the scar left behind from Donavin."

Skyler gasped. "Breach it all. Does it hurt?"

Nin's dark eyes sparkled. "It's a quick procedure, and one I thought you'd be interested in, Skyler. How long did you go before trying to cover up his design?"

"A month. Less, even."

Nin rested a hand on his desk and arched his palm upward as a small section of the white metal blobbed upward into his hand. He lifted it away, flipping his hand up as he did. The white blob shifted and solidified into a triangle shape, flat on one side, rounded on the other.

"Would you like to have it done?" Nin's question seemed directed to both of them.

Skyler spoke up first. "Yes."

Tugging her shirt off her shoulder, Skyler revealed the spiral tattoo and the scar hidden within it. Nin nodded to the floor. Skyler knelt, back to him, trusting him completely. But, Mia gathered, this man had saved her life. Both their lives. Of course they could trust him. She let go of Cassidy and moved closer, needing to see what this technology could do. Nin rested the triangle device atop Skyler's skin. The device glowed white, light encompassing the entire tattoo. Skyler gritted her teeth, a wince scrunching up her face. The light stopped, and he lifted the device. A section of the spiral disappeared, the scar entirely gone and leaving an imperfect tattoo behind. Mia gaped at such technology.

"How is that possible?" Cassidy asked.

Was that a waiver in her voice? Skyler's skin seemed impossibly smooth. Not a trace of the scar remained. Mia ran her fingers over the puckered flesh of her palm. Easy. It would be so easy to wipe away that remnant of her past.

"It is not a normal scar." Nin put the triangle down. "It was made by picobots being injected into the skin. The mark you see isn't marred flesh, it is the core of bots if you will. Where they spread into your system. Since yours are no longer active, I can reverse the process and heal the scar."

Skyler rubbed a hand over her shoulder, eyes wide as her fingers ran over her tattoo, then stood. Beaming, she hugged Nin. "Thank you, once again."

He simply nodded to her and turned to Mia. "I can do the same for you."

Would she want that done, too? Her first instinct was to say yes, shout it, scream it even. To remove the scar on her hand would just be one step closer to breaking Donavin's hold. In her heart of hearts, the deepest part of her soul, uncertainty tugged at her. If she got rid of the scar, removed the proof of what had changed her forever, would she still be herself? She had lived with this scar for many cycles. It had become a part of her. Mia had almost accepted his offer when Cassidy grabbed her hand and pulled her back a step. "No," Cassidy mumbled.

What? Mia turned to argue with her. Her voice disappeared, chased away by the sight before her. Cassidy stood next to her, almost in tears. Her cheeks grew pink and lines crinkled the skin by her eyes.

"Please. She's been through enough. You've been through enough for one day." She grasped Mia's hand with both of hers. "If you want to do it later, fine, but for now." She hesitated, took a breath. "For now, let's just sit together. Please."

Taken aback by Cassidy's emotions, Mia drew her in for a hug and nodded. Cassidy was upset, and finally Mia could console her. The smile that grew on Cassidy's lips could brighten the galaxy better than any star.

Nin gave them both a soft grin. "Very well. If you go through the archway and take a left, there'll be a place where you can sit together. Sleep, if you're interested. You will not be disturbed."

Mia started to lead Cassidy away when a look on Nin's face stopped her. "Is there something else you wanted to say?"

"I must monitor your condition."

Mia could swear the man's bald head turned pink as he said those words.

"No." One of Cassidy's hands slid down Mia's arm. Tingles followed her touch. "I'll monitor her for you."

The man nodded. Ignoring Skyler's mutter of "I'm sure you will," they walked through the archway and took an immediate left. Another archway melted open to reveal a small circular space lit by four glowing orbs. The lights shimmered in a cozy way. A section of the floor pushed upward and formed a couch and two end tables. It looked comfortable, although Mia had her doubts. How could metal be anything but hard?

Cassidy dragged her inside and settled down. She grinned. "Come sit. It's nice."

Mia glanced back. The archway flashed white for a moment and formed an opalescent door. Nin had said they wouldn't be disturbed. She arched an eyebrow and turned back to Cassidy, sinking into the couch next to her. The gleaming substance flowed around her form and solidified into an imitation of a cushion. Comfortable enough. Their legs touched and Mia's breath caught. Maybe too comfortable.

Cassidy laced their fingers together and lifted Mia's hand to her lips. The slight touch ignited a passion too deep for Mia to manage. Her free hand rested on Cassidy's leg, but when had she put it there? Heat crept up the back of her neck. She swallowed her questions and leaned back. Now wasn't the time for such actions. Grinning slyly, Cassidy rotated Mia's palm upward. Her fingers traced the outer edges of the scar. Warmth raced up Mia's arm, and she glanced down at the old wound. It seemed less harsh in this light, less traumatic.

She cleared her throat. "Why did you stop Nin from healing it?"

Cassidy traced the scar four more times before answering. "It's a part of you, and I fell in love with all of you. To you, it might be a reminder of your past. To me...to me, Mia, it's a symbol of your strength. You overcame Donavin, even though he tried to break you."

Her explanation did nothing to resolve the heavy beating of Mia's heart or the aching desire in her soul. If anything, it amplified them. She curled her fingers around Cassidy's hand. "I love you, too."

Love. The last thing Mia had ever signed up for when she found this crew. But after being hunted for so long, after pushing so many people away, after Donavin's onslaught to her soul, Mia knew above all else that she loved this woman sitting next to her. Though when Cassidy pulled Mia in for a kiss and heat pulsed in her core and settled lower, she still felt like now wasn't the time. With great effort, she broke away and stilled.

Cassidy didn't feel the same way as she nuzzled Mia's neck, reaching under Mia's shirt and resting her hands on Mia's sides. The warmth of Cassidy's hands on her skin nearly drove Mia into recklessness. A familiar kick jolted through her. Desire wanted to take over, to pursue the feeling humming in her soul. Still, she nudged Cassidy away. Heat crept up to her ears.

Voice deeper than expected, Mia said, "We can't. Not here."

"Why? We both want to." The longing in Cassidy's eyes almost melted away her resolve.

"True." She caressed Cassidy's cheek. "But we're in someone else's home. We're on a strange planet. The Acedians are still after us. The military is still after us. This isn't the right time."

"When will it be?" Cassidy whispered.

A strange sense of gallantry awoke in Mia, one she hadn't had until now. "I want our time to be more special than this, Cassidy. I want you to feel special."

Cassidy smiled at her. A lover's smile. She leveraged herself onto one knee then straddled Mia. She kissed Mia's forehead and ran her hand through Mia's hair. "The only thing I need to feel special is you."

That's all Mia needed. Surrendering to her desire, Mia traced the line of Cassidy's jaw, grazing her fingers against the soft skin of her love's throat. Her fingers hovered over the buttons of Cassidy's shirt for a moment. She glanced up, needing approval. Warm, brown eyes met her gaze, and Cassidy nodded. Yes, more than okay. The black shirt slipped from Cassidy's shoulders easier than water over rocks. She stood, and her pants and undergarments slid off just as easily. Mia's eyes widened at the beautiful sight before her. Gorgeous, pale skin and soft curves. An adorable blush spread on Cassidy's cheeks, and she glanced back at the door.

Mia wished they had some kind of locking mechanism, something to be sure that they wouldn't be disturbed, but Cassidy pulled her up from the couch and over to a white bed she hadn't noticed before. With a feather-light touch, Cassidy removed Mia's clothing, drifting over her skin, her touch searing warmth as they went. Mia gasped for air. She gently pushed Cassidy down onto the bed, no longer caring about the picobots, the Acedians, or the crew beyond the shimmering door. All she cared about was Cassidy.

She ran a trail of kisses from Cassidy's lips down to her stomach, sliding her hands down Cassidy's body, exploring the trembling form of the woman she loved and tasting the saltiness of her skin. Cassidy moaned softly, and Mia loved that sound, wanted her to make that noise over and over again. She cupped Cassidy's breasts, running her fingers gently around the brown tips already hard then giving her nipples a slight pinch. Cassidy's breath hitched. The blush spread across her neck now. Mia couldn't believe how adorable that blush was, or how wonderful it made her feel. She was no longer the cause of pain, or confusion, or worry. She'd make Cassidy feel loved, wanted, needed instead. She moved lower, intending to do much more, when Cassidy pushed Mia onto her back. The lights shifted in Mia's new position, throwing shadows onto Cassidy's curves.

"Hey," Mia whispered. "I'm in control here."

"Not right now," Cassidy teased, arching an eyebrow.

Cassidy leaned down and nipped Mia's neck as if to reaffirm her statement. Light kisses fluttered down Mia's chin, her collarbone, her abdomen. Cassidy's tongue swirled elegant designs on her skin. On the nape of her neck. On the curves of her breasts. On the swell of her hips. Mia's heart pounded, but Cassidy didn't stop. Her hands wandered as well, cupping Mia's breasts and squeezing, running down her sides, gently spreading her legs but never going where Mia wanted her most. Everywhere Cassidy touched burned. Mia's core fluttered. She gasped, her muscles tightening, her back arching of its own accord. Wanting Cassidy closer, the place between her legs pulsed. Mia's grip tightened on the bed, then because she didn't quite like knowing this softness was actually picobots, she reached for Cassidy instead, tangling her fingers into her love's hair. It didn't surprise Mia that the moans filling the room were her own.

She needed more. She pulled Cassidy up to her. "Cassidy," she breathed.

A passion sparked in Cassidy's brown eyes. "Yes, Captain?"

"Just—" Mia was nearly shot to pieces by the intensity of Cassidy's kiss.

Cassidy's hands drifted lower. She broke the kiss and again traced a line down Mia's stomach with her tongue. It was agony, sheer blissful agony, but still Mia waited, waited for Cassidy to do more, wanting her to move faster but loving the slow, teasing way Cassidy moved. Her fingers trailed up Mia's inner thighs. She twisted her fingers through the curls between Mia's legs and tugged, pressing her palm against Mia's clit while she did so. Mia stiffened. Her heartbeat sank to Cassidy's palm. Cassidy hadn't even done anything big yet, and still Mia's stomach coiled with anticipation.

She closed her eyes, but Cassidy's warm hand on her cheek made her open them. She stared at her lover and understood. Cassidy wanted permission, too. Mia nodded. Cassidy's smile disappeared, and Mia immediately felt the softness of her tongue between her legs. One long lick on her folds, and wetness brimming there immediately spilled from her. Mia moaned, felt Cassidy kiss her inner thigh once. Twice. Teasing her more. Then Cassidy moved to her clit and swirled her tongue around it.

At first, Mia tightened with such direct pressure. Her body adjusted. Her stomach coiled tighter. The pressure built. She couldn't take this much longer; she wanted to writhe beneath her lover, but Cassidy held her still. The steady hands Mia had come to know and respect now held her solid as a rock. Cassidy's tongue darted over Mia's clit, again and again. Teasing her, giving her some, never enough. The wonderful agony spread, left Mia out of breath, anchoring her hands into Cassidy's hair as an anchor as waves of pleasure crashed over her. She opened her legs wider, giving her lover more space, needing more. Needing so much more, needing to be filled.

As if Cassidy knew, she kissed Mia's folds once more and slipped her fingers deep into Mia. Gasping at the fullness, Mia cried out Cassidy's name, more a yelp than anything resembling a word. Cassidy's fingers rocked in and out, in and out. Pleasure coursed through Mia, the bliss building so fast she could hardly contain it. Cassidy curled her fingers, hit a sensitive spot that made Mia see stars, and Mia's breath stopped altogether. Frozen, this time in passion, this time in love.

"Let it go, Mia," Cassidy whispered, and Mia locked eyes with her. The sly smile on Cassidy's lips and the desire clear in her eyes pulled Mia over the edge. Her muscles drew taut as a string, finally snapped, and she came in waves over Cassidy's fingers. A hot and lovely release, one that made her see stars, see the universe even. Her muscles finally uncoiled, and shaking with afterwaves, Mia felt tears run down her cheeks but she didn't care. Cassidy ran her hand down Mia's stomach until the trembling ceased.

Mia finally relaxed, came back to the present and stared at Cassidy. Mia had never felt this way before. She was so vulnerable in this moment—naked and ravished, heat spreading across her cheeks—but she was protected and in love. Her legs still splayed open, breathing still ragged, pleasure still rippling through her body, she tried to grab hold of Cassidy's hand, the one currently drawing circles around her nipple. Cassidy pushed her hand down on the bed. She kissed Mia hard on the mouth and slipped her fingers inside Mia again. She started slowly, rocking gently and pulling the last of Mia's cares away. The ache returned, and Mia grasped Cassidy's hand tighter.

"Wait, Cass, wai—" The kiss had left her breathless, and the way Cassidy moved stole the words right from her lips.

Cassidy had pulled Mia's nipple into her mouth, tongue circling. She bit down ever so gently, and Mia arched again. Sparks of electricity jolted through her, causing her skin to tingle, her insides to burn. Cassidy curled her fingers inside Mia, hitting the spot that almost sent Mia to the stars. Nothing else mattered now, nothing else aside from her and Cassidy. Cassidy lifted her gaze, and Mia lost all control, swept away by those beautiful, brown eyes. And this time, she didn't mind one bit.

When the waves finally drifted away, Cassidy removed her fingers and licked the wetness off them. She curled up beside Mia, one leg resting over both of Mia's, one hand thrown over Mia's stomach, pressing their bodies close together. Sharing warmth even though Mia was desperately hot. Welcoming the closeness, Mia tugged Cassidy up a little and kissed her.

"You're going to let me be in control next time, Cass. That's an order," she whispered, pushing back a lock of Cassidy's soft hair.

Cassidy chuckled. "I look forward to it, Captain." She nuzzled closer. "My love."

Mia wrapped an arm around her. "Me too, love."

Chapter Sixteen

MIA LAY CURLED NEXT to Cassidy, the warmth of her lover seeping into her core. After being cold and lost for so long, the touch reassured her that she still existed. Mia tucked a strand of violet hair behind Cassidy's ear, resting a gentle hand on her neck. She couldn't take her hands off Cassidy, couldn't stop staring at her lithe body sprawled in shadows, couldn't believe how lucky she was to be in love with such an amazing woman and to be loved in return. A tendril of happiness curled in Mia's chest, lifting her lips into a smile. For the first time in a long time, she felt calm, at peace with the universe, and weightless. She drank in Cassidy's form, the darkness curving over the spots Mia desired most. After a moment, she shook herself from this peaceful place and stirred, meaning to lift herself from the bed, but Cassidy grabbed her hand and pulled her back. A sleepy smile settled on Cassidy's lips and she kissed Mia's right palm.

Even that slight touch sent a jolt through Mia's system. "We should probably see what the others are up to," she whispered, ignoring the feeling.

"They can wait." Cassidy wrapped her leg around Mia's waist, holding her in place.

Mia gave her a look she hoped portrayed seriousness rather than desire. "We have responsibilities, Cassidy."

Cassidy sighed, unhooking her leg. "I suppose we do." Her voice took on a tone of mock gravity. "We could die at any minute though, you realize that, right? Don't you think one more go would help us carry on?"

"The memory of you could carry me anywhere." Mia kissed Cassidy on the nose then rose from the bed. Saying something like that a few cycles ago would've been impossible, now the words hummed inside her, begging to be released.

They slipped into their clothes in silence. The dark fabric seemed constraining. Nothing could match the softness of Cassidy's skin. Mia hooked an arm around Cassidy and brought her close for a kiss that lingered too long and left them both breathless.

"Are you sure you want to leave, Captain?" Cassidy smirked, arching an eyebrow.

"No." Mia fingered the silver-edged collar on Cassidy's shirt. "But we have to face them sometime. And you, my love, will lead the way."

Chuckling, Mia nudged Cassidy toward the door. It dissolved, revealing the open archway once more. Voices came from the living area, so Mia and Cassidy headed that way. As they entered the room, Mia appreciated her friends' efforts to keep the conversation going. Skyler did grin, though it slipped from her lips faster than it had appeared. They had all gathered around, munching on some kind of brown bars. Cassidy took Mia's hand, pulled her over to the silver desk and grabbed two from the bowl, handing one to Mia and biting into one herself. As Mia chewed on the fruit and grain bar, a memory flashed of Skyler's spiral design disappearing. She thumbed her own scar. Did she want that? It shocked her that she didn't quite know the answer yet.

"We need to work out a plan." Will rubbed his chin. A fresh bruise reddened his cheek.

Mia caught his eye, and he looked away. Where'd he get the bruise?

Before she could ask, Cassidy spoke up. "We're talking about escaping the Acedians, I hope."

Nin frowned. "A plan has already been set in motion. He is coming."

The old man didn't need to explain who the *he* referred to. She looked up at the circular door in the ceiling, the one leading up to the labs. A chill raced down her back at the thought of Donavin bursting through it.

Nin stared evenly at the group, his dark eyes narrowing. "He knows where I am now."

Her first instinct was to run. She tried to calm the adrenaline surging through her body, but her legs ached, wanting to move. Cassidy linked an arm through hers now, edging closer, and Mia's body stilled.

Skyler swiped the crumbs off her mouth. "He can't find me any longer and, unless he was right behind us, he doesn't have Mia's signature to home in on either."

"You speak the truth, but he has another," Nin said, his shoulders slumping, making the little man even smaller.

"Another Acedian?" Will yelped, dropping the breakfast bar he held. It smashed onto the floor, nuts and dried fruit scattering.

Mia remembered before Nin even raised his hand to point. She swiveled toward Jeff, pulling away from Cassidy's hold. The Dee brother stiffened and backed away.

Cassidy gasped, her hands flying to her mouth, and Will shook his head, but only they seemed shocked by Nin's revelation. Skyler glanced at Mia, eyebrows raised, as if needing confirmation. At Mia's nod, sadness wrinkled Skyler's features.

"No," Will muttered. "You're mad! My brother's not an Acedian."

Jeff halted his backward steps, and his jaw tightened. Mia stepped closer, staring into his green eyes as if she could still link with him. "I remember Donavin talking to you. I remember the fight we had on the *Escambia*. You were faking it. Donavin hurt you to cover his tracks, to cover the fact that you're turning. He knew I'd be saved. He knew he wouldn't be able to reach this planet without another scar to track. He used you."

Jeff nodded, a short jerk of a move.

Will pushed Mia out of the way and grabbed his older brother by the shoulders. "It's not true."

"I tried to tell you in the kitchen," Jeff replied, eyes clouded yet still holding Will's stare.

Will's features tightened. "No, you punched me."

Jeff shrugged out of Will's grasp and Mia thought, for only a second, that he would do something reckless, something stupid, something Acedian. Instead, Jeff tilted Will's chin up so the bruise caught the light. The red mark spread across Will's cheek toward the corner of his mouth. Jeff let go. "It's the only way I could tell you something was off, Will."

Will kept shaking his head, his voice cracking. "But...but you can't be turning into one of them."

"I am," Jeff whispered.

Mia bit her lip, thinking fast. He seemed resigned to his fate. She searched Jeff's blank face, studied his too-calm movements. He seemed too resigned, and the memory of her own apathy surfaced, how nonchalant she must've appeared to everyone else even though that wasn't how she'd truly felt. Worry clenched her stomach. She didn't say anything, her tongue held captive by her fears.

Will's face paled. His expression crumpled then hardened, jaw set, eyes narrowed. He shoved his brother away and stalked over to Nin. "Fix him." His voice held a sharpness Mia had never heard before, one that could cut through the strongest metal.

Nin held up his hands, his expression crestfallen. "My machine can turn the bots off, but I'm sure by now Donavin has the coordinates to this world."

"Do you think I care about your blasted little world?" An ugly look tightened Will's lips. He spit out his next order. "Fix my brother, now."

At that, Nin input the commands, the hatch spiraled open, and he led the way up the ladder. Will forced his brother up next and turned to Mia.

"Come on." He gestured for them to follow with a short jerk of his hand.

Mia climbed the ladder after him, the hard metal unyielding under her palms, thoughts still swirling. Why was Jeff so resigned now? He'd resisted Donavin during the trip here. She reached the top and made room for the others. Cassidy followed close behind, and Skyler soon after. They both looked worried, making Cassidy's shoulders tighten and Skyler's eyes flit about. Jeff stood in the corner, muttering to Will.

A ping-ping-ping sounded, and Nin hurried to one of the monitors. It flashed to life with a steady, red warning. A chair bloomed up from the floor, and Nin sank into it. He glanced sadly at Jeff. "They'll be here soon."

Another memory shook Mia. Jeff had hesitated when crossing the force field. He couldn't go through easily. Nin had narrowed his eyes. He had seen Jeff hesitate. Nin knew right from the start about Jeff and didn't warn them. Anger surged through her, propelling her to his chair, towering over him. "You wanted the Acedians to come. Why?"

Nin stared up at Mia for a moment. "You look so much like his daughter, you know. So much like her."

The hairs on Mia's neck stood up. Something felt wrong. "So what?"

A whimper escaped Nin's lips. "I just want to help Donavin."

"Why did you help me then?" Mia asked, disgust churning her insides.

Nin seemed to wither, crumple in his chair, a sob shaking his body. "No one should become a drone unwillingly, but perhaps, if you meet him once more as yourself...perhaps you'd want to stay with him."

Almost there...ten minutes out...multiple biosigns. Thoughts jumbled in her mind, thoughts not her own. Acedian thoughts. How could she be hearing the Acedians? Mia shook her head and scoffed. "Why in the known universe would I want to stay with him?"

Nin's voice came mumbled from between his arms. "He might stop all this madness if you stay with him. All the killing. You could save people, and I thought if I gave you to him, he might set my Pira free. A child for a child."

Words left her, scattering like leaves on the wind. A child for a child? But she wasn't a child any longer, and whomever this Pira was probably wasn't a child either, if he was even still alive. She'd been betrayed by the Vespa government and sentenced to a life of fear by the Acedians. It was only fit that she was a bargaining chip for this old man. The one who saved her.

Skyler huffed and brushed past Mia to Nin. She grabbed him by the shoulders and propped him upright. "He took your son long ago. We both know there's nothing you can do about it. You can help us now."

All at once, Nin seemed to be an old man. A balding, shirtless, barefooted old man. The bags under his eyes shadowed a darker purple. The wrinkles around his eyes deepened. Tears slipped down his cheeks. He grimaced, turning his gaze to the crimson screens.

"Yes. Yes, Donavin has done enough. I do want to help you." He shook himself and wiped his nose with the back of his hand. He turned to Mia. "But don't think you're safe just because the picobots are deactivated. You must leave this world."

"Everyone's leaving." Cassidy moved closer to Mia.

"I'm not," Jeff whispered, though the whole room could hear him.

"There's nowhere to hide," Nin said, staring at the Dee brother in shock.

"I won't need to," Jeff replied.

Skyler stiffened beside Mia, and she waved her hand as if swatting his words away. "Breach it, Jeff, you're not actually saying you want to become a drone, are you?"

Mia's gut stopped churning and turned to stone instead. That couldn't be possible. No one wanted to be a drone. Then she remembered how influential Donavin could truly be, how appealing what he promised could be. Surely, Jeff couldn't believe him, though. He wouldn't.

Jeff shrugged. "It might be better than—"

Mia socked him on the chin. Pain radiated up her hand and arm from the blow, and she winced. At least she felt the throbbing this time. He stumbled, couldn't regain his footing, and cracked his head on the table, thudding to the floor. She stepped closer, but Will yanked her back.

"What the blast do you think you're doing?" he yelled.

Mia pried his hand off her arm. "Do you think that was Jeff talking? It was Donavin. He wants another drone, another tool to use. And we don't have time to deal with that. We have Nin's machine. We can just treat the idiot and be on our way. Now, come on, help me."

The last statement came out as an order, and, much to her surprise, her crew obeyed. Will and Skyler grabbed Jeff and hauled him to the table. Mia grasped Nin by the collar and followed them, slamming the hood down over Jeff's upper body. The voices entered her again. *Mountain range. The rock. Energy.*

"Fix him," Mia ordered.

Nin stepped back, but Cassidy moved behind him. He couldn't get away. Nin's lower lip trembled. "It may take too long—"

In the back of her head, Mia knew he was right. They didn't have much time left. Her crew had gone through too much for her to leave one behind. She towered over the old man. "Not that long. Fix him. Now."

Nin wired Jeff in then punched the top of the hood. The machine thrummed, brightening with multicolored lights, burning a brilliant green. Mia's shoulders tightened, recalling the painful procedure, but at least Jeff would be himself again. His yells filled the lab, and he bucked against the table's straps. Will moved toward the head of the table, worry narrowing his eyes. When the thrumming finally ceased, Jeff's heavy breathing filled the room. Not just breathing, something else. Was he crying? The moment the procedure finished, Will pushed back the hood, revealing Jeff's dazed expression and the tears spilling down his cheeks. Cassidy glanced at Mia, but Mia didn't have an explanation. The machine hurt but not that much.

"Why did you do that?" Jeff shouted, eyes darting from side to side and face scrunching up.

Skyler dragged Nin from the table and murmured a quick word to him. He grasped the square machine he'd used to test Mia, pulled a sample of blood from Jeff with a needle, and inserted the blood into the device. The metal melted, solidified.

"He's clean," Nin muttered.

Then what the blast was wrong with him? Mia stared at Jeff, trying to understand. He squirmed against his bonds, and they slipped free. Jeff pushed himself off the table and stumbled. Will steadied him, but Jeff shoved his brother away.

"Why did you do that to me?" Jeff yelled again. He went over to the cabinets and threw the doors open, smashing the contents onto the floor. He swiveled to Nin. "Fix me. Put me back. I want to go back to the way I was."

"The way you were was wrong, Jeff," Will said quietly, holding up his hands in front of him.

Jeff turned to him. "No, Will, I was calm. I didn't need to feel anything anymore, and I liked it."

Mia's eyes widened. "What do you mean you liked it, Jeff? He would've used you."

Charging over to Mia now, Jeff stopped short of her. "I didn't need to feel a blasted thing. Not Sarah's death. Not guilt. Not pain."

A wail escaped his lips, and he crumpled to the ground. Unsure what to say, Mia stepped back. Emotions did overwhelm her when the machine deactivated the picobots but not this much. Even Skyler, who had gone through the same process long ago, looked confused. She lingered next to the machine, a hand resting on the metal. Cassidy shook her head. It seemed even she didn't know how to respond to this outburst. So Mia looked to Will, hoping he'd have some way to help his older brother.

Tears brimming in his eyes, Will took a deep breath then kneeled beside Jeff and placed an arm around his shoulders. "I know it's hard. It's the most difficult thing I've had to deal with, but you have to deal with it, Jeff. You can't just run away from things. Life doesn't work like that."

Knocking Will out of the way, Jeff stood and strode from the room into the next lab. Will followed quickly behind, a hurt look settling on his face. Mia slipped one of her hands into Cassidy's, but even that small comfort couldn't remove her apprehension. If he truly felt this way, how could they change his mind? Skyler looked as if she might speak, but Will rushed back into the room, grabbing Mia's arm and yanking her away from the others. "He says he doesn't want to come with us. Mia, you have to convince him."

The broken sound to his voice cracked Mia's heart, and she allowed him to lead her into the other lab. Jeff stood in the corner and stared out the broken window, his features hard. He looked so solid, so sure. How could they—how could she—convince him otherwise? The voices came again. *Seven minutes out.* They didn't have much time left.

Going over to the window, she looked out. Dirt and rock spanned the area around them, brown and black, drab as the mood in Nin's home. She drew in a breath. "They'll make you kill people, Jeff. He'll make you murder innocent people."

His mask faltered for a moment. "Like you did?"

Mia grimaced. Emotions. Pain, sorrow, guilt. Her true emotions flooded her system, but after having Donavin control her, she relished feeling them.

"Yes." Mia locked her gaze onto Jeff's. "Like I did."

Jeff sneered. "And how do you deal with it?"

His words stopped Mia cold. By isolating herself, manipulating others, not well and he knew it. The ping-ping-ping of Nin's warning grew louder. Dread caused Mia's hands to shake, and she shoved them in her pockets. Donavin was headed this way. The voices seemed more insistent, excited, too. The Acedians could be hovering over them right now. She wanted to leave, wanted to run. Her crew crowded around Jeff.

Cassidy's hands lifted in a calming gesture. "What if you hurt us? Or even Will?"

Jeff didn't even look in his brother's direction. A muscle in his jaw twitched. "Everyone hurts someone."

Cassidy reached out. "If you just listen—"

"No!" Jeff elbowed her aside, causing her to lose her balance.

Mia caught Cassidy, arms wrapping around her. Her first mate didn't really need the extra support, but Mia did it anyway, just to feel her warmth, just to comfort herself. She drew them both back a little, letting Will step closer to his brother. Sunlight bathed the pair and sparkled off the slivers of glass on the floor.

"You have to come with us," Will said.

Jeff shook his head, still staring out the window. "I don't want to."

"Why not?" Will pulled Jeff around to face him, his tone pleading and desperate. "Why?"

"Because I don't want to feel Sarah's death any longer." Jeff's voice deepened, the Paradousian accent elongating his s's into a slight hiss. "I want that hole in my heart to vanish like it did before."

Will dropped his hand and took a step back. "What about our parents? What about Elizabeth? How do you think she'd react to this?"

"You can comfort her. She always preferred you as a brother anyway." Jeff swiveled to face the window again. "I just can't take it anymore. I keep seeing Sarah die over and over in my mind, and I don't want to feel that pain. I want to be empty, Will. I need to be."

Will frowned. "You'll be joining Donavin. He destroyed our home"

"I know."

Again, Will pulled Jeff around to face him. "He tortured you."

144

"I know." Jeff balled his hands into fists.

"He murdered Sarah." Will's voice boomed now, filling the space with his anger, his worry, his fear.

"I know," Jeff yelled back.

Will shoved his brother, sending him back against the window and a few more glass shards sprinkled to the floor. A disgusted look crossed his face. "Then how can you stay? You'll be joining his side. You'll be helping him. And you'll just be another blasted threat to us."

Then it hit Mia. Will was right. Jeff might not be a drone anymore, but Donavin would find a way to use him just like he'd used Nin. Her stomach knotted. Donavin might even take Elizabeth away. Or their parents. Or Will, even.

"You're worried about me being a threat, huh?" Jeff pulled out an energy gun. Harrison's gun.

Mia shifted Cassidy behind her and motioned Skyler to step back as well. When had he gotten Harrison's weapon?

"If you're so worried about me being a threat, why don't you just kill me now?" Jeff flung the weapon at Will, who caught it double handed. A crazed look flashed in Jeff's eyes. "I won't struggle. In fact, it'll probably be better this way."

Will glanced at Mia as if she'd have the answer to the standoff. She didn't. Raising the weapon, Will pointed it at Jeff, hands shaking but at this range, even a badly aimed shot would easily kill.

Jeff straightened to his full height. "Just get it over with if you're so worried. Kill me!"

Cassidy gasped and buried her face in Mia's shoulder, and Mia had to force herself to watch, to acknowledge the panic swirling like a tornado in the room.

Tightening his finger over the trigger, Will stared at his older brother. He closed his eyes. Jeff stilled. Then, with a sob, Will lowered the gun, and Mia knew where he would look next. She readied herself, as Will's sad eyes met her own.

"I can't. Captain, I can't do it. He's my brother. I could never. But we can't leave him here, either. And we can't let Donavin get him. Can you…" Will's voice broke. He lifted the gun, handle facing her. Mia took the weapon.

Cassidy murmured into her neck. "No, please, Mia. Don't."

Gently removing Cassidy from her, Mia replied, "I have to, Cassidy. We can't leave them here."

"Them?" Nin drew backward.

Mia looked at Skyler, who grabbed Nin and shoved him over to Jeff's side. The old man blanched and raised his hands.

"Is this really what you want, Jeff?" Mia asked.

Jeff nodded. And as if that wasn't enough, he said, "Yes, Mia. It's what I want."

"Then I'm sorry." Mia swallowed. She raised the energy gun level with Jeff's chest. It shouldn't be so hard. She'd killed others before, after all. She survived by doing this, for blasted sake, taking out others before Donavin could get to them. This shouldn't be so difficult. Still, her throat tightened. Guilt squeezed her chest. It got harder and harder to breathe.

"Just kill me. Please," Jeff whispered.

"I won't give you away," Nin said. "I know better now. I won't betray you."

How could they be sure? Maybe Donavin could find a way to probe into his mind, their minds, to find the information in another way. She couldn't be sure. Mia's gaze flitted to the rest of her crew. To Will, silently crying by the screens. To Skyler, grim faced but determined. To Cassidy, fingers still grasping Mia's arm, still connecting them together. She stared at Jeff and Nin, both pale.

Slowing her breathing, Mia tried to quiet her body, tried to stop the pounding of her heart, tried to ease the pain in her chest. But she couldn't. Committing murder, that's what she'd be doing, committing murder. And it wasn't her right to decide their fate for them. It was Jeff's choice to stay behind, not hers. She lowered the gun.

"I'm sorry," she said again and turned to the rest of her crew. "I can't do it either."

"Then I'm staying," Jeff said.

Two minutes out. The voice sounded positively thrilled.

Tears lingered in Cassidy's eyes. Skyler's glare could've opened a hull breach. Mia had had enough. The Acedians were close, close enough she could somehow hear their thoughts. She couldn't have her entire crew be captured by them, not again. "Let's go."

"What? No." Will spun to her.

The ping-ping-ping grew more insistent.

"We have to go, Will." Mia laid a gentle hand on his arm and squeezed. "He's made up his mind."

"But..."

The expression Will gave her, a look so full of hurt, almost caused her to break. To stay, to somehow fight. They didn't have weapons, though, not enough to take on Donavin and his army. A wild thought skittered across her. What if they stayed inside Nin's force field? No, it would only hold for so long, only delay the inevitable. Will tugged on her, drawing her attention back to him. Tears streamed down his face. Of course he wouldn't leave, what she asked was unthinkable. But he had asked the unthinkable as well.

"We're leaving now. Help me." She directed the command to Skyler and Cassidy.

Mia pulled Will away from his older brother. Will struggled and shouted, and she steadfastly ignored his yells. Skyler and Cassidy helped shove him outside, across the shimmering force field she could still somehow see, and into the shuttle.

Standing next to Jeff just inside the flickering field, Nin called out and threw something into the air. She caught the device. An archivist.

"Use it." Nin tapped his temple. His comp-tact glowed.

Mia nodded and took one last look at Jeff. His usually animated face had morphed into a mask of indifference. Voices bombarded her. *One minute. Scanning surface of planet. Mountain range looks promising.*

She shouted to them, "Hide under the lab. Maybe they won't find you in there."

"He won't let me live either way. It's time I faced my friend." A tiny gun morphed in his palm. "And I'll finish fixing Jeff."

Boarding the shuttle, Mia looked at the archivist resting in her palm. With it, she would see what happened when Donavin came. She would see Donavin murdering Jeff...or using him, transforming him into something else. Something evil. Her gaze landed on Will, hunched over in the corner of the shuttle, sobbing into his hands.

"Skyler," Mia quietly interrupted the nurse in the middle of the starting sequence.

"Mia, we have to leave. Right now." Skyler turned in her seat, eyes wide.

"Wait. Just one more second." Mia opened the hatch again, running out. No way would she be responsible for another death. No way would she see another one of her crews suffer because of him. Her thoughts turned to Sarah Dee. Suffer more because of him, because of her. She got to Nin and Jeff a moment later, breath heaving from her lungs, guilt twisting her stomach, bile rising in her throat. No way would she leave another one of her crew members behind. Not again. Not ever.

Shock registered on Jeff's face moments before it happened. Shock, not worry, not anger, not fear. Shock, perhaps, that Mia had returned. And Mia, surprised even by her own actions but thankful she'd finally made one right decision, punched him on the jaw so hard he toppled to the ground. Dirt puffed up around him. Mia wondered how she was supposed to haul him inside the shuttle before the Acedians reached the surface. Before she could finish that thought, Cassidy, Will, and Skyler had all reached them, grabbed hold of Jeff, and helped her drag him inside.

Mia looked once over her shoulder at Nin. Even as she slammed the hatch closed, even as Skyler rushed to the control panel and made the shuttle jettison into the atmosphere, and even as Will sobbed over his brother while he and Cassidy lashed him down, she could swear the old man gave her a smile. She could swear his thoughts entered her mind and said *thank you.*

Chapter Seventeen

MIA RUBBED HER ACHING knuckles and stared at the hatch. Nin said *thank you* to her with his mind, like through the link. Was Nin an Acedian? It was his tech, though, using his picobots. Maybe there was a different reason. There had to be.

"Thank you." Will shook Mia's arm, dragging her out of her thoughts. She stared at him. He motioned to Jeff, still unconscious and strapped tightly in one of the chairs, much like Mia had been before. "Thank you for saving him."

"I just couldn't…" Her voice broke, and she coughed to cover it. "I couldn't let Donavin hurt you again."

Will grinned and nodded, leaving her side to sit next to his brother and hold his hand. Mia didn't know what would happen when he woke up, screaming maybe. He'd wanted to stay, and Mia had stolen that choice from him. It might've been stupid to save him, a stupid reckless decision. He may even hate her in the long run, but at least it had been right. Mia took comfort in that and sat down on the bench facing them. When Cassidy slid next to her and squeezed her hand, Mia gave her a small smile.

"Why isn't he waking up?" Will asked.

"Because he's…" Mia stopped herself. She was going to joke about how he was obviously a weakling, going down after one punch like that. The man was all muscle. Still, he should be awake by now. She frowned and got up from her seat, rummaging around in the pods for a medical kit. A bright-yellow device caught her eye. "This is a scanner, right, Skyler?" At Skyler's nod, Mia pulled it out. "This will let us know if anything is…if anything is wrong with him."

Even those words sounded bad to her. Of course something was wrong with him, he wanted to be a blasted Acedian, wanted to turn on all of them. Still, she went over to Jeff and clicked the device on next to his head. Identical yellow legs spidered out from the machine and latched onto Jeff's forehead and neck, holding itself inches away from the side of his face. Mia shuddered. The spidery legs reminded her too much of Donavin's testing machines. A light suddenly glowed from the device, washing the side of Jeff's face in a pale yellow hue. A moment passed, and another. Will leaned forward, staring at it, as if willing it to go faster. Finally, the device pinged. Mia removed it from Jeff's head and looked at the results on the screen that covered one side of the scanner.

"What does it say?"

Mia chuckled, relief washing over her. "That he's fine. No brain damage. Not even broken bones. He should wake up pretty soon." Hopefully not too soon, though, Mia didn't want him to be awake when Donavin reached Nin's home.

Only after Skyler activated the shuttle's MP Drive and they were away from Nin's world did Mia feel safe enough to turn on the archivist. She shoved the storage pods out of the way and gathered her crew around. They would tell Jeff what happened later.

After turning the archivist on, she placed it on the seat next to her. The device hummed before projecting a white cube above it, waiting for the link to be initiated.

Cassidy cleared her throat. "How long will we—"

The holoimage blinked once, twice, an image of Nin spread across the square like water over a flat surface. And even though she barely knew the man, Mia's throat tightened, knowing what would come next. Should she have tried to save him, too?

Nin looked at himself in a small mirror, a smile still resting on his lips. He lowered his hand and looked up to the cloudy sky. The clouds parted. Mia gasped, as she recognized the ship steadily descending toward the planet. With the busted up engine coil and scratches on the side of the hull, it had to be hers.

"It's the *Eclipse*," Cassidy murmured. "How's that possible? I thought you said he destroyed our ship."

Mia shook her head. "I...I don't know. The *Eclipse* blew up. I saw it happen."

The memory took hold of Mia for a moment. How she'd pressed up against the viewport, her heart beating frantically in her chest. How the light flashed green so she could see better. How the *Eclipse* had exploded and drifted away, and how Mia thought her crew had drifted away as well. It had exploded. She saw it. Then she remembered another flash of green light. The same green light that had projected her bunk back on *Hekate*, the bunk that couldn't be there while she was trapped and strapped down in the Acedian ship. The green light that had washed over her to project her holoimage to how far the picobots had traveled in her body. It was a trick. A deception. She shook herself free from the memory.

The *Eclipse* drifted down to the surface, the aft hatch spiraling open. Mia expected swarms of people to exit her ship, but only Charles Donavin stepped into the light. Clad in plain brown attire, he pushed the sleeves of his jacket up his arms. His silver eyes glinted. The man said nothing as he walked across the dirt toward Nin's home, and he stopped short of the force field.

Donavin frowned, staring at the air between them. "Now, this won't do."

His voice reverberated through the archivist's tiny speakers. At first, Mia couldn't understand why Donavin would say such a thing. They watched the field between Donavin and Nin shimmer. Of course, he could see the force field, all Acedians could. Her bots were deactivated though. How could she see it? She'd have to ask Skyler about it later on. Donavin's image grew sharper, and Mia noticed a trail of red snaking from Donavin's left ear to behind his jacket collar. Blood? Good, she hoped he'd bleed even more.

"It took you long enough to find me, Charles," Nin said in a high, clear voice.

Donavin ignored him. "This won't do at all, this wretched field."

"Are you going to destroy my research?"

Again Donavin ignored him. He placed a hand on the field and grimaced. "Fascinating." Donavin's hand filled the square as Nin focused on it. The field glinted, moving in waves around Donavin's touch.

Nin slid his gaze back to Donavin's face. "Are you going to kill me, Charles?"

Cassidy shifted in her seat. Mia took a sideways look at her. Cassidy rubbed one finger over the other, an odd gesture until Mia remembered the ring that used to be on that finger. It would probably be twirling furiously by now. Wanting to comfort her, Mia reached for her, hand resting on her arm. Cassidy's face had whitened, and she nodded at the square. Donavin finally made eye contact with Nin. Silver eyes glared at them, and even here, far away from him, Mia's heart pounded. Her mouth dried. The air suddenly seemed heavy. Why hadn't Nin used the blasted gun already? Maybe it couldn't shoot through the force field?

"I don't need to do anything." Donavin's gaze drifted to Nin's left. "Not when he'll do it for me."

Nin followed Donavin's gaze so fast the square blurred. When it cleared, a man Mia didn't recognize filled one side of the archivist's square.

But Will gasped. "That's Rika Wes."

The name jarred a memory in Mia, when they had been running from the Acedians, going across the cabin full of new drones, Will had shouted that name. Said it was one of his friends from Paradous. The man looked barely Will's age, with green hair bright against his dark skin. His eyes glinted silver, just like Donavin's. The man stood at attention, hands linked behind his back, staring straight ahead.

Guilt boiled in Mia's stomach. This man was an Acedian because of her, because she had led Donavin to Paradous, led them to Will and Jeff's home world. And even though the list was long since destroyed, she added Paradous to it. A place she would have to apologize to. To the families. To anyone Rika Wes left behind. She thought his name over and over, determined to remember. She would remember. Movement in the cube caught her eye.

Sidling over to stand in front of him, Donavin smiled. "Are you ready to complete the process?"

"Yes," Rika Wes said.

Donavin's lips twitched, a smirk spreading across his lips. He looked to Nin. "You may have created the first generation. The one residing in this drone's body." Donavin reached into his breast pocket and pulled out a syringe filled with silver fluid. "But I have a new generation. A better generation."

He injected the substance into Rika Wes' arm. The man winced and closed his eyes.

When Donavin's gaze traveled down, Rika hunched forward. His arms flailed at his sides, hands opening and closing. His legs buckled, though he didn't fall. Donavin's intense stare traveled up, and Rika arched his back, his head shaking. Finally, he straightened. Stilled.

The two Acedians stared at each other, but Nin seemed no longer concerned with Donavin. He stepped closer and focused on Rika. The silver in Rika's irises swirled an impossibly bright color, one that seemed to shine. Glow, even in the brightness of the day.

Nin frowned. "So quickly. That's not possible."

It wasn't possible. It took weeks to become fully Acedian. Maybe it had been accelerated because he already had picobots in his system? Because he already was Acedian? By the horror of Nin's expression, Mia knew her theories were wrong. It would be that fast with anybody, everybody. There'd be no chance to stop it.

Donavin swiveled on his heel, and Rika did the same. Two pairs of silver eyes glared back. Donavin arched an eyebrow. "Like I was saying."

Rika lunged.

The image swung upward as Nin stumbled back. A humming sound began. Nin looked down at his attacker. Rika had overshot his target, overbalanced, and crashed to the dirt. He righted himself and lunged again when a yellow light flashed, blinding the archivist.

Will moaned. "No."

The light cleared. Rika had sunk to the ground, dust settling around him. Not even a muscle twitched. The shot had made it through the force field. A low wail came from Will. Another piece of his home world gone, ended, just like that. Mia glanced over, air catching in her throat. Will had buried his head in his hands once more. Unable to face his grief, she turned back to the square.

Nin faced Donavin but didn't lower his weapon, the tip still glowing yellow. "Surely you didn't think I wouldn't have a means to protect myself, Charles?"

"It was worth the time to decipher your little defense system." Donavin tilted his head. Another dribble of blood leaked out his ear, bright against his skin.

Had he cracked Nin's defenses already? Mia sagged forward, closer to the archivist. A chill settled in her arms, and she rubbed it away. The field flickered, flashed. Something was wrong. Donavin placed a hand on the weakened structure. It disintegrated, and he stepped through. Nin positioned himself between his home and Donavin; the hand holding the weapon trembled.

Donavin smirked. "You honestly don't think that little machine of yours will work on me?"

"It worked on him," Nin said. The view swiveled to Rika then back to Donavin.

A shadow moved behind Donavin, but Nin didn't focus on it. Mia's heart pounded in her ears. Sweat slickened her palms. Why didn't Nin focus on the shadow? There could be more Acedians!

"He was nothing." Donavin stared at Nin, his eyes narrowed into slits.

"You won't find her." Nin's voice cracked, moving backward.

"Of course, I will," Donavin whispered. Even though he couldn't possibly touch her, Mia's chest tightened, and fear tried to regain its hold on her. Warmth suddenly surrounded her hand, and Mia glanced down at Cassidy's hand resting over her own.

Nin squeezed the trigger. A burst of yellow light shot from the gun. The light balled on Donavin's chest, shimmered then disappeared inside him. He still came forward. Nin fired again. The second shot proved no different.

"What's that about?" Skyler muttered.

Donavin stopped. Frozen? No, a crooked grin crept over Donavin's lips. His gaze drifted to the side. An arm fell into view and the square blurred as the angle suddenly changed. They faced Nin's home now. Nin must've glanced sideways. For a moment, the image filled with Harrison's features, his arm wrapped around Nin's throat.

"Thank you, Harrison." Donavin's voice came from behind. "Take one last look, Nin."

Harrison's smiling face swam up into Mia's vision, and she swallowed a lump forming in her throat. Her stomach seemed to drop from her, and she curled her fingers around Cassidy's now, needing that anchor. Harrison was one of them? She added his name to her list of apologies.

A shadow fell over the house as the *Eclipse* hovered over it. Twin cannons protruded from the base of her, their tips glowing aqua. The weapons charged and fired one steady aqua burst into the building. The house crumbled to the ground then fell further as the underground rooms swallowed the wreckage. A wall of dust swamped them. The square went dark a few times as Nin blinked. When he opened his eyes, the square seemed dirty, smudged. One corner showed complete darkness.

Donavin stepped into view. He held the tip of a dagger up to his chin, the same snowflake dagger he had taken from Mia. "I know you can hear me, Mia. There's a beacon on your ship that activated the moment you lifted from this planet. I'm tracking it. Don't bother trying to shut it off. You won't be able to. I will find you, Mia Foley. You and your precious crew. You can't escape me."

The dagger disappeared. Nin must've struggled, for the image jerked back and forth, showing dirt, Harrison's profile, Donavin. Finally, Nin grunted. The image swung downward, a dagger piercing Nin's clothing, a bubble of blood gathering around the blade. The holoimage blinked off, and Mia added his name to her list.

.

Chapter Eighteen

"YOU SHOULD HAVE LEFT me on the planet," Jeff's voice broke the silence that reigned after the holoimage turned off. They all turned to him. He sat up straight, eyes narrowed at the now-empty space. "I asked you to leave me on the planet."

"You asked me to kill you," Will said quietly.

Jeff stared at him. "And you couldn't even do that, could you, brother?"

"I'd never do that, Jeff." Will grabbed Jeff's shoulder and shook it a little. "We will get through this. I swear it."

Jeff didn't move, didn't respond, didn't even blink. He shifted his gaze from his brother, looked past Mia and Cassidy, to the hull behind them. His features hardened.

Cassidy moved as if to speak, but Mia held her back with a shake of her head. After all the deaths she had behind her, she knew Jeff was trying to put up a shield of his own, trying to protect himself from the grief of his sister's death. Of Rika's death. It wasn't fair to Will. It wasn't fair to any of them. But she understood why. She also knew it wouldn't be long before the shield cracked. Harrison's jovial face once again swam up into her mind and her stomach seemed to bottom out. Her own shield had started to crack.

There was a bigger danger than grief now. Somewhere on this shuttle, a beacon called to Donavin. He was right. She would never escape him, but she had to try. For the safety of the crew, she had to push them to run. A sudden hand on her shoulder roused her from her thoughts. Cassidy brushed Mia's cheek with the tips of her fingers.

Mia frowned. "I don't care what Donavin says. We need to find the beacon. Suggestions?"

Skyler leaned forward. "We could try to scan for it, see if any anomalies or energy surges appear." She squeezed past them to the command chair and brought up the diagrams of the ship. A gray line drifted over the schematics as the scanning began. The lines stayed clear, the energy constant.

Cassidy shifted closer, peering at the screen. "What does that mean?"

"It means Donavin isn't an idiot," Skyler replied. "He probably knew the first thing we'd check for is an energy signature."

"Maybe the beacon emits a signal only Acedians can notice. Like the force field around Nin's home," Cassidy suggested.

Mia glanced around. Command panels, viewport, narrow deck. Had she noticed anything out of the ordinary since they lifted off? Nothing seemed amiss, and yet something called to Donavin. Could it be Jeff? She eyed the man, still glaring at the bulkheads. No, Nin had fixed him. Donavin couldn't link with him any longer. And even as a sliver of doubt curled in her, she told herself this over and over again.

"I haven't felt anything," Skyler closed her eyes, waited a moment then opened them again. "Or heard anything strange."

"Neither have I." Mia looked at Will, still sitting next to Jeff, eyes now only for him. She slid an arm around his shoulders. "Will, we need your ingenuity right now."

He shook his head, as if pulling himself from somewhere far away, and he rubbed a hand over his face, hard. "We could try hiding from them."

Mia nodded. "How?"

Will eyed the viewport, looking past the warped stars. "We could try finding a magnetic storm and hunker down, shutting off all critical systems. That might disrupt the beacon."

Cassidy chewed on her lip. "Wouldn't the magnetic storm disrupt our shuttle?"

Will frowned, rubbing a hand on the back of his neck. "Well, yeah, but we'd compensate. This is a military-grade shuttlecraft. I'm pretty sure it can take a beating. Does the ship have rotating shields?"

Skyler punched a few commands into the control panel. "Yes."

"If it's protecting us, wouldn't the Acedians detect the shield?" Cassidy asked.

Will paused for a moment. He gave a reluctant nod. "Yeah, that's a possibility."

Still, it seemed like a good option. They could chance it. "Where's the nearest storm?" Mia asked.

Will settled into the chair next to Skyler and brought up the navigation system. "It's close. Right—"

The shuttle lurched to the side, throwing Mia into the bulkhead and sliding the pods toward the aft hatch. Pain blossomed on her shoulder, and she grunted from the sudden jarring. The MP Drive shut off and the stars righted themselves, pinpricks in the darkness.

"We've been knocked off course," Will said.

Mia slid up behind him and studied the viewport, trying to see if the *Eclipse* followed. "How did they sneak up on us? Blast it, do we have any weapons?"

"The scans were directed internally. And yes." Skyler keyed the controls. A panel ejected from the bulkhead, sliding around Cassidy and glowing a steady red. "Fire only when needed."

"Got it," Cassidy replied.

Another blast rocked them. Mia grabbed the backs of both Skyler and Will's chairs. Would this shuttle hold against an Acedian attack? Probably not. "Will, bring up anything you have on the navigation system. We need to find a planet close enough to pull us out of this. And fast. Skyler, activate the shields. Cassidy, I don't care if it's the *Eclipse*, shoot her out of the black."

Her crew followed her commands. Another shot connected with the aft shields, the blast creating ripples that made their way all the way to the bow, sparking with aqua light. The shuttle jerked forward, but the shields held.

Relief washed over Mia, and she sent a word of thanks to the military. At least the shuttle didn't break. "Skyler, bring us around for a clear shot."

Skyler maneuvered so they faced their attackers. *Eclipse*'s bulbous shape peered back, showing the Acedian double-barreled energy guns welded to her hull.

Mia tightened her hold. "Fire."

A red blast burst from their shuttle and flashed past the viewport, heading straight for the Acedians. The shot exploded, radiating outward and lighting the shields surrounding the *Eclipse*.

"Of course they'd have shields." Sweat beaded on her forehead. She wiped it away.

The *Eclipse* fired again. The shot connected with their shields, puncturing through on the starboard side of the viewport. The shuttle rumbled. Skyler brought up a scan of the ship.

"Shields down to fifty percent, Captain." Skyler swiveled to her. An alarm sounded, high, beeping, annoying.

Mia grimaced. Apparently the shuttle couldn't handle that much. "Fire!"

Cassidy charged the weapons and two red lines sliced their way to the *Eclipse*, but *Eclipse*'s shields held, the shots bursting across it.

"Damage?" Mia asked.

Skyler scanned the screen. "None. And we can't take another hit like that. The emergency pod was nearly sheared off with our hull."

Shock rippled through Mia and her eyes widened. "Emergency pod? This tiny shuttle has an escape pod?"

Skyler frowned. "Of course. All military-grade shuttles do. They're collapsible hubs."

"What if we—" Mia didn't have time to finish. The *Eclipse* fired again. The shot buckled the starboard side of the hull, crushing one section inward.

No use for an escape pod now, and who knew how many people it could carry. Certainly not all of them. She pointed to the screens over Will's shoulder. He had been typing madly away at the keys, trying to locate a planet for the MP Drive to latch onto. "Any planets that'll work for us?"

"Yes!" Will brought up some coordinates on his screen. "This one. The pull is strong. We should reach there in half an hour. If *Eclipse* follows, she'll be faster than us, though I bet she'll have a hard time navigating through that." He pointed to the asteroid field blocking the path to the planet. "With a shuttle this small, we could get through no problem then zip away again before they arrive. Like when the Acedians first tried to attack us on the *Eclipse*."

Mia nodded, remembering that moment clearly, how they'd used Pargon's rocky field to protect them while the *Eclipse* was able to slip through. It was almost poetic how they'd do the same in this tiny shuttle, trying to get away from the *Eclipse*. "Activate the MP Drive."

"Activating," Skyler replied.

The magnetic field formed, blurring the *Eclipse*. The engines whirred. The stars warped as the MP Drive took hold, and they left the *Eclipse* behind, heading for the asteroid field. Will leaned back in his chair, rubbing a hand over his face and groaning. Cassidy pushed the weapons panel back into its holding cell and closed her eyes. Skyler kept her gaze on the viewport, staring at the bright, white tails from the stretched out stars. Mia didn't need to look at Jeff to know he still glared at the hull.

Her heart pumped against her chest. Her hands shook. She couldn't catch her breath. Sitting down, she forced herself to be still. Her body wouldn't listen. Those blasted little picobots had starved her of emotions for so long, shielded her from her own feelings, she couldn't contain them now. Without the Acedian technology swarming inside her, locking her away, the full weight of her past slammed down. The pain she had caused. Sarah, Rika, Harrison. All the people from Paradous. All the people from Pargon. All the people on her first four ships. Even in her mind, the list grew heavy, threatening to pull her down, to hold her captive. Her chest tightened. She couldn't be weak. Not now. Worried the others would notice, Mia stood up.

"I'm going to check the emergency pod, in case we need to use it."

Skyler waved toward the back. "The entrance is by the aft hatch."

Mia nodded, but Cassidy grabbed her arm. "Are you okay?"

Throat too tight to answer, Mia just shook her head and pulled away. She'd already failed Will and Jeff. Their entire world suffered because of her. What if she failed Cassidy? She reached the hatch and looked up at the panel above her. Not knowing how to open it or even how to activate the emergency hub, she lingered there. The panel slid away and, through the circular viewport, Mia watched as the emergency pod activated and expanded before her, hissing and cranking as it did.

She glanced back. Cassidy stood behind her, hand against a control panel built into the bulkhead. Her brown eyes searched for answers Mia couldn't give. The viewport popped open, and a ladder lowered to her feet. Without another word, Mia pulled herself into the emergency pod. She crashed her head on something and closed her eyes against the pain, tumbling into the pod and shuffling backward until she found the other side. She pulled her knees up to her chin. Her body shook.

When she opened her eyes again, the sight before her took her breath away. Gleaming solid walls sloped to form a dome at the top, a single chair built into one bulkhead. A control screen loomed in front of the chair. How it managed to inflate and form this, Mia didn't know and didn't care. It was the perfect getaway ship.

As if on impulse, Mia clawed her way into the chair and searched the screens. It seemed easy enough to understand. Her vision blurred. She could just leave. She'd done it before. She could do it again. Her head ached. She could run. Hope the beacon stayed with this shuttle. Donavin still followed that blasted beacon, maybe he'd never find her, maybe she would finally be free.

Pain lanced though her at the thought. At the stupid, cowardly action, and at her past self. Of course she couldn't leave. This crew had saved her and Cassidy. She would never leave Cassidy behind. But she had failed so many of them, and Donavin still came. Some insane part of her had thought if the bots in her system were stopped, he wouldn't be able to find her but that wasn't the case. He still came. He still chased her. Her heart pounded. She wiped her sweaty palms on her thighs, eyes darting around, focusing on nothing.

Her mind raced back to the list, the one in her old captain's jacket, the one she'd lost on the Acedian ship. The one with *Eclipse* penned at the base, and the one she had mentally added to since then. She had destroyed ships, families, lives. The ache loomed so great, Mia almost wished for the Acedian technology to be back in her system to drive it away. Almost. She hugged her knees and squeezed her eyes shut. She had to be strong. She had to be a captain. She shouldn't cry. Not now.

Hot tears coursed down her cheeks. Each heaving breath sent spikes of pain through her chest. It seemed like she couldn't get enough air. Why couldn't she get enough air? Her fingers scraped over her legs, pulling her knees closer.

A soft voice startled her, halting her sobs. "Were you going to leave?"

Mia didn't need to see who it was. "No."

"Then you're actually checking the system to see if the pod works?" Cassidy's voice softened.

"No," Mia replied, her voice cracking like a fearful child's.

"Ah." Cassidy's voice sounded closer this time.

Mia wished she would leave and wished she would stay. A warm hand touched the back of Mia's neck and stroked small circles between her shoulders.

"Talk to me, love," Cassidy murmured. "Let me help you."

Mia shook her off, slid from the chair and stumbled over to the other side of the pod. She pushed her palms against the metal, welcoming the cold surface. Gooseflesh prickled her skin. Her muscles tightened. She pounded the metal with her fist, half expecting it to buckle. Of course, it wouldn't. She wasn't Acedian any longer. Cassidy wrapped her arms around Mia's waist, but Mia couldn't face her. Not yet. Tears still streamed down Mia's cheeks.

"I've caused so much pain," she said at last.

Cassidy nodded, leaning against Mia. "True, but you're different now. Better."

"I should've stayed behind and killed Donavin." Mia's hands tightened into fists. "Protected Nin. Saved Harrison, somehow."

"You can't save everyone, Mia."

Mia's breath caught. "That's right. I can't. Now they're gone."

Cassidy leaned closer, hugged her tighter, her chin tucked by Mia's neck. Still, Mia couldn't look at her. "You protected us, Mia. You saved Jeff."

Mia's lip trembled. "Jeff wanted to die. He asked me to kill him, and I couldn't. Wouldn't."

"And I'm glad for that, love," Cassidy whispered, her breath tickling Mia's cheek. "We'll figure out a way to help him."

A thought struck Mia. One she hadn't even considered before. "But what if he turns into someone like me?"

The pod seemed to shrink. The bulkheads darkened. Everything seemed to move in on her. Even Cassidy blurred. Mia sank to the deck, hiding her face behind her hands and pushing her back to the metal now, facing outward, seeing darkness. Her heart thudded painfully and what little air she had managed to inhale left her in a rush.

"He won't." Cassidy's whisper filled the quiet. She tugged Mia's hands away from her face. Cassidy knelt before her, a small smile crossing her lips. A lock of hair fell over her eyes. "Because you won't let him. We've all lost someone. It's what you do afterward that shows who you are. You'll help him by being an example for him."

Mia gave a bitter chuckle. "I lost my parents then killed other parents. What kind of breached-up example does that make me?"

Cassidy kept quiet for a moment, searching Mia's face as if the answer could be found there. "A person who made the wrong decisions in her past."

The disappointment in her voice nearly crushed Mia. She dropped her gaze to her knees.

Cassidy tucked her fingers under Mia's chin, lifting her head and gently cupping her cheek. "But I also see a person who made the right decision in saving Jeff. Even if he doesn't believe it now. And a person who can continue making the right decisions in the future."

A small flicker of hope loosened the tightness in Mia's chest. She had made the right decision, and she'd help that idiot Jeff any way she could. She had to.

Cassidy rummaged around in her pocket for a moment before showing Mia the memory chip from the military ship. "I think it's time you saw this."

She rose and placed the memory chip into the emergency pod's comm system. Pulling Mia to her feet, she touched the comm. A holoimage of the boy who'd helped them escape the *Escambia* flickered into view.

Mia blinked once, twice. What was the boy doing? "What is this?"

"Just listen, love." Cassidy went behind her, wrapped her arms around Mia's waist and rested her chin on Mia's shoulder. The warmth. The strong embrace. The soft tickle of Cassidy's breath on her cheek all calmed her.

With the flicker of hope still in her chest, Mia watched. The boy recalled how they had known each other on the *Oasis*, how they had talked only once or twice, how he had been so frightened, how he remembered the girl who threw the bomb that saved their lives. He thanked her. Another person appeared, the medic who helped calm her when Commodore Bay had leered over her. She did the same, recalling how they knew each other, thanking her for saving her life. Then another person came on. And another. And another still. Thanking her for saving them. Thanking her for saving their friends. Their family. Their loved ones. Thanking her for doing her best to protect them. And in each thank-you the gift of forgiveness shone through, so much that it felt like a hot bead of it dripped through her soul. So much that it lifted the crushing doubt, the agony, the fear of her past. The flicker of hope grew into a glaring fire. Weightless, once more, Mia allowed herself a small smile.

The holoimage ended, and Cassidy faced her, hands still resting on Mia's waist and grinning. "So what's your decision going to be now?"

The simplicity of her question shocked Mia. Now? Cassidy kept their eyes locked, her stare burning deep into Mia. What would she do now? She stilled, the answer forming clearly.

"What I should've done a long time ago," Mia replied.

.

Chapter Nineteen

MIA DREW CASSIDY IN, molding her arms around the soft contours of her body, letting Cassidy's gentle heartbeat calm her own. Facing Donavin would be difficult, but she had to do it. And she had to do it alone. She couldn't risk the others getting hurt, not anymore. She released Cassidy and went over to the hatch, mapping out the *Eclipse* in her head. How would the others take her decision? Probably not well. Lowering herself to the main shuttle, Mia grabbed a heavy weapons pod twice her arm's length and joined the others at the front. Skyler swiveled around, wincing at the scraping noise as Mia dragged the pod over. Will leaned over the control panel, his features illuminated by the stars warping outside the viewport. Even Jeff stopped his brooding mood and watched.

Mia let the pod crash onto the deck. "Skyler, I keep hearing Acedian thoughts. Why?"

Skyler stared at the weapons pod. She touched the metal, fingers spreading wide across its surface. "It's residual. The bots had already embedded themselves in your brain, altering pathways, before Nin deactivated them. I used mine to my advantage. Donavin didn't know about me, since I kept up the ruse. But he knows about you. Don't focus on the voices. They'll fade. Mine did."

"Good," Mia said. "Take us out of Drive."

Skyler jerked her hand off the metal. "Is the emergency pod—"

"It's fine. I need you to drop out of Drive. Now."

"They'll catch up to us." Skyler gaped at her, as if she had never heard of a crazier request, and Mia figured, perhaps she hadn't.

Mia nodded. "That's what I want."

"You're giving up?" Will spoke in a quiet tone.

Cassidy, ever her shadow, appeared beside Mia. "Of course not."

"Of course not," Mia echoed. She frowned. How could she explain her plan without sounding crazy? Maybe she was crazy for thinking she'd survive. She chose her words carefully. "Donavin's obsessed with finding me. He's been chasing me since this first began, and I'm not going to run anymore."

Skyler hooked an arm over the back of her chair, shirt bunching up at the elbow. "And what are you going to do after we drop out?"

"I'll surrender," Mia said.

"What?" Cassidy yelped, pulling Mia around to face her. "You can't be serious. When I asked what you were going to do, I didn't mean for you to—"

"It's the perfect attack plan." Mia grabbed Cassidy's hand and eased the grip, squeezing tight and turning back to the others. "If I surrender, he brings me onto the *Eclipse,* and I know that ship better than anyone. I don't have activated bots in my system now, so he can't control me."

Will leaned back, rubbing his forehead. "But he'll just inject you with the same picobots he used on Rika."

She hadn't thought of that. The new bots Donavin had might be an issue and some of the confidence building inside her dissipated. She pressed her lips together and thought for a moment. "I doubt it. He doesn't know how Nin stopped the original picobots in the first place. I'm betting he'll want to use me to figure it out. He'll have to get close. When he does, I'll kill him."

Cassidy dropped onto a seat, shaking her head. Mia sat across from her with the weapons pod on the deck between them. She leaned over and lifted the hinged cover. A yellowed slab of foam lined the base with several guns, spark knives, and a single syringe resting within it.

Mia's confidence rose again as she ran her hand over the weaponry. "It's not like I'll be going in unarmed."

Cassidy eyed the weapons and hefted a stocky, single-barreled magma gun. Her pale fingers seemed to glow against the dark surface. "You really think they'll let you smuggle these onboard?"

"Of course not. The guns are huge. These aren't." Mia selected the smallest spark knife, its serrated blade no longer than her thumb. With her other hand she picked up the multi-needle syringe filled with blue sedative.

Cassidy's features tightened, and she put the weapon back in the pod. Her voice lowered. "Mia, you're seriously considering going into Donavin's territory with those pathetic things?"

"Yes. They're small, easy to hide." Mia rested her boots on the bench across from her. She plucked the accompanying sheath from the pod, slipped the spark knife inside, and slid the weapon inside her right boot. Uncomfortable, but better than nothing. "See?"

Will poked her boot, pressing where the spark knife was hidden. "Not to be selfish, but if you surrender, what's to stop the Acedians from shooting us?"

She grinned. "I'm counting on this shuttle getting shot." An outburst from her crew stilled Mia for a moment. "Skyler, can you mimic biosignatures in here, to make it seem like there are life forms and the emergency pod is still connected?"

Skyler fumbled around with the controls for a moment. "Yes, only for ten minutes. After that, the energy disintegrates."

"That's fine. I only need it for a short time."

Cassidy rubbed her temples. "You want him to think we've died."

Mia nodded. "You take the escape pod. I'll deal with Donavin."

Silence. Cassidy's gaze fell to the deck, and the simple action stabbed Mia's heart. Knowing Cassidy, she'd follow Mia anywhere. And a part of Mia wanted that but not this time, not into Donavin's grasp. They needed to follow her plan. She fingered the syringe still in her hand, the liquid that could save them all. The smallest drop would knock anyone out for an hour or two, even Donavin. Mia would have to use it on him in order to survive. What would happen to the rest of the Acedians onboard? Or herself? It didn't matter. Once Donavin died, Mia could go peacefully. Except for Cassidy. How could she leave her love—her heart and soul—behind, alone?

Will glared out the viewport. Skyler stared at the syringe, and Mia tightened her fist over it. Perhaps she could tell them all her plans. Maybe they could help. Mia's head began to pound. The muscles in her neck tingled. No, she had to go alone.

Cassidy cleared her throat. "And you think we'd just leave you to deal with the rest of the Acedians because..."

Mia sighed. "I can't face another person dying because of me."

"Well, tough," Skyler snapped. "Tough! We didn't go through all the breaching trouble of saving you just so you could kill yourself on some stupid revenge kick."

Mia rubbed the back of her neck, trying to ease the building tension. Part of her was relieved, grateful even. Of course her crew would want to help. It might not be a suicide mission if they were there. They could even the odds, surprise Donavin while he focused on her. A sneak attack. But they'd have to be unconscious to be truly safe from the *Eclipse's* scans. The drug could do that. Still, she couldn't shake the image of Cassidy strapped to the Acedian table. Cassidy had been there before, and Mia never wanted her to be in that position again.

Protectiveness surged within her. "You can't come with me. It'll be more dangerous."

"Blast it all! We've almost gotten killed plenty of times. For once, I'd like it to be on our terms." Will glared at her. "You need our help. You're just too stubborn to ask for it."

"No," Mia shot back. "I wouldn't be able to concentrate with you onboard. I'd be too concerned for your safety to pull any sort of backup plan."

He raised an eyebrow. "How many plans do you have?"

Mia scowled. Truly, she only had one backup: blow up the *Eclipse*. It was a good plan, though. "One I know will work."

"Will's right. You're being stubborn, Mia." Cassidy leaned forward and gave Mia's arm a squeeze. "Of course, we're going to come with you. Of course, we're going to help you. We'll stop Donavin together."

Mia sighed, allowing herself a small smile. Loyalty and love might doom them all, but she couldn't help feeling glad that her crew wanted to help. Her finger grazed the cap of the needle still in her hand. She glanced down at the blue liquid. If she used it now, she'd have little to protect herself from Donavin. She could use it on her crew, force them to sleep, put them on the emergency pod, and jettison them away. It might be the only way to protect them. But if they came back and helped, what would she do then? Mia lifted her gaze to Cassidy.

Cassidy's brown eyes watered and she lifted her hand, curling her fingers around Mia's chin. "I can't let you go alone. I won't let you go alone."

Mia gritted her teeth, torn between what she wanted and what she needed to do.

Cassidy took one of Mia's hands in her own, slipping her fingers around the blue syringe as well. Of course she knew what it could do. Of course she had figured out Mia's plan before Mia had even figured it out for herself. "We can help you. Trust me, please."

Trust. Mia broke Cassidy's intense gaze and stared out the viewport. The shuttle rumbled underneath her boots. Dependence on someone other than herself? She had gone so long alone, taking care of herself, trusting only herself. After all, no one else could be depended on. No, that wasn't true, not anymore. Not since the *Eclipse*. It wasn't just her. Cassidy, Will, Skyler, even Harrison and Jeff had helped her. They believed in her enough to save her. Did she trust them?

Her gaze wandered. Will leaned forward in his chair, hazel eyes blazing as if challenging her to deny their help. Skyler cocked an eyebrow, black hair falling over one of her silver eyes. Even Jeff's features had softened, if only a little. And Cassidy. A surge of love rushed through Mia. Cassidy still stared at her, brown eyes burning through her, as if she could see through Mia's defenses, see the depths of her uncertainty. And, of course, she could. Did Mia trust them? A smile tugged at the corners of her lips. For the first time in a very long time, she could honestly answer yes.

"I do." Mia held the syringe up. "Skyler, is there an antidote for this drug?"

"Not an antidote." Skyler clicked open the storage pod beneath her seat and pulled out a small, oval medical kit. She flipped it open and selected another multi-needle syringe filled with white liquid. "This adrenaline is its counterpart. It can activate automatically after a time and shorten the duration. It's used for stealth missions. Why?"

Mia took one of the syringes from Skyler, narrowing her eyes at the white liquid. "You're going to activate the fake biosignatures to fool Donavin and inject you, Cassidy, Jeff, and Will with the adrenaline. You'll go into the emergency pod. I'll need to give you the sedative so your biosignatures will be weak. Hopefully, you won't show up on Donavin's scans after you jettison. How much time will that adrenaline shave off the sedative?"

Skyler bit her lip. "Well, it depends on the person, how quickly their bodies break down the medication, how strong the sedative is to begin with."

"Fine." Mia took a deep breath. What if they never woke up? She shoved the concern away, pieces of her plan locking securely into place. "When the adrenaline takes hold, you sneak back onto the *Eclipse* and find me. Look for me in the infirmary. I bet he'll be taunting me for a good while before anything actually starts, so there's your window. It's not much…"

"But it's enough," Cassidy whispered, leaning over to kiss Mia on the cheek.

The place she kissed burned, and Mia grinned. The plan could work. With her friends' help, they could win.

Will grabbed an energy gun from the weapons pod. "You mentioned a backup plan?"

"Yes," Mia said. "If my plan fails, then I'm going to blow up the *Eclipse*. I'll give you the signal and we'll take the *Eclipse*'s emergency shuttles down to the planet. We're close enough, right?"

"Five clicks, not bad." A smirk even crossed Will's lips. "The planet's just called 03-K64. Stupid name, but it can support life. If we do need to use the *Eclipse*'s shuttles, we can land on the planet no problem."

Cassidy jerked back. "Wait. How will you even be able to plant bombs on the ship? You said you didn't plan on destroying the *Eclipse*."

Mia winced. Of course, Cassidy would remember that conversation on Paradous, even though it had taken place after so much had happened. She'd confessed to keeping a list of all the ships and people she had destroyed. Her blood debts. The memory of writing *Eclipse* on her piece of paper, of jotting down that fate, pained Mia. They all deserved the truth, and it shocked her that she hadn't told them before, on the *Eclipse*, when she'd divulged so much else. "I put bombs on all my ships. It's the first thing I do. They were in place even before you arrived, hidden very well. Even Will never found them. When the Acedians killed Sarah, I thought about destroying the ship."

"You would've blown us up?" Cassidy's voice grew louder.

"Of course not, love." Mia couldn't bear the shock widening Cassidy's eyes. The explanation sounded bad, a horrible reminder of what Mia was once capable of. Now, it could be their perfect plan. She reached out and held one of Cassidy's hands in both of hers. "I never would've activated them with you onboard. Any of you. It was part of my past life, one that's over and done with now. You know that." Mia squeezed Cassidy's hands tighter. "And for this attack, we'll be long gone before the bombs go off. It's a simple fuse, quick and easy, and the entire ship explodes."

The tight lines around Cassidy's lips smoothed, and she let out a breath. "If we can't have the *Eclipse* as our home...at least he won't be able to have it either."

"Fine." Will swung around and activated the controls. "We're going to have a second backup. The military should still be following us, right? When we're in the emergency pod, I can contact them. We're still in a military shuttle so the pod must have some beacon to attract the rescue vessels."

Mia sighed. "That would be a good plan, Will, but Donavin is using the military. He's infiltrated Commander Bay, and I bet Donavin's commandeered the *Escambia* by now."

"What about the *Bell*?" Skyler straightened in her chair.

"The who?" Mia asked.

"*Escambia*'s sister ship, remember?" Skyler pulled up the information on her screen and projected it as a holographic image. The *Escambia* floated next to a shockingly similar vessel. Mia didn't recall hearing the name before, but she'd lost a good chunk of time during Donavin's control. Skyler pointed to the vessel beside the *Escambia*. "Admiral Boreas was scheduled to visit the *Bell* and transport her to a new location out in the Helix solar. I was informed of his schedule when we first visited *Escambia*."

Mia shook her head. "We don't know if he's been compromised. We could be calling more Acedians to our location. I think I can handle Donavin, and with your help, the crew on the *Eclipse*. If the *Escambia* is following us, I don't want to pull another military-grade Acedian vessel into the brawl."

Will straightened. "I can find out who's in the Drive. Hold on."

He fiddled with his controls and replaced the *Escambia* and *Bell* images with a replica of the MP Drive. A slipstream appeared, inside it two blinking, purple lights. A red square tightened over the first ship.

He pointed to the square and glanced back at his screens. "That's the *Eclipse*."

The square shifted to the next ship.

"And that's the *Bell*. It's a stroke of good luck the *Escambia* isn't around." Will huffed out a breath, but Mia's thoughts darkened. If the *Escambia* wasn't following them, she might be taking more people, ruining more lives. "The *Bell* is following the *Eclipse*. Maybe she can attack it instead of us. It might not be such a suicide mission then."

Mia shoved her hand through the hologram and shut it off. "If you don't want to help you don't need to, Will. No one's forcing you to attack Donavin."

Will leaned back in his chair. "Lots of people are, actually. I'm with you all the way, Captain."

Mia nodded, knowing he referred to Sarah and Rika and everyone else on his home world. And probably Jeff as well, since Will kept looking over at him. Jeff. Mia swiveled to the older Dee brother. What were they going to do with him? He'd wanted to die earlier today, wanted to become an Acedian, wanted to be left planetside. Her crew seemed to sense this issue, because they faced him, too.

Jeff scowled. "I won't help you destroy the *Eclipse*. I won't stop you either. And I won't try to kill myself or call Donavin or anything."

This sudden shift of attitude made Mia suspicious. It must've shown on her face, because Jeff glared at her. Pain creased the lines in his face. "Do you think I'm so cold hearted I'd willingly put my brother in danger, Captain?"

She already knew the answer, so she slid down the bench to sit directly across from him. After a moment's hesitation, she reached out and touched his arm. It was a mark of how confused he was that he didn't shy away. Mia knew he wouldn't know what he should feel, and she could certainly relate. "I know you'd never do that, Jeff. And for what it's worth, I'm glad you're still with us, angry as you may be."

"Well, considering I'm tied up," he nodded to his binds, "there's really nowhere else I can go, is there?"

"Nope." She grinned and patted him on the cheek. "You're stuck with us, Navigator. Deal with it."

She walked away, back to the bow of the shuttle. It might not have been the best move, saying he was stuck with them when, with this current plan, he could theoretically slip away anytime he wanted to. Quietly move the opposite direction from the rest of the crew. Kill himself even, somewhere in the bowls of the *Eclipse*. But when Mia snuck a quick look back his direction, it was clear by the way he stared at Will, he wouldn't dare leave his brother's side. Not on a ship filled with Acedians.

"Well, it's settled." Will stared at the place where the *Bell*'s holoimage once was. "We can't go by maybes, though. If the *Bell*'s been overrun, we'll have both her and the *Eclipse* to deal with."

Skyler reactivated the hologram, pointing to the ships' destinations. Their slipstream stopped right over the shuttle. "We'll have two ships to deal with either way."

A chill settled over Mia, and she tried to rub it away. Could she trust the entire crew on the *Bell*? She had to.

"Fine, call the *Bell* when you're out of range of the *Eclipse*, but just a coded distress call, nothing more." Mia handed Skyler two sleek, single-barrel energy guns. "I'll want to have a weapon bigger than my knife once you sneak onboard. According to that holographic slipstream, the *Eclipse* is almost here. Activate the biosignatures."

Skyler did so, then strapped the gun to her leg and hefted the other in one hand. She grabbed the white syringes. "How are you going to transfer yourself to the *Eclipse* if we take the emergency pod?"

The question stumped Mia for only a moment. "The beaming technology. I bet Donavin's commandeered the *Escambia*'s beaming technology by now, like the one Harrison used to get us off of Fissure. I'd bet anything he outfitted the *Eclipse* with it, but they need to drop out of Drive before they use it."

Will rose. "And if they altered the *Eclipse*, what if they found your bombs?"

Mia stared at him for a heartbeat. "Well, I'll have you guys, won't I?"

Nodding, Will grasped her shoulder and squeezed. He slipped in between Cassidy and the weapons pod and started undoing the bonds that held Jeff in place. Skyler flashed her a grin and moved to the men, leaving Cassidy and Mia by themselves. Or as by themselves as they could be with the rest of the crew a few paces away. Still, Cassidy pulled Mia in for a hug, arms wrapping around her shoulders, head resting in the nape of her neck. Mia leaned into her, melting into the softness of Cassidy's form. She wanted to stay there, right there, like this forever. She broke the embrace and tilted her head to the others.

Her crew had moved over to the emergency pod, and Skyler lifted the white syringe. "This first."

She injected herself, Cassidy, Jeff, and Will. Turning unexpectedly to Mia, she held out her hand.

Mia frowned, eyeing the multi-needled device. "Why me?"

Skyler sighed. "You haven't had much rest these past few days. You'll need it."

Mia nodded, wincing when the needles poked her skin. A stinging sensation traveled up her shoulder. She shook it off. When the escape pod's ladder slipped down to the deck, her crew climbed in. She followed, clutching the sedative in her fist. Not having the drug to use on Donavin would make her job of surviving the *Eclipse* infinitely harder, but the chance of protecting Cassidy overruled any doubt. When her crew awoke, they would come for her. Or she'd be gone, and they'd be safe. Either way, she'd get Donavin. Either way, Cassidy would be safe. Cassidy and Will sat on the deck with their backs to the hull and strapped themselves in, Jeff right next to them.

Skyler positioned herself in the command chair, drawing the safety belts around her shoulders. "Let's get this sedative thing over and done with."

A small smile pulled at Mia's lips. "You're nervous about going under?"

Skyler scoffed. "Only to the extent that I'm going to be floating unconscious in enemy space."

"The adrenaline will wake you soon enough." Mia injected Skyler with the sedative, and she slumped immediately in her bonds. Mia hoped the revive would be just as quick.

She knelt by the others. Will's jaw clenched tight, his arms quivering. His eyes widened, as she nudged back his shirtsleeve. "I wish she hadn't mentioned enemy space."

Mia squeezed his shoulder. "No one will be looking for you until you call on the *Bell*. After that, it's a short jaunt to the *Eclipse,* and you'll be back with me."

"Yeah, we'll be safe there," he grumbled. "You're causing a ton of trouble, Captain."

"I always seem to," she whispered. "Thanks for putting up with it."

Will rolled his eyes, although a ghost of a grin softened his features. She pressed the needle into his arm and pushed some sedative through. He relaxed.

She moved to Jeff next. He merely nodded and looked away. Still, Mia rested a hand on his arm and muttered, "Keep your brother safe, Jeff. That's an order."

A slight grin, much like Will's, appeared on Jeff's face. "Yes, Captain."

Mia plunged the needle into his quivering arm and gave him some sedative, making sure he slumped in his bonds before moving on.

Cassidy placed her palm on Mia's cheek, and Mia kissed it, the skin soft against her lips. They linked hands, and she rested her forehead against her love's. "Come get me, Cassidy."

"Always, love. Always," she whispered.

Mia kissed Cassidy, short—too short—but gently, too. The contact sent sparks through Mia's body, warming her to her core. Lifting Cassidy's arm, Mia pushed the needle into her skin and emptied it. Cassidy closed her eyes, leaned back, and fell asleep.

Hands shaking, Mia brushed a strand of hair off Cassidy's forehead and straightened Will's shirt. She tucked Jeff's pant legs back into his boots. Then she stood and went over to Skyler, tightening the straps across her shoulders. Mia backed away. Her legs felt like lead. Air rushed from her lungs. She turned and dropped through the hatch.

Closing it quickly on the other side, she charged to the shuttle's control panel and dropped out of Drive. The rumbling ceased. The stars pulled back into pinpricks of light. The planet beyond filled the viewport with mottled purple. She pulled up the jettison sequence on the emergency pod, ejected it from the shuttle then initiated the highest speed. Only when the emergency pod left the sensors, could she really breathe again.

Then it happened. Acedian thoughts invaded her mind. She ignored them, hoping they would fade. They didn't. The *Eclipse* dropped out of MP Drive directly in front of her, swamping the viewport. Charles

Donavin's voice filtered through the comm system. "You can't run forever, Mia."

Speaking in what she hoped was a clear voice, Mia replied, "I'm not running."

"What?"

She straightened. "I won't run anymore. On one condition."

The comm's static filled the shuttle. Donavin's voice burst through. "Oh? Name it."

"Let my friends go free."

Static again filtered through the comm.

Finally, Donavin answered. "Very well. I will not harm them."

Liar. Mia tensed. She wanted to yank this blasted shuttle around and run. Instead, she focused on her love for Cassidy and that night they'd spent together. "Then beam me onto your ship."

Her skin tingled, the shuttle faded, and the *Eclipse*'s bridge appeared. Twin aqua beams lanced toward their shuttle drifting outside the viewport. It shuddered and seemed to fold in on itself where the shots connected. In less than a heartbeat, it burst apart, throwing pieces of metal outward like a supernova. A shard bounced off the *Eclipse*'s shields. Playing her own part, Mia twisted her features into a fit of rage and smashed one of her fists into the nearest Acedian. He doubled over. She managed to punch two more before they subdued her. Once captured, Mia sank to her knees and dropped her head into her hands, covering her smile. Her friends still lived. Cassidy still lived. They would return. They would save her again.

Kellie Doherty

Chapter Twenty

MIA TRIED TO KEEP her expression passive as she walked through the corridors, but a frown tugged at her lips. Two Acedian guards, a man and a woman, prodded her forward. The bulkheads seemed shinier than she remembered. The deck gleamed. All the hatches stood open, so she snuck glances inside as they made their way through the *Eclipse*. The living quarters looked cleaner, too. Will's weights stacked nicely in the corner instead of strewn around. Even the kitchens had been tidied, no more boots on the deck, no more cups in the sink, no more cabinets open wide for all to see. Her muscles tightened as she moved, warning her something wasn't right. Warning her to run. The guards shoved her into the infirmary.

The table, stools, and cabinetry, once locked into place, had been removed. Bare bulkheads loomed overhead. The lack of the sharp disinfectant scent seemed off in a place that used to be an infirmary. One guard left and returned with a simple metal chair, which he placed in the center of the cabin. The base of the legs melted then fused into the deck.

Mia swallowed. Just like in Nin's living room. His place had been this clean and shiny as well. Perhaps she didn't have the upper hand. The guard stared at her, a scar traveling across both cheeks and over his nose, creating the mimicry of a smile where there should be none. The other guard pushed her into the seat. With dark hair and a similar jaw line, Mia guessed the pair to be siblings. Did they even remember their family ties? The woman's breath fanned hot on Mia's cheek and carried a sour hint, like hazii fruit. She clamped down on Mia's shoulders, pushing her back into the chair. The woman's thoughts swarmed inside Mia—*she's ready for you, sir*—and Mia ignored the words, hoping they would fade away. She couldn't be distracted at a time like this. Besides, she didn't want to give herself away to Donavin.

Donavin entered the cabin, a lazy smile spreading across his lips. His brown jacket was still bunched at his elbows, but a dark stain now marred his left pant leg. A stain that looked like blood. "Why hello, Mia, how are you doing this afternoon?"

Her pulse quickened at the sight of him. She needed him to be close by to do what she should have done a long time ago. Still, every thought vanished from her. Panic bubbled up her throat. Her stomach twisted. She stared at the smooth panels above her, averting her gaze to give herself more time to compose herself, to calm her beating heart. She had to be calm, or appear to be, and think up a plan of attack.

She lowered her head and stared at Donavin, her voice as light as she could force it. "I'm doing quite well, thanks." If the idiot quasar wanted a conversation, he'd get one. At least it would give Cassidy and the others more time to wake up. The other guards backed off, stationing themselves beside the hatch.

Donavin swept his hands around the room. "Allow me to welcome you to my humble ship." Mia's hands tightened into fists at that comment. His ship? Not likely. "I see my guards have accommodated you nicely, though they did miss one thing."

His silver eyes shifted to the deck. Mia sensed movement then a solid pressure on her boots. She tried to jerk away, but the pressure held her down. The pressure wound up her legs, cinching them to the chair. A chill seeped through her pants. Acedian technology. Silver liquid crept up to her wrists, pushing them into the armrests, before continuing upward toward her forearms like vines around a tree. She'd never be able to reach the spark knife hidden in her boot.

Mia's stomach churned. She forced herself to take up a conversational tone, as if the substance solidifying over her arms didn't terrify her. "How are you?"

"I'm doing well. I must say I am impressed with your courage. I didn't think you would have it in you, facing me." Donavin blinked rapidly as if to clear his head. He linked his hands behind his back and advanced until he stood directly in front of her.

She had to crane her neck to look at him. "Took me long enough, right?"

"And yet, in some senses, just the right amount of time." Donavin's silver eyes bored into hers.

After a few seconds, she glanced away, tilting her head to the bulkheads. "I like what you've done to the place."

Donavin chuckled, moving to one side and tracing his fingers on the smooth metallic surface. "I figured you would hate all this space, actually, considering the state your cabin was in when I found it."

The thought of him rifling through her belongings sickened her, but

176

she let it pass, focusing instead on the man before her. The blood by his ear had been smeared, darkening his earlobe and the entire side of his neck in the process. Another drop welled from his ear and made its way to his collar.

"You're bleeding," she said.

Donavin wiped the fresh blood away with the back of his hand, staring at it. "It's astounding what a little ingenuity can do."

She flexed her hands, testing the bonds. The Acedian tech allowed little movement. "And what do you plan on doing with your ingenuity?"

"Take over the government, of course." He turned away.

That couldn't be it. No, she'd seen his memory of his daughter, the pain he felt, the flash of sorrow when Nin deactivated Mia's picobots. Donavin had even called her Elanora. No, this wasn't about the government.

"This is about your daughter." She struggled, trying to move her legs. The vine-like substance didn't budge. She had to get to the spark knife. "This always has been about Elanora."

Donavin whirled around, towering over her once more. "Don't you dare mention her."

Darting his hand into the folds of his jacket, he brought out the same dagger he'd used to kill Nin. The same dagger he'd stolen from her. The silver bonds tightened, whitening the skin on her arms. Donavin pointed the tip of the dagger at Mia's chest. Fear clasped her throat shut, blurred her vision, dried her mouth. It took all she had not to cower away. A bead of sweat traced a path down her back. He was so close, so close, and she couldn't do a blasted thing about it. But her crew would help set her free. They would come for her. They had to. She forced herself to be still.

"You'd never kill me." Mia glared at him, trying her best to remain calm while the dagger hovered inches from her shirt. "You never could. I look too much like her for you to even come close. You want me to stay with you. That's why you keep hurting my friends, keep turning the ones I love, keep trying so blasted hard. It's because you want me to turn to you."

Donavin smiled. "Like Jeff nearly did. Before you knocked him out."

A hot ball of fury rose in her throat. She let her anger wrinkle her features, but Donavin had done her a service. At the mention of Jeff, Mia's mind darted to another ex-Acedian, one who had survived Donavin's brutal takeover. Skyler. The residual. Skyler managed to communicate with Donavin and fool him by using the residual from her picobots. Mia stared at the weapon by her chest, then past it at the bonds wrapped around her arms. Perhaps she could communicate with the metal substance.

"Yes, just like Jeff almost did. I stopped him."

"True. A fruitless gesture in the end." Donavin moved the dagger's tip in a circular motion, ripping a swath of black fabric open. "You did sacrifice yourself for your friends. That seems like progress. Coming to me instead of running away again."

Mia lurched backward, grimacing as the bonds cut into her skin. She met his gaze and kept to the story. Her voice grew louder with each word. "And you blew them to pieces! Can you honestly think by killing them I'll want to join you? After you murdered my crew, I'll suddenly be on your side?"

He brought the dagger up and Mia's skin burned white-hot as he traced a thin cut across her cheek. "You must've known I'd never let them go free. Didn't you think of using the emergency pod?"

Now was the time to throw him off. She widened her eyes and allowed her jaw to go slack. "There was an emergency pod?"

Donavin chuckled again. "Stupid girl. There's one on every military shuttle. But, of course, you'd have to be involved with the military to know that. And you've spent your life running away from them, haven't you? I didn't need your friends, anyway. I only need you."

He straightened and closed his eyes. Odd timing until Mia figured out he was communicating with someone. Perfect. Concentrating on the substance holding her down, Mia allowed the Acedian thoughts to permeate her. There seemed to be more than last time, so much more her head stung listening to them. She narrowed her focus and heard Donavin's thoughts.

Bay, Harrison, come to me.

She glared at the vines. The substance seemed to grow colder. *Move,* she thought. *Move.*

One tiny section jerked, pulling away from her arm only to snap back in place. She winced. A rustle of movement distracted her. Donavin had turned to the hatch. Harrison and Commodore Bay had come, but so had a handful of others, maybe ten in all. Mia recognized some from the screens on Paradous, including the woman in the red coat Harrison seemed so fond of. The Acedians, usually still in the presence of Donavin, shifted from side to side, milling about. The woman's hand flew to her lips then drifted down again.

"What are you all doing here?" Donavin drew himself up and

stalked to Commodore Bay's side, shoving a hand into his breast pocket, and grabbing a syringe. He popped the cap off the needle. Methodically, almost too methodically, Donavin injected each of the ten Acedians with the silver liquid. The milling ceased. Donavin glared at Commodore Bay. "Has it been done?"

Bay blinked, once and very slowly. "The *Escambia* has been overrun. The ship is yours."

Donavin swiveled back to Mia, a grin wrinkling his cheeks. "You see, Mia, I will take over the government. I wanted to destroy the military for doing what they did. With Admiral Boreas at my fingertips I can control it instead. I can—"

Commodore Bay's monotone voice cut through Donavin's. "Admiral Boreas wasn't on the ship. We couldn't locate him in time to administer the new generation."

Donavin jerked around. "And you didn't think of transferring this data to me sooner?"

While his back was turned, Mia frantically tried to connect with the vines again. Her crew had to be onboard by now. The distress call couldn't have taken that long. A hollow pit formed in her stomach, unless the adrenaline hadn't worked. Mia gritted her teeth. Of course the adrenaline worked. Cassidy would come back. She just needed to give them more time.

She narrowed her eyes at her bonds, ordering simple commands. *Retract wrist, forearm, boot.* The pressure subsided on her foot. The vines on her right forearm slackened. The conversation continued around her.

"I wasn't able to, the connection—"

Waving a hand, Donavin spoke over Commodore Bay's mumbling. "Enough. I'll deal with you later. Have you located him?"

The vines on her wrist eased.

Harrison replied this time. "We think he went over to the *Bell* moments before you gave the order to spread the generation."

"And where is the *Bell* now?" Donavin spoke slow and clear, as if to a child.

His drones didn't answer. The vine retracted halfway down her forearm.

"Find them. Order *Escambia* to meet up with the rest of the fleet and administer the new generation. I want every confirmed ship I can get." The drones scurried off. Mia glanced up, halting the movement of the silver substance. Only Commodore Bay remained.

Donavin sighed, rubbed his forehead, and faced Mia. "You see, I must overrun this corrupted government and start anew. No one has to die. No one has to suffer. The military won't kill people, because there'll be no one to kill. Everyone will be in my control."

But the *Bell* had escaped. Mia could almost sing. "The only reason you want to do that, Donavin, is because the military killed your daughter in order to cover up their weapon radiation. You want revenge. That's all this is."

A glob of blood pooled again in his ear. Why did Donavin keep bleeding? Had something gone wrong? He wiped it away before it could fall and moved close to her, now inches from her face. He seemed disoriented though. His eyes seemed...empty, almost.

Mia pushed further. "I always thought you were this great mastermind. You're not. You're just a father who doesn't know how to mourn his daughter's death."

Donavin's lips curled downward, as he turned to Commodore Bay. Mia kept her eyes trained on Donavin, but her mind on the metal substance. Bay reached into his pocket, brought up a capped syringe filled with silver liquid, and handed it to Donavin. It had to contain the new generation, the same one they'd used on Rika. Maybe Donavin wasn't as concerned with how Nin stopped his original bots after all. They didn't need her for testing like she'd originally thought. Donavin uncapped and raised the syringe, leaning over her with an odd grin parting his lips.

Terror raced through her, sparking her into action. She tore her eyes off Donavin and glared at the vines. *Melt.*

The vines dissolved. Mia jerked up her hand, knocking the needle from Donavin's grasp. She pushed a hand into his face, shoving him away. He fell back into Bay. The vines dug into her left arm, one more command melted the rest of the bonds. She grabbed the spark knife hidden in her boot and thumbed it on. The serrated edges crackled, pale yellow arching from one edge to the next. She lunged at the two men. Donavin sidestepped the attack, and Mia plunged the dagger into Commodore Bay's neck, thumbing a shock wave into him, and yanking it free. Bay fell, electricity stunning him to the deck. She turned to Donavin.

Although he stood in one corner of the cabin, directly across from the hatch, he seemed calm. Too calm. Mia started toward him, a few quick steps and she'd wipe that blasted smirk off his face. The deck liquefied around her feet, and she stumbled. The substance rose to her boots, calves, and finally her knees, freezing her in place. Mia tried to make it let go, but she couldn't connect with it. Her head started to pound. She still had the spark knife. She could throw it. The aim would have to be perfect. He walked slowly toward her, his thoughts ebbing into her.

Tricky, Mia, very tricky.

Before she could reply, other Acedian thoughts crashed into her mind.

A ship.

She's here.

Guns are charging.

Donavin's eyes widened, the smirk sliding off his face. The *Eclipse* jerked to the side, wrenching her legs. She cried out from the sudden pain, but the weapon's fire could only mean one thing. The *Bell* had arrived. Her crew's distress call had gone through. Alarms sounded through the corridors. Donavin locked eyes with Commodore Bay. Mia glanced behind her, catching a glimpse of Bay, a hand slapped to the side of his neck. Blood leaked beneath his fingers. Mia took a deep breath and concentrated, trying to hear their conversation through the other thoughts. Finally, only two voices remained.

Hull breach, multiple casualties.

Destroy them.

A jumble of Acedian thoughts burst through again. Her head spiked with pain, so Mia unfocused and let the thoughts drift away. The stabbing subsided. Bay rushed off, stumbling to one side when the *Eclipse* shuddered again. Another barrage rocked them. The sibling drones from before came into the cabin and stood by the hatch, but they twitched as they guarded the entrance.

Donavin glared at Mia. "It seems we have company. *Escambia*'s sister ship doesn't want to go down without a fight."

"Neither will I," Mia said.

His gaze shifted from her face to the deck. The deck changed beneath her, liquefying for a heartbeat before solidifying. Not enough time for Mia to do anything, but enough time to wonder what the heck was happening to Donavin's tech. To Donavin himself.

"You're in no position to make threats," Donavin muttered.

"Neither are you." Cassidy's voice rang through the cabin.

Donavin, slower than usual, blinked a few times and looked beyond Mia to the infirmary hatch. Mia twisted around, warmth rushing through her at the sight of her crew. She grinned like a blasted fool.

Cassidy pointed her gun at Donavin. Will and Skyler aimed their guns at the guards. Jeff stood to one side, arms crossed tightly across his chest and eyes darting between Cassidy and Donavin. One sibling watched the newcomers. The other stared at Donavin.

"How..." Donavin seemed stunned by this turn of events. He backed away, further from Mia, further from her crew.

Will's face twisted into a grimace. "Admiral Boreas found us and was kind enough to give us a ride." He fired his gun. The weapon sizzled as sparks shot from its barrel and connected with the Acedian guard. Will swung his gun around and shot the other guard. Sparks burned a hole through her shirt and flesh. Both guards dropped, wounded but certainly not dead. Mia knew they would get up. They should get up. Yet they didn't. Mia gawked at the pair. Why weren't they getting up? Or fighting at all? Then it dawned on her, an impossible thought. Maybe Donavin was losing control of his drones.

Swiping at his ear, Donavin eyed Will's gun. "If you kill me, thousands more will die. Can you live with that?"

The tip of Will's gun dropped a few inches.

Skyler's gaze skipped from Donavin to Mia. She stepped forward a pace and aimed her weapon. "I won't have a problem with it."

The weapon's vibrant crimson pulse shot through the cabin so close to Mia hairs rose on her neck.

Chapter Twenty-one

A SECTION OF THE overhead panels melted, fusing with the deck and creating a wall in front of Donavin. Skyler's shot sparked off it. The picobots holding Mia in place liquefied, and she stumbled toward the new bulkhead and slammed her hands upon it. Cold, ice cold and impossibly smooth. She pounded on it, frustration boiling inside of her. The bulkhead spanned the entire length of the cabin, effectively hiding Donavin behind it. Where would he go? The back of the infirmary was against the outer hull. She pressed her ear to the barrier, but a hand yanked her back. Just in time, too. Tendrils of silver curled toward her. Cassidy wrapped one arm around Mia while the other raised her gun. The tendrils sucked back into the bulkhead, rippling its surface before hardening.

The *Eclipse* lurched sideways, throwing Mia to her knees. The little spark knife spun away from her hand, clattering onto the deck. Pain spiked up her legs. Blasted *Bell*. Mia immediately clamped down on the thought. The *Bell* had saved her.

Cassidy helped her to her feet. "What's happening?"

The deck had come alive, it seemed, the metal rising and falling like the ship itself breathed. The infirmary creaked and groaned. Then, just as suddenly, the deck flattened to its usual shape. Mia's tiny weapon had vanished.

She pointed toward the bulging paneling above Skyler. "Move!"

Skyler threw herself forward, and the panels crashed down, covering the hatch, trapping them inside. "How the—"

Mia cut her off. "Donavin."

"We have to get out of here." Will pointed his gun at the bulkhead.

The fear in his voice heightened Mia's own anxiety.

Surprising them all, Jeff grabbed Will's arm and pushed it down. "And you think shooting will help? You'll only hit yourself, idiot."

Probably because of the shock more than anything else, Will consented. Mia nodded a quick thanks to Jeff and moved toward the new wall. If Donavin could block them inside, he could easily crush them entirely. The overhead panels quivered. Was that his plan all along? Crushing them like bugs? Stopping an arm's length away, she waited for the tendrils to emerge.

When none came, she brushed her fingertips over the surface. If she could communicate with the bonds, she should be able communicate with these bulkheads as well. "I can get us out."

The bulkhead seemed solid. Imposing. Yet somehow, Mia knew she could move it. She placed her hands on the surface. The metal grew colder under her palms, so cold she wanted to pull them away, but she kept still, allowing the chill to permeate her arms and shoulders.

A crashing sound thundered behind her. Cassidy cried, "Mia, sooner would be better."

Melt. Mia ordered.

At first, nothing happened. Then, all at once, the bulkhead disintegrated into silver shards and fused into the deck. Cassidy shoved Mia out into the corridor, followed close by Will, Jeff, and Skyler. The infirmary, and the hatch that led to it, disappeared behind them as if they'd never existed. A smooth bulkhead remained in their place.

"Too close," Mia muttered. "We need to get to the bridge and find out where Donavin went."

Skyler unstrapped the gun from her leg and handed it to Mia. "How did you do that?"

"I don't know. I just speak to them."

Skyler shook her head. "You're a natural."

"At controlling Acedian technology? Oh good, all my dreams have been answered." Mia hefted the weapon, bulky, heavy, and so much better than the tiny knife. "Let's go."

The corridor seemed smaller than before. Tighter. An explosion flashed white from the hatch straight ahead, the one that led to the kitchen. She flattened herself against the metal. Sparks danced over the deck panels. Mia inched forward, charging her gun. A steady crimson glowed from the barrel. Another explosion radiated through the ship and the deck rippled beneath her. Maybe the *Bell* wasn't helping after all.

Stopping beside the kitchen hatch, she glanced in. A group of Acedians huddled together, silver eyes wide and worried, lifted to the overhead paneling. How could they be afraid? She held up four fingers, indicating the number of their opponents.

Will pushed past Mia. "Blast it all, we can't wait any longer."

Mia tried to grab his shirt. Missed. "Will!"

Gun drawn, he stepped into the kitchen and fired. Four obvious thumps followed. He backed out again. "Come on."

Mia passed the hatch without looking inside. "We didn't know if they were a threat."

"I didn't kill them," Will said over his shoulder, leading the way.

Mia glanced behind them. The Acedians should be following them, chasing them, trying to catch them. She shook her head at the empty space. She should be happy, thrilled even that they were having an easier time than she had anticipated coming on an Acedian-controlled ship, but unease twisted her stomach. Did Donavin have something even more terrible up his sleeve?

"Mia," Skyler yelled, grabbing her arm.

Mia glanced over just in time to see the kitchen collapse in on itself. The metal screeched, forming a solid wall where the hatch had been, burying the occupants inside, killing them anyway. The bulkheads behind them crushed closed, forming a wall that slid ever closer. Donavin had retrofitted the entire *Eclipse* with picobots. How could he do such a thing? How was that even possible? Mia couldn't fathom it and didn't have time now, anyway. Heart thudding in her ears, she shoved Skyler forward. They passed her cabin, barely giving it a second glance, as a new bulkhead formed over the hatch. Donavin was altering the ship, morphing it into something different. They had to get off it. They had to get off it now.

The bridge loomed ahead. With high-backed chairs and a curved structure, she couldn't see much. She threw out her arm to stop the procession, and another blast shook the *Eclipse*, throwing them to the side. Her shoulder took most of the impact. Letting her crew compose themselves, she counted on her fingers—one, two, three—then motioned her crew to move. They charged onto the bridge.

Donavin stood by the navigation system and spun around, hand hovering by his cheek. Blood coated the side of his face, splattering across his cheek and trailing down his neck. His eyes widened, but a smirk pulled at his lips. Mia raised her gun and fired. The deck rose up like a wave, shielding him, and dropped back down again. Keeping her gun trained on him, Mia stalked closer. If she could get near enough, maybe she could stop him from using the picobots. The shots would connect if he didn't have all the blasted bulkheads blocking them. Another shot ripped past from behind her. A thick tendril sprouted from the deck and blocked that shot.

"You can't go anywhere, Donavin," Mia said.

Donavin's smile grew wider. "So it would appear. But you know what they say about appearances."

Mia rushed forward. The deck billowed and dipped, swallowing Donavin in a silver bowl. The deck hardened, as she skidded toward him. A hole appeared in the center of the silver bowl, so deep it swallowed the light. Footsteps echoed from down the narrowing corridor. Acedians, silver eyes glinting, charged toward them, weapons raised. Where had they come from? Aqua pulses ripped through the air. Cassidy dropped to a knee and fired into the crowd. A shot connected with Will's arm, slamming him into the deck. Jeff bellowed and grabbed the gun from his brother's hand, taking out the Acedians one by one but not fast enough. Shooting to kill.

Time for her backup plan. She dropped her gun and slammed her hands onto the deck, cold coursing through her fingers, hands, and arms. *Rise.* The picobot metal followed her command, forming a narrow bulge directly in front of the oncoming enemy. *Rise.* The picobots rose and slammed into the overhead panels, creating a solid thin barrier between the Acedians and her crew. The Acedians pounded on the new wall, and the substance shivered.

"Cassidy, Skyler, check the sensors. Find him." Mia went to Will but Jeff was already there, tearing off a piece of his shirt, and helping him wrap up the wound. She knelt next to them. The wound was painful but, thankfully, not deep. Will gritted his teeth. She patted his cheek and pried open the panel beside the weapons system behind him. A bundle of purple wires lay underneath. She pushed her hand in, feeling around for the hidden compartment toward the back of the space and clicked it open, lifting the bomb closer to the opening so the brothers could see. A flash of bright yellow lay underneath. A tiny multi-paneled window showed its pulsing white, liquid heart.

She looked at Will. "Do you know what this is?"

Will nodded, eyes cloudy with pain, mind still seemingly sharp. "A plasma bomb tied into the weapons system. It'll only take a few minutes to—"

Cassidy's yell sliced through his explanation. "He's off the *Eclipse*. Heading away from the planet."

Mia rose. "How'd he get off the ship?"

"I'll figure it out, hold on." Cassidy typed in commands, and a holographic image projected above her screen. The bulbous *Eclipse* looked sleek, narrow. The dual engines had melted into a point, a single needle-like aft. The coveted Acedian weapon flashed in Mia's mind. The gash in her thigh, how the spokes had ripped her flesh apart. Could Donavin replicate those, too? A backup plan, just like she had.

Skyler gestured to the base of the *Eclipse*. "Somehow, he modified it so the escape shuttles are directly under the bridge. Only one's ejected, with three biosignatures inside. He's changed them though, the shuttles, they look more like capsules now, used for short distance flights at best." Skyler's fingers flew over her control panel, pulling up more holographic images, showing orbed capsules with two narrow guns jutting from the bow.

Acedians shouted behind Mia and the barrier shuddered but stayed in place. She grimaced, knowing it wouldn't stay in place long. "He's heading away from the planet?"

"Affirmative," Cassidy said.

Jeff latched onto Mia's arm. His voice cracked. "We have to stop him. We can't let him get away."

"We won't," Mia said, staring into his wild eyes. "It's time to go."

Skyler and Cassidy readied their weapons, though Cassidy's grip seemed far too tight.

"Go where?" she asked.

Mia stepped close to the hole. "In there. After him. Skyler, you said it led to the capsules. Are they far?"

Skyler pounded the controls, bringing up the route. "No."

"Good. We won't have long once I activate the bomb."

A screeching noise came from the corridor. The new wall already seemed weak and, with so many Acedians trying to break through, it wouldn't hold. Her barrier screeched again, bending inward.

"Can't you strengthen that?" Will asked, rising to his feet, gripping his shoulder tightly to help staunch the wound. Jeff stepped between him and the Acedians. One more shield against an attack.

"No," Mia muttered. "You four jump down first, I'll be right behind you." She knelt once more and pushed her hand into the wiring, feeling her way through until she reached the bottom of the bomb. Her finger paused over the button that would set it off. "Go."

They didn't move. The bulkhead twisted, cracks spidering around the dent.

"Go, blast it. Go," she shouted.

Cassidy swung her gun toward the weakened barrier, grabbed Mia, and pulled her into a quick kiss. A hard one, just what she needed. Once they parted, Cassidy whispered, "Not without you, love."

With one last angry screech, the metal gave, splaying open first before shattering completely apart. The shards melted into the deck, and her crew fired into the oncoming horde. Mia pushed the button. She rolled away from the open panel. An aqua shot grazed past her head.

"Come on!" She leapt to her feet, grabbed Cassidy, and wrenched her to the side. Another shot hissed through the empty space where Cassidy had been. A third skated by Mia's face, tearing open a gash that bled down her chin. Will and Skyler shot a few more rounds off then jumped first, the hole swallowing them. Jeff followed. A bald Acedian charged, spittle flying from his mouth, eyes wide. Mia's shot tore the man off his feet, hurtling him into the crowd. Cassidy grabbed Mia's free hand, and they leapt, jumping into the darkness together, sliding down a chute that seemed to curve way from the *Eclipse*.

Light punctured the black at the end. Mia slid out of the chute and onto a dark, cushioned seat. The capsule swiveled a quarter turn, knotting her stomach with the sudden jolt. Cassidy landed with a thump, and the chute closed behind her. Straps flew from behind Mia's shoulders, crisscrossing over her chest and snapping into place by her waist. Her knees jammed against the monitor in the center. The silver deck curved inward, forming a sphere. Will sat facing Cassidy, clutching his own straps as they creased his shirt. Jeff sat next to him, staring at his brother, staring at the trickle of blood running down Will's arm.

Skyler, catty-corner from Mia, bent over the screen. "Eject in three, two, one."

The capsule lurched, the force of its engines shoving Mia back in her seat. The straps tightened. A steady hum filled the air. The overhead paneling brightened with a searing, white light and turned transparent. The *Eclipse* trembled, its hull writhing, transforming into something else. Something deadly. The capsule still moved farther away. Above the *Eclipse* loomed the *Bell*, sleek in design, just like its sibling. Its cannons charged, glowing a steady red, but before it could fire, Mia's bomb went off.

The explosion rocked the *Eclipse* back, ripping the hull to shreds, tearing the needle-like shape apart. Spheres of red, yellow, and blue rippled around the destruction.

Mia looked away. The *Eclipse* had been a good ship, and more than that, it had been her home. She found Cassidy's hand and held it tight. It was time to end this once and for all. "Follow Donavin."

Chapter Twenty-two

THE FLAT MONITOR BETWEEN them glowed, filling the capsule with a steady light. Mia leaned close. One yellow dot stayed consistent, moving to the right side of the screen, the other yellow dot blinked, following the first. A large red orb shimmered toward the bottom.

Skyler pointed to the crimson. "That's the planet. We're flying slightly above its magnetosphere." She jabbed a finger at the first dot. "That's Donavin."

Mia scowled. "Can we shoot him?"

Skyler nodded. "He's retrofitted these capsules with a weapons system. Basic, one shot at a time and then it needs to charge."

"It's so he'd have a defense." Mia tightened her hold on Cassidy's hand, still glaring at Donavin's blasted yellow dot. "He planned his escape all along. It's why he morphed the *Eclipse* into an Acedian needle. He couldn't have the *Bell*'s soldiers so he created a backup plan. I bet it would've sunk right into the *Bell* if my bombs didn't destroy the *Eclipse* first. Are we in range to fire?"

"Yes."

She glanced up at Skyler. "Do it."

Skyler traced a finger from their capsule to Donavin's, inserting the trajectory of the weapon into the screen. The pod's hum increased, charging for the first blast. Mia held her breath. Could that really do it? End it after all this time? Her stomach clenched. The capsule jerked back, and the humming ceased. Mia stared at the screen. A tiny white light traversed the darkness and smashed into the yellow.

"Direct hit." Skyler smiled.

Will whooped. "He's losing altitude. Entering the planet's atmosphere."

Mia couldn't take her eyes off the little yellow light speeding to the planet. Had they done it? It seemed easy, though, uncomfortably so.

"Captain?" Skyler's sharp tone jarred Mia back.

Mia tore her gaze from the screen. "What?"

Skyler raised her eyebrows. "Should we follow him?"

"Yes," Mia replied. "We need to be sure. Will?"

"Confirming our trajectory. Aligning it with the quasar's." The smile on Will's face crinkled the skin around his eyes. Even Jeff leaned for a closer look. "Entering atmosphere."

A sudden jolt sent Jeff careening into his brother, who yelped when Jeff hit his injury. Jeff took a quick glance around, meeting each of their eyes in turn before ending on his brother's.

"I'm sorry," Jeff muttered.

A blush stained his ears, and something clicked in Mia's mind. That apology, though directed at Will, was for everyone. Could it be that simple? And even though they hadn't said anything more to him about his actions on Nin's home world, even though Mia hadn't had a chance to talk with him about how to deal with such things, even though the mood still tightened with the aftermath of the battle and what was to come, the air seemed lighter. Clearer. Sweeter. When Cassidy and Skyler both reached across their seats and placed a hand on Jeff, squeezing only for a moment before letting go, Mia knew. It was that simple. Jeff eyed her, and she gave him a nod. Of course she would forgive him. There was nothing to forgive, really, everyone acted differently in the face of death. Still, Jeff grinned, straightened, as if a weight had been lifted off him. Simple.

"No worries. You're still an idiot, though," Will replied, giving Jeff a shove in return.

The scenery outside the viewport changed from the black, star-patterned space to fiery-red as the capsule heated from entry. The light filled the pod, washing everything out in crimson. The viewport vanished behind a glaring white. When the light dimmed, a slate of metal remained.

You make this too easy, Mia. Donavin's laugh suddenly permeated her.

"Wait," Mia cried, her hand darting to the control panel and yanking it from Skyler. But she couldn't stop the capsule, didn't understand the controls. "Donavin just spoke. Wait!"

Frowning, Skyler pulled the controls back, the screen lighting up her cheekbones. Fear pitched her voice. "I don't know what's wrong. I can't stop the trajectory. I can't slow us down either. We'll crash."

You'll do more than that, Mia.

"Mia." Will nudged her, pointing to the overhead. It trembled. Bulged. Screamed as the metal shifted. Cassidy grabbed her hand. The deck panels changed as well, pushing toward them like a silver tongue.

Jeff shouted, his legs rising as his section of the deck bulged upward.

Skyler's voice rose above it all. "Our hull's losing integrity. Weakening. The metal's shifting."

"He's made these capsules out of picobots," Mia murmured.

She untwined her hand from Cassidy's and pushed her palms against the metal below her seat. Her skin cooled, tingles racing down her fingers. She concentrated on the deck panels, and they sank back into place. The overhead still bulged, though, almost touching Skyler. Mia concentrated on those panels, too, forcing them back. Slowly, they receded back to their original shape. She removed her hands, breathing hard. Took a lot out of her this time, more than usual. Her hands shook. She pressed them under her thighs, forcing the chill away.

"Better." Skyler brought up an image of the capsule, scanning its surface. The hull glowed a steady white. "Integrity has returned. Wait, look."

A flash of blue pinpricked the white. Will yelped as the hull beside him swelled outward, pulling him into the pocket. Jeff twisted and grabbed his brother, shouting for help. Mia's mouth ran dry. The heat from reentry would rip the bulge right off. She palmed the metal again. The cold chilled her up to the wrist this time. Her head ached, each breath harder to take in, but she concentrated anyway, and the protrusion flattened back into place.

Donavin's thoughts webbed across her. *Let's see how long you can keep this up.*

Skyler's voice broke through. "Another weakness in the starboard hull."

"Help me," Mia cried, panic now knotting her stomach, making it even harder to concentrate.

Skyler mimicked her, pressing a hand against the hull. She closed her eyes. "I can't."

Mia groaned. "You were an Acedian before me. Try harder!"

"I'm sorry," Skyler cried. "I don't know how you're doing it."

Trying to calm herself, Mia focused on that starboard side, forcing the picobots to follow her commands and strengthen the hull.

Cassidy grabbed Mia's shoulder. "Another by the port."

As Mia focused on that weakness, the chill crept up to her shoulders.

Donavin laughed. *If it reaches your heart, Mia, you'll die.*

Her thoughts darted to her crew. To Cassidy. Mia clenched her teeth. She had to keep them alive, whatever the cost, keep the hull strong enough to survive the impact. Shaking, she still ordered the picobots to follow her will. The capsule jerked. Dropped.

"We're through the atmosphere, entering the skyline," Jeff said.

A clap sounded throughout the capsule, and a whooshing sensation pulled at her legs. The straps cut into her shoulders, chest, and sides. Cassidy's lips parted in a silent scream. A hole appeared in the deck as long as her arm. Billowy mauve clouds streamed past outside. Mia tried to pull picobots into the void. The hull still weakened. She narrowed her focus, a vein by her eye throbbing. *Move, now. Move.* The silver metal moved sluggishly, filled the hole. Thinner than the last, but it would hold.

"I've increased the oxygen levels. Another section's about to be—" Skyler said. The hull by her shoulder ripped loose, a square foot of metal spinning off into the distance.

Cassidy burrowed closer. Mia narrowed her eyes. The cold traveled over her neck. The metal surrounding the hole rippled, tendrils shot out and widened, filling the empty space. Back aching, muscles rigid, Mia tried to keep her position. The new hull beside Skyler seemed thin, too thin to remain during impact.

She gasped against the frozen grip, darkness creeping into her field of vision. Something warm and wet leaked out of her nose. She ignored it. "How close are we to the surface?"

"One thousand feet," Will replied. "We won't survive the impact. The engine isn't responding."

"I'll fix that." Mia stared at the column below the control screen. *Show me.* The picobots melted back, displaying the knee-high, orbed engine. It still seemed intact. Had she been controlling the picobots, trying to kill them, it would've been the first thing she'd destroy. "What needs to be repaired?"

Jeff's voice seemed far away when he replied. "The fuel's not reaching the engine."

Mia flitted her gaze to the base of the orb. Numbness filtered over her collarbone. A bulge of picobots blocked the energy tank. *Move.* The silver substance drew back and power surged forward into the engine. It sputtered, hummed to life. *Close.* The picobot metal flowed back into place, protecting the system once more.

Will nodded. "I've got control of the engine. Five hundred feet. Activating reverse."

The capsule lurched, reducing speed. Mia sank back into her chair, rubbing her hands together. Gooseflesh prickled her arms.

You can't think I'm done, Mia.

"Hull's weakening again." Jeff pointed to the white scan.

A blue pinprick appeared on the starboard side. The color spread to the port. The panels around them started to shake. Clatter. Fill the space with an unending noise like metal boots dancing on a deck. They moved closer to the monitor, close as they could get, gripping the monitor tightly with white-knuckled hands. The blue stretched further, darkening the overhead. The panels above them trembled.

"Two hundred feet," Will yelled.

Mia tightened her jaw. "We'll make it."

The overhead metal licked toward them then bulged outward. It ripped partially away from the hull, screeching and exposing them again to the outside. A rush of air filled the compartment, pulling at them. She flinched. It felt as if a spike drove itself through each eardrum as the pressure changed. Her body tensed. The straps cut deeper into her skin. Slamming her palms onto the metal, Mia mended the hole with a thin sheet of picobots. If the bulkheads pulled away, her crew would be yanked away. An image of Cassidy spinning through the air, strapped down to a disconnected shard of hull flashed through Mia's mind. She forced everyone's clips to unbuckle. Will reached for the useless bonds.

"Don't," she shouted, and Will stopped, his hand still outstretched.

Mia stared at the monitor. Blue spread down the port hull. The bulkhead behind the brothers weakened too rapidly to fix. She wrapped her fingers around Jeff's wrist, signaled Skyler to do the same for Will, and crammed her legs harder under the monitor. The thin metal overhead burst apart, widening and peeling away like a ripe banana, taking his seat and straps with it. A whoosh of air threatened to wrench them out of their seats, but Cassidy had locked their elbows together and jammed her legs under the monitor, keeping Mia and Skyler in their seats. Mia pulled, yanking Jeff over to their side, while Skyler did the same for Will. They huddled together now, clinging to each other and to what remained of the capsule, fighting against the suction that threatened to pull them away from each other. Easy targets, Mia knew. All in one area, Donavin could end it right now if he knew. The cold dropped below her collarbone. Their capsule spun from the force of the explosion. She glared at the gaping hole, at the sky rushing past, at the ground speeding ever closer. She couldn't fix an opening that big. There weren't enough picobots left to mend it.

Her body trembled from the effort of controlling the ones that were left, the pounding in her head blocked out all sound. Her vision blurred, concentration wavering. Something wet and warm leaked from her left ear, and she dared not wipe it away. She grasped hold of the monitor and of Jeff. Cassidy squeezed her eyes shut and pressed harder into Mia's shoulder, locking them tighter together.

Her closeness calmed Mia. *We will survive this.*

Really, Mia?

Donavin's jeer gave her a burst of strength. She pooled all of the picobots she could manage beneath them. *Yes.*

The hull behind them yanked free with a screech, but she was ready. Mia arched the picobots behind her crew, thickening with each passing heartbeat. She closed her eyes to concentrate entirely on this task. The whooshing of air grew louder, the pull stronger, filling her ears, tearing at her eyelids, whipping her hair around her face. Nothing else of the capsule remained, just the seat they occupied and the shield behind them. She forced the picobots to harden. They fell. The cold slithered to the center of her chest.

The capsule jerked to a stop, shoving Mia into the seat and breaking her concentration. The cold snapped away from her body. She opened her eyes. Sunlight blinded her for a moment, and sweet, warm air filled her lungs. Gasping, she lifted the hand still in contact with the metal. The bulkhead shattered behind them, causing them all to topple off the seat and to the ground. The air smelled a little too sweet, like freshly cut fruit, and bright-purple grass pinpricked Mia's face, but she didn't care. They had made it safely to the ground. Safe and sound. Slowly, they all rose to their feet. Skyler stared at yellow flowers covering the meadow. Will laughed, shaking his brother. Jeff whooped.

Cassidy came over and kissed Mia's check. "You're amazing."

Mia couldn't celebrate. Not yet. She swiped her ear with the back of her hand and wasn't shocked when it came back red. Blood. From overusing the picobots, like Donavin. Donavin's capsule lay across the field, three dozen paces away. His hull remained intact. A landing ramp slid to the ground and two men—Mia recognized Harrison's shock of black hair and Commodore Bay's rigid stance—stepped into view. Charles Donavin followed.

Without thinking, Mia lifted her gun and charged toward her enemy, confident her crew would be right behind.

Chapter Twenty-three

MIA FIRED FIRST, ADRENALINE pushing through her earlier exhaustion. Her gun's red beam sliced Commodore Bay's shoulder, drawing forth a spurt of equally crimson blood. Commodore Bay held a palm over the wound to staunch the flow. It didn't hurt him. It wouldn't, not with Donavin's technology controlling his body. She fired again. Bay ducked under the beam, dropped to a knee, and shot back. Mia hurled herself sideways, away from the burst. Another shot sliced through the air, twisting directly above her. She flattened. Pebbles jabbed her cheek. Footsteps pounded toward her, stopped. Cassidy helped her to stand, while Skyler fired at the Acedians. Mia glared at Donavin, but the quasar stood next to his capsule and smiled.

Cassidy aimed her gun at Commodore Bay. "You take Donavin, Mia. We'll take care of the other two. Skyler, with me. Will—"

Will and Jeff had reached their side, breathing hard. Will's knuckles whitened as he gripped his gun. "We've got Harrison."

They moved forward as one. Commodore Bay darted off to the left side, and Skyler blasted him in the knee. He tripped, though in a heartbeat, he stood again and fired. The shot burrowed harmlessly into the ground. Cassidy put on a burst of speed and skirted wide, aiming to get between Bay and his escape, the strange purple and black woods towering to their left. Will and Jeff headed toward Harrison, dodging weapon fire. Will reached him first, slamming the butt of his gun against Harrison's temple. Harrison jerked to the side, falling to the dirt. Jeff threw himself bodily atop Harrison, pinning him to the ground.

Mia let out a small sigh of relief. The Acedians seemed disorganized. Weakened. She turned her attention back to Donavin in time to watch him sprint behind his capsule, but he wouldn't get away. She wouldn't let him. She dashed after him, swinging wide around the machine, her weapon steady. Its barrel glowed a deep burgundy. Donavin waited on the other side of the capsule, still grinning, his weapon lying on the ground next to him. What the Helix was he doing? She fired, and a burst of crimson energy barreled to him. The capsule shuddered, falling over, creating a sleek silver barrier in front of Donavin. He wouldn't face her? Coward.

Mia pushed her hands onto the capsule's surface. The chill seeped into her body, edging closer to her heart. The pain in her temple spiked. She ignored it. *Melt away.* The hull weakened, vibrated, then splashed onto the ground and sank into the grass. The smile faded from Donavin's lips. With the shield out of the way, Mia rushed to him, her anger and fear and hatred combining to form a single solid punch to his jaw. He toppled to the ground, but Mia wasn't done. Far from it. Her boot connected with his stomach. Grunting, he flipped to his back, and Mia loomed over him. Moving his gaze away from her, Donavin stared at the sky. Mia's hands shook. After all this time, after everything he put her through, he wouldn't even look at her? Then she'd just blasted well make him.

She dropped to her knees and straddled Donavin, one hand wrapping around a wrist and pushing it down, the other dropping the gun and grabbing his face. Her fingers curled under his chin, slipping across fresh blood on his cheek and neck. She tightened her hold on his chin, nails digging into his skin. Finally, Donavin met her gaze. His silver eyes stared into hers. Her heart thudded, each pulse shoving the cold away from her core. Hatred spiked in her, tightening her grip until her fingers shook. Her vision clouded, darkened, narrowed until it was only them. Only her and Donavin. Waiting. Waiting until he lashed out. Waiting for him to strike, like he always did. He didn't struggle underneath her. Grime covered his forehead and dirtied his hair. The scar on his neck, still visible through the blood, marred his skin. She let go of his face, grabbed her gun, and pushed the tip of it against his temple instead. She pushed until his flesh puckered. He winced.

"Mia, it's how you act now that matters." Cassidy's call lifted her gaze. Cassidy stood in front of them, still gripping her gun, pointing it at Donavin. Harrison and Commodore Bay sat upright behind her, tied together with the same shackles her crew had used on her. The rest of her crew stood over them and watched Mia and Donavin's fight.

Mia turned her attention back to the man beneath her. Donavin lay motionless, an empty shell. Overpowering him had been easy. Without his drones to protect him, Donavin was feeble. But he had killed her parents. He'd tried to kill her, tried to kill her crew, tried to kill Cassidy. She shoved the gun harder into his temple. Her hand trembled, but she couldn't call up the anger from moments before. Cassidy's words drove a spike between her and her bloodlust.

How she would act right now would determine how others would see her. Would determine how Jeff would see her. He'd said from the start she was a killing machine, always angry. He was always raging against her, always fighting her at every turn. If she killed Donavin now, she'd prove him right. And after causing so much destruction in her youth, after swearing to Cassidy she'd do better, after swearing to herself she'd do better, would she honestly be able to face herself if she killed him? The answer flared up clearly in her, a brilliant blue glow that had been inside her all along, burning away the fog. No, she wouldn't. Donavin didn't deserve to live, not after all the destruction he had caused. But it wasn't her choice to make. Not anymore.

She stared at the man beneath her. Dirty. Bruised. Broken. A father who couldn't face mourning his daughter. And for the first time in Mia's life, the fear she'd carried since the moment they'd met disappeared. The weight lifted from her, uncurling her spine, relaxing her tight muscles, loosening her grip on her weapon. Somehow, some way, Mia knew the weight would never return again. Still pointing the gun at him, Mia rose.

He coughed up a bit of blood, smiled. "I can help you."

"Killing isn't strength, Donavin," She lowered her weapon. "Strength is the power to deal with your emotions. Something you don't have. Something you never had. Your daughter died, and you've been running from that pain ever since, deluding yourself into thinking this technology is helping people. You're not. You're not honoring her life or her death."

Donavin's face scrunched, wrinkling the skin on his forehead and around his mouth. He closed his eyes.

"And, besides, I don't need your kind of serenity. I have my own." She looked at Cassidy, feeling the familiar tug toward her, seeing the love in her beautiful, brown eyes.

Cassidy smiled. She brought out another shackling device and twisted it open, tossing the halves to Mia. Mia knelt, grabbed Donavin's shirt, and jerked him upright. Pulling his hands behind his back, she clicked the shackles together. Light poured around his wrists, the energy freezing Donavin in place.

"What're you doing?" Hovering over Bay and Harrison, Skyler waved her gun at them.

Cassidy stepped in front of her. "We're tying him up, Skyler. The military can deal with him now."

Skyler scoffed, her features hardening. A glint came into her eyes

Mia had never seen before. "We are the military, and we have to follow orders, Cassidy."

"And what are the military orders, Skyler?" Mia rubbed a hand over her face, trying to scrub away the throbbing that still lingered in her head. With everyone tied up, they could just wait for the *Bell* to arrive. Let them deal with these Acedian quasars.

Skyler stalked over, pointing the barrel at Donavin's head. "This."

"Skyler, wait!" Mia threw out a hand, too late.

The weapon charged. Fired.

Chapter Twenty-four

THE POUNDING IN MIA'S skull ceased instantly. Donavin slumped over, shackles dimming before plopping to the ground. Blood pooled under his broken skull, bones catching the light like some macabre display.

Mia pushed Skyler's weapon down. "He was contained." Her voice came out quieter than usual. "You didn't need to do that."

Skyler wiped a hand across her eyes, rustled around in her pocket, and drew out a communicator, the same style as Harrison's. She cleared her throat before speaking. "Admiral Boreas, the threat's been neutralized."

Admiral Boreas' voice filtered through the device. "Very good. We'll take care of the rest."

Five soldiers in crisp orange and gray uniforms blurred then sharpened beside them. Mia stood back, moving away. She couldn't wrap her head around what had happened. Dead, Donavin was dead. No amount of picobots, or any healer for that matter, could bring him back now. And how did she feel about it? Numb, but not as happy as she thought she'd be.

Frowning, Cassidy linked her arm through Mia's, rubbing her shoulders, pulling her gaze from the gruesome sight. A smudge of red marred Cassidy's cheek. Mia wiped it off with her thumb, resting her fingers on her love's neck. "He's gone, Cassidy."

A slow smile now spread across Cassidy's lips. "Yes, he is."

"He's gone." Mia swallowed a lump forming in her throat.

Will appeared by their side, giving them a wink. "Now don't go celebrating just yet, you two. Not in front of the stiffs."

Mia sighed, stepping back from Cassidy and settling for holding her hand instead. She had to hand it to Will, the man knew how to diffuse any situation. Jeff sidled up to his brother and socked him on the shoulder, careful to avoid his injury. Will nudged him back, grinning.

Skyler walked with the soldiers, pointing to the capsule and to the sky, before joining them. She tossed the communicator back and forth in her hands.

Mia eyed the device. "Thank you for calling the *Bell*."

Skyler shrugged. "I was just following orders."

"Admiral Boreas ordered you to kill him?"

"Yes." Skyler paused, gaze drifting to the ground. When she lifted it, Mia had never seen such intensity in her silver eyes. "But I would've done it without the orders."

Mia nodded, a small part of her wishing Skyler hadn't done it. Donavin's death would haunt her for the rest of her life. The soldiers started placing a small round device on each fallen Acedian, spending extra time with Harrison, checking his pulse, opening his eyes. One soldier spoke into a communicator, the round devices glowed white, and the Acedians disappeared. The soldier lifted the communicator to his ear. He smiled and grabbed another's shoulder, speaking quickly. The party whooped.

The excited solider parted from the rest and stopped inches from Mia's shoulder. A lock of red hair curled over his eyes. "Bay is dead. But Harrison's still alive and himself. We're hopeful about the others as well, now that their link to Donavin has been cut. Maybe others survived this mind control." The soldier faltered and took a breath. "Admiral Boreas is prepared to take you four to any planet you want. Unless any of you still want to serve the military."

One by one, Will, Jeff, Cassidy, and Mia shook their heads. Surprisingly, even Skyler declined.

The soldier saluted and hurried off to his group, relaying the message.

Mia turned to Will and Jeff. "What are you going to do now?"

Jeff answered for the both of them. "Help the ex-Acedians back to Paradous. Help rebuild. Maybe go back to Pargon and help them."

Mia beamed. She expected nothing less from the Dee brothers.

Cassidy swung an arm around Skyler's shoulder. "What're you going to do now?"

"I don't know." Skyler stared up at the sky and hooked her fingers into her belt. "It's been a while since I've been home. What will you two do?"

Mia took a deep breath of the fresh, crisp air. This planet had a new feel to it, one that hadn't been tainted by humans or technology. The forest to their left looked unhindered, strange as it was. Dark vines of green, blue, and pink curled around the trees and matted the ground beneath. Black trunks jutted skyward and dark purple leaves waved gently in the wind. She followed the trees upward, staring at the mauve-tinted sky, and could almost see the darkness beyond. Without Donavin, she was free, truly free. The galaxies had never seemed more welcoming.

She moved closer to Cassidy, sliding a hand down to twist their fingers together. "Anything we want."

Chapter Twenty-five

"IT'LL DULL IN TIME, Jeff, I swear." Mia reached out and touched the holoimage of Jeff's hand. Even though they were planets apart and he couldn't possibly feel it, Jeff gave her a small smile.

"But how long?" he asked again, the same question he had asked since the moment Donavin had died and he hadn't felt the relief that he—and even Mia herself—had anticipated. The same question he had asked each month after, five in total. Mia had finally been able to open up to Jeff, to give him advice on how to deal with the death of a family member, to help him transition from wanting to kill himself to wanting to live. It had been a slow process, especially since Jeff couldn't distract himself now that Will wasn't in constant danger.

"Honestly, Jeff, it never goes fully away. I still think of my parents. I still think of the *Hekate,* of my old home, of what my life used to be before everything went to Helix." Mia's voice cracked, and Jeff's lower lip began to tremble. As Mia had opened up, Jeff had also, showing her the softer side of his usually harsh angles.

Even though Jeff was planets away on a mission for more supplies to help rebuild Paradous, Mia still felt a tug on her heartstrings for him. For the pain he was feeling. And, if she was completely honest with herself, for the pain she felt as well.

"Everyone has pain. Everyone has sorrow." Mia echoed Cassidy's words from so long ago. "The trick is to understand that pain, to reflect on it, make it a part of yourself, then let it go. To remember the good parts about their lives." Visions of her parents running through the *Hekate,* chasing after a younger Mia, flashed through her. How their brilliant, blue eyes used to crinkle at the sides when they smiled. How they linked hands and leaned into each other when they thought Mia wasn't looking. How they kissed her on the top of her head before tucking her in each night. "And if you remember the good parts, the sad parts won't hurt you so much anymore. If your home is destroyed, you have to make a new one."

Mia found she couldn't go on anymore and smiled. She had long since accepted that her emotions ran closer to the surface than before, a trait many of the ex-Acedians had discovered. She didn't mind. After being trapped in her own body, after feeling emotions that weren't hers, she enjoyed these. Jeff looked away from her, swiping at his eyes, and Mia took this moment of privacy to steal a glance of her own. Her gaze skated away from the holoimage, past the dark metal plating that made up this small room, and fell on Cassidy. She was sitting on the porch outside and looking up at the sky. The curve of Cassidy's back, the way her brown and purple hair spilled over her shoulder, the light glinting off the decorative gold designs woven in her orange dress made Mia's heart skip a beat. Her new home.

She turned her attention back to Jeff. Will had entered the holoimage, his bulk filling the rest of the frame with the white and black Paradousian officer's uniform so like his brother's. "Hello, Will.".

"Hello, Captain." Will gave her a lazy salute and winked. "Sorry to cut this short, but we've been called on rotation again, something about heading back to Paradous as we have all the supplies now."

Jeff's features brightened. "What? Really?"

Will chuckled. "Really. Now come on, we're shoving off in a few."

"Wait! Did you get to speak to Admiral Boreas and deliver all the notes like I requested?" Mia leaned forward, closer to the holoimage. She had asked the military to give her the names of all the crew of her four ships and had personally written a letter to each of the crewmembers' families, confessing her part in what had happened to their loved ones. It had helped ease the guilt, and the weight of the list had lessened with each letter she'd written. She had written to *Jubilee*'s families two weeks ago, the last bunch of letters sent out via the military's communication tech.

Will tilted his head. "I thought someone would've contacted you about it already. They all reached their destinations. Admiral Boreas personally made sure of it, even urging some of the reluctant ones to open the notes."

The last of the guilt lifted from Mia. The weight of her list, so ingrained in her being, dissipated. She grinned, a rush of happiness filling her instead. "It'll be good to see you two again, and have you see how far we've gotten on repairing the city. I'll let your mother know to expect you. We'll have some Paradousian tea waiting when you get back."

"Make it a double." Will reached around Jeff to shut off the communication device. They faded from view, and the room darkened.

Mia rose from her seat and headed for the porch. She passed the living area, an open space with one large fireplace on the side, a metal table brightened by the tech inside it, and a simple couch with orange cushions. The fireplace had been Cassidy's idea, something to remind her of her own home on Skadi, though they rarely used it here on Paradous. Mia passed the kitchen, a gleaming space filled with the usuals; a disintegrator, a convec, a bowl of carotas and hazii, and even some xarianflower tea cubes. A simple setup, almost like the *Eclipse* in design, though that had been Cassidy's doing, too. Mia snatched a bright-pink laria fruit from one of the nearby bowls and made her way through the open doors to Cassidy's side.

"How's Jeff doing?" Cassidy asked, leaning on Mia's shoulder as soon as she sat down and grabbing the fruit to take a bite.

"Better. Still asking. But better," Mia replied. "Will seems to love the guard."

"I knew he would. He was built for it, really, and they're doing so much good these days. Helping to fix what Donavin broke here on Paradous. Even on other planets, when we can spare them." Cassidy took another bite of the pink fruit, some juice sliding down her chin.

Mia laughed and wiped the juice away with her thumb, slipping it into her own mouth and enjoying the burst of tartness on her tongue. "They're coming here, by the way. I told them we'd tell Arai."

Cassidy shifted away, her eyes brightened, a grin growing on her lips. "That's wonderful news. They're going to be amazed by how much we've done with the place."

Areas of Paradous were still in ruin. The larger buildings would take ages to clean away and rebuild, but the smaller neighborhoods were salvaged pretty easily. Mia had pushed for them to stay here and help clean, figuring she could at least help rebuild these people's lives after having a hand in destroying them and keep her promise to Will and Jeff. Cassidy readily agreed, claiming that she had wanted to spend more time with the Dee family, anyway, and how they needed to work to gain funds so they could restart her business. In her heart, though, Mia knew it was because Cassidy wanted her to be happy. Cassidy would've gone anywhere to make that happen, and now Mia would do the same for her.

"Isn't Skyler supposed to call in soon?" Cassidy asked, breaking the peaceful silence that had fallen over them.

"Yes," Mia replied, wrapping an arm around Cassidy's shoulder and pulling her close, loving the feeling of heat shared between them. The peace between them, the stillness.

Even though they were no longer technically a crew, her friends still touched base with Mia every month. And still called her 'captain.' Skyler was due for a call any day now. She had traveled back to her home world, Gyre, to reconnect with her family. She had linked up with the medical agency and apparently had risen fast in her chosen field, claiming the title of head nurse within two months' time. Even Harrison checked in, though admittedly fewer times than the others and just to say he was doing well on Pargon, taking care of a herd of fillies with his bride-to-be, Ellen.

The good news seemed to continuously fly in these days. A few weeks after Donavin's defeat, the military had called them, saying they had found Nin's son, Pira, alive and well. The Dee family had bonded closer than ever, rebuilding their family home and holding a proper burial for Sarah, which the whole city attended. At Mia's insistence, and both Harrison and Skyler's agreement, Sheyla, Clin, and Viv had their sentences wiped clean and were now living on Skadi, much to Cassidy's joy. During a burst of good will, Admiral Boreas had even set them up with their own housing and fifty thousand units. It seemed everything had been righted in Mia's world. She laughed, unable to contain herself.

Cassidy threw the last of the fruit to the chittering red birds nearby and nudged Mia. "Let me in on the joke, love."

"No joke, I'm just so happy."

Rising to her feet, Cassidy pulled Mia up as well. "I'm glad to hear that, love."

Mia wrapped her arms around Cassidy, pulling her close again. "Are you happy, Cassidy? With me? With this?" Her gaze pulled away from Cassidy's and took in the scenery around them, the simple home they had settled into next to the Dee household, the tiny, red birds flitting this way and that, the cloudless sky.

A warm hand caressed her cheek and drew her attention back. Cassidy rubbed a thumb gently over Mia's lips. "I've never been happier, Mia."

Mia pulled Cassidy in for a kiss, tender at first then deepening. Mia needed this, needed her. When they finally parted, Cassidy's eyes flashed with desire, and Mia knew hers reflected the same. "Remember that order I gave a while back when we were in Nin's house?"

Cassidy burrowed her face in Mia's neck, her breath tickling Mia's skin. "You mean how you want control this time?"

Mia tightened her hold. "Yes. That. I say we follow it right now."

Laughing, they made their way inside, leaving behind the bustle of the outside world and ducking into their sanctuary once again.

The End

.

About Kellie Doherty

Kellie Doherty lives in Portland, Oregon, though she spent her childhood in Alaska. In June 2016, she graduated with a Master's in Book Publishing from Portland State University. She is also a freelance editor, taking jobs whenever they come her way.

Kellie has been writing since she was young. Her work (fiction and non-fiction) has been published in *Flight* (Mischief Corner Press), *Mission 20* (Back of Beyond Press) *Pathos, Alaska Women Speak, F Magazine,* and *The Chugiak-Eagle River Star,* as well as the blogs of 49 Writers and Ooligan Press. Her debut novel—*Finding Hekate*—came out in April 2016. She is currently working on a fantasy series.

When not writing or editing, she enjoys reading, taking walks, playing video and board games, and hanging out with her friends.

Contact Information

Website - http://kelliedoherty.com/

Editing - http://editreviseperfect.weebly.com/

Twitter - https://twitter.com/kellie_doherty

Facebook - https://www.facebook.com/KellieDoherty89

Email - kellie.f.doherty@gmail.com

Other Fantasy and Science Fiction from Desert Palm Press

Cicatrix Duology by Kellie Doherty

Finding Hekate

ISBN: 9781942976073

Mia Foley is running away from the attack that changed her life. She's captain of a new spaceship when the Acedians find her and try blasting her peaceful crew from the black. She must sever her bonds in order to run, again. But she's grown fond of this crew, particularly Cassidy Gates. Staying with them will jeopardize their safety, and they have much closer fears than the Acedian hunters. Mia's time is running out. She's becoming one of them.

Amendyr Series by Rae D. Madgon

The Second Sister

ISBN: 9781311262042

Eleanor Of Sandleford's entire world is shaken when her father marries the mysterious, reclusive Lady Kingsclere to gain her noble title. Ripped away from the only home she has ever known, Ellie is forced to live at Baxstresse Manor with her two new stepsisters, Luciana and Belladonna. Luciana is sadistic, but Belladonna is the woman who truly haunts her. When her father dies and her new stepmother goes suddenly mad, Ellie is cheated out of her inheritance and forced to become a servant. With the help of a shy maid, a friendly cook, a talking cat, and her mysterious second stepsister, Ellie must stop Luciana from using an ancient sorcerer's chain to bewitch the handsome Prince Brendan and take over the entire kingdom of Seria.

Wolf's Eyes

ISBN: 9781311755872

Cathelin Raybrook has always been different. She Knows things without being told and Sees things before they happen. When her visions urge her to leave her friends in Seria and return to Amendyr, the magical kingdom of her birth, she travels across the border in search of her grandmother to learn more about her visions. But before she can find her family, she is captured by a witch, rescued by a handsome stranger, and forced to join a strange group of forest-dwellers with even stranger magical abilities. With the help of her new lover, her new family, and her eccentric new teacher, she must learn to gain control of her powers and do some rescuing of her own before they take control of her instead.

The Witch's Daughter

ISBN: 978131672643

Ailynn Gothel has always been the perfect daughter. Thanks to her mother's teachings, she knows how to heal the sick, conjure the elements, and take care of Raisa, her closest and dearest friend. But when Ailynn's feelings for Raisa grow deeper, her simple life falls apart. Her mother hides Raisa deep in a cave to shield her from the world, and Ailynn must leave home in search of a spell to free her. While the kingdom beyond the forest is full of dangers, Ailynn's greatest fear is that Raisa will no longer want her when she returns. She is a witch's daughter, after all—and witches never get their happily ever after.

The Mirror's Gaze

ISBN: 9781942976196

In the final sequel of the Amendyr series civil war has broken out in Amendyr. With undead monsters ravaging the land, an evil queen on Kalmarin's white throne, and the kingdom's true heir missing, Cathelin Raybrook and Ailynn Gothel must join forces to protect their homeland. They hope to gain the aid of the Liarre, a reclusive community of magical creatures, but some of their leaders are reluctant to join a war that isn't theirs. Meanwhile, Lady Eleanor of Baxstresse thinks she's safe across the border in Seria, but when a mysterious girl in white arrives in an abandoned carriage, she finds herself drawn into the conflict as well. Together, they must find the source of the evil queen's power, and discover a way to destroy it before it's too late.

Desert Palm Press

Dark Horizons Series by Rae D. Magdon & Michelle Magly

Dark Horizons
ISBN: 9781310892646
Lieutenant Taylor Morgan has never met an ikthian that wasn't trying to kill her, but when she accidentally takes one of the aliens hostage, she finds herself with an entirely new set of responsibilities. Her captive, Maia Kalanis, is no normal ikthian, and the encroaching Dominion is willing to do just about anything to get her back. Her superiors want to use Maia as a bargaining chip, but the more time Taylor spends alone with her, the more conflicted she becomes. Torn between Maia and her duty to her home-world, Taylor must decide where her loyalties lie.

Starless Nights
ISBN: 9781310317736
In this sequel to Dark Horizons Taylor and Maia did not know where they would go when they fled Earth. They trusted Akton to take them somewhere safe. Leaving behind a wake of chaos and disorder, Coalition soldier Rachel is left to deal with the backlash of Taylor's actions, and soon finds herself chasing after the runaways. Rachel

quickly learns the final frontier is not a forgiving place for humans, but her chances for survival are better out there than back on Earth. Meanwhile, Taylor and Maia find themselves living off the generosity of rebel leader Sorra, an ikthian living a double life for the sake of the rebellion. With Maia's research in hand, Sorra believes they can deliver a fatal blow against the Dominion.

Desert Palm Press

Chronicles of Osota – Warrior by Michelle Magly
ISBN: 9781311834324

Alina knew that one day she would return to the heartland of Osota, even after eleven years of isolation. But how could she know her return to the capital would coincide with the arrival of young Warrior-in-training Senri? Beautiful and strong, Senri makes for a pleasant distraction from Alina's troubles. But as the prospective ruler of a nation, Alina can hardly devote time to pursuing a romance. As a new threat looms over the kingdom of Osota, she is left with little choice but to turn to Senri for help.

Desert Palm Press

Journey To You by AJ Adaire
ISBN: 9781311571854

What do you do if you are one of the few who remain alive after a mysterious, flu-like virus claims most of the global population? This is a question Kim Robins and Peri Henderson have to answer when the world changes and society falls apart. Violent gangs of looters make it unsafe to remain in the city. Hoping to improve their chances for survival, Kim and Peri decide to hike into the remote forest area of Maine. Dangerous circumstances along the trail cause the women to join forces with another hiker and her dog. The longtime friends and their new companions set off on a daunting trek filled with both menacing and kindhearted survivors. With evidence of the illness everywhere they go, will this journey bring each of the women the happiness and safety she seeks?

Desert Palm Press

The Broken Coil by Sy Itha

ISBN: 9781972976042
Secluded in the Dainlock Woods, Jacquelyn Fletcher makes her living trading furs and occasionally escorting travelers through the dangerous forest. Disguised as a man, she hides from the mistakes of her past. As a favor to an old friend, she finds herself agreeing to guide Avalon, a Paladin of Sel, through the woods to safety. All Avalon has known is the temple life. When her fellow Paladin is murdered, Avalon is framed for the crime and must flee her home to find the source of the attack. Her only clue is an ancient tome that she is unable to decipher. Traveling with the ranger Fletcher, Avalon thinks she is safe. Neither of them realize the danger that follows them.

Cover Design By : Rachel George
www.rachelgeorgeillustration.com

Note to Our Readers:

Thank you for reading a book from Desert Palm Press. We have made every effort to edit this book. However, typos do slip in. If you find an error in the text, please email lee@desertpalmpress.com so the issue can be corrected.

We appreciate you as a reader and want to ensure you enjoy the reading process. We would like you to consider posting a review on your preferred media sites such as Amazon, Smashwords, Bella Books, Goodreads, Tumblr, Twitter, Facebook, and/or your blog or website.

For more information on upcoming releases, author interviews, contest, giveaways and more, please sign up for our newsletter and visit us as at Desert Palm Press: www.desertpalmpress.com and "Like" us on Facebook: https://www.facebook.com/DesertPalmPress/?fref=ts.

Bright blessing.

Made in the USA
San Bernardino, CA
06 March 2018